A
SHIPWRECK
in FIJI

ALSO BY THE AUTHOR

A Disappearance in Fiji

A SHIPWRECK in FIJI

NILIMA RAO

Published by
Soho Press, Inc.
227 W 17th Street
New York, NY 10011
www.sohopress.com

Library of Congress Cataloging-in-Publication Data

Names: Rao, Nilima, author.
Title: A shipwreck in Fiji / Nilima Rao.
Description: New York, NY : Soho Crime, 2025.
Identifiers: LCCN 2024055028

ISBN 978-1-64129-547-5
eISBN 978-1-64129-430-0

Subjects: LCGFT: Detective and mystery fiction. | Novels.
Classification: LCC PR9619.4.R37 S55 2025 | DDC 823/.92—dc23/
eng/20241122
LC record available at https://lccn.loc.gov/2024055028

Interior design by Janine Agro, Soho Press, Inc.

Printed in the United States of America

10 9 8 7 6 5 4 3 2 1

EU Responsible Person (for authorities only)
eucomply OÜ
Pärnu mnt 139b-14
11317 Tallinn, Estonia
hello@eucompliancepartner.com
www.eucompliancepartner.com

*To Zain, Gwen, Eshan, Stirling
and all those who come after*

THE FIJI TIMES, SATURDAY, MAY 1, 1915.

Patriotic Cricket

Old v Young Players

A cricket match on quite a novel scale will be held tomorrow after-noon—weather conditions permitting—at Albert Park between Old and Young players. The proceeds are to be handed to the Fiji Contingent Fund.

The conditions of the match are:

1. All players must contribute 5d each.

2. For every run scored the batsman must pay 8d.

3. For every catch made 1s.

4. For every decided catch missed 2s.

5. For every block, 5s.

6. Batsman after making 50 must retire.

7. For every wicket credited to the bowler 2s.

8. Every man stumped or run out 2s.

9. Every player who deliberately misfields a ball 1s.

CHAPTER 1

"WHAT DID I MISS?" Dr. Robert Holmes asked, sounding out of breath.

Sergeant Akal Singh raised a hand to his forehead to shield his eyes against the brilliant sunshine. Even so, he had to squint as he looked up at the doctor, who had arrived at the cricket ground twenty minutes later than he had promised. Akal looked with envy at the hats of the men around him. Not an option with his turban in place.

"Nothing much," Constable Taviti Tukana replied. Taviti had questioned Akal about this game they called cricket many times, but still didn't understand why the British and the Indians in Suva were all so mad for it. As far as Akal could tell, Taviti came along to these Sunday matches to flirt with the ladies in attendance. "Sergeant Singh hasn't had his turn hitting the ball yet."

"Batting," the doctor and Akal corrected in concert. Taviti shrugged indifferently.

"We are waiting for the inspector-general before we can start. And half of the other team are missing," Akal explained to the doctor. The match today was ostensibly to raise money for the Fiji Contingent Fund, which would pay for a small group of British subjects to make their way to Europe so they could enlist to fight in the war. It was also a grudge match, the Suva Constabulary versus the civil service—the officers of the Fijian colonial administration.

"Ah, well, they were all with me, stuck in a last-minute meeting with the governor. Some war updates came in over the telegraph," Robert informed them gravely as he sat down on the bench next to Akal. "That disastrous battle in Turkey last week. There were a lot of Australians killed. The names have started coming through, and the Australians here are worried about their people."

Akal had heard that there were Indians in that battle as well, but it seemed the governor didn't think they warranted a mention. He wondered if any of his friends had lost their lives. While he worked within the British Empire by going to Hong Kong and joining the police service, some of the boys in his village in the Punjab had joined the British Indian Army. Could they have been part of this battle? Akal quickly dismissed the thought, pushing away the lurking sense of dread. He would likely never know.

"I think they might be a while. I don't have the stomach to dwell on it all, but a lot of the others stayed back to talk about it," the doctor continued. "You've probably got a bit of time before your famous bowling arm is required, Akal."

"Batting," said Taviti cheekily.

"No. Bowling," said Akal, rotating his arm through the bowling motion. Taviti shrugged indifferently again, while Akal turned to Dr. Holmes. "What other information did we receive on the war?"

Dr. Holmes grimaced, clearly reluctant to revisit the topic, but filled them in on what he had learnt of the battle. The Australian and New Zealand Army Corps had landed on a beach, somewhere called Gallipoli, and had met strong resistance from the Turkish troops. Despite heavy losses, they had dug in and were at a stalemate with the Turks.

"It all feels very far away from here," the doctor concluded, gesturing towards the crowd who had gathered for the long-awaited game of cricket.

Everyone was in their Sunday best. The well-heeled Europeans, sitting on chairs in the shade of a cluster of trees, had trickled over from their post-church lunch at the adjacent Grand Pacific Hotel. Dominated by British, Australians, and New Zealanders, these were the elite of the backwater colony of Fiji, one of the last acquisitions of the British Empire. Many were part of the colonial administration, and a few were plantation owners who had come to Suva for a break in the nearest thing they had to a cosmopolitan metropolis.

The ladies sat gossiping under parasols and hats, protecting themselves from the sun as best they could, drinking lemonade brought across on trays from the hotel by uniformed waitstaff. The men stood plucking gin and tonics from the same trays. The planters were easy to identify, sporting the leathery, tanned faces of men who couldn't avoid the sun.

Across the field from the Europeans, the Indians, sitting cross-legged on woven mats, were largely the shop owners in Suva, the more prosperous of the Indians in the colony. Most of them had paid their own way from India to seek business opportunities. There were one or two who had made it through their five years of indenture and had scrambled their way to the top of the food chain in their own community.

Akal, Taviti, and Dr. Holmes were an anomaly in the

crowd, which was segregated along racial lines. Taviti was the only Fijian present, and Akal the only Sikh. Add an older, dignified British doctor to their little trio, sitting apart from everyone else, and the incongruity was complete. They ignored the occasional curious glances cast their way. This friendship was Akal's lifeline in an otherwise unfriendly environment, so he was beyond grateful that the other two had thrown their lot in with him.

"Who are they?" asked Taviti, nudging Akal and nodding in the direction of two women who had just arrived, one who looked to be in her early twenties and the other perhaps approaching fifty. They were clearly related, both sporting the same red hair, though the young woman's shone fiercely in the sun and the older lady's was more muted with grey.

Akal shook his head with a small frown. He didn't recognise them, which was unusual; with so few Europeans in Suva, he recognised everyone, even if he didn't know them by name. They could have come in from a plantation, but he thought he would have heard if there was a beautiful young woman living on a plantation. It seemed more likely that they were new arrivals. Akal and Taviti both looked questioningly towards the doctor.

"No, no idea. Though that is Hugh Clancy they are joining. Looks like he may have some family visiting."

Hugh Clancy was the editor of the *Fiji Times*, the best source of news and a powerful institution in the colony. Clancy was not afraid to criticise the administration and report on things the governor would prefer to remain quiet. Last year, the *Fiji Times* had published claims made by a Catholic priest, Father Hughes, that an Indian coolie woman had been kidnapped from a plantation. The inspector-general had reluctantly sent Akal out to investigate, instructing him to close the case quickly and quietly. Akal's failure to follow these instructions had cemented his commanding officer's already poor opinion of him.

The two unfamiliar ladies had settled into some seats and were looking around, the younger woman more animated as she pointed at various objects. The older lady seemed content to nod indulgently, occasionally adding a comment of her own. Akal followed the young woman's gestures, seeing the scene with fresh eyes.

This was the very image of a British colony. The cricket stumps set up and waiting for the match to begin. The natural environment of the tropical island ruthlessly tamed to allow for a game which was transplanted from half the world away. The fair-skinned Britishers who were not meant for the Fijian sun wilting in the humidity. Behind, the graceful edifice of the Grand Pacific Hotel. And beyond all of that, the endless ocean.

"Here they come. Time to shine, young man," declared the doctor. Akal turned to look over his right shoulder towards the road. The missing cricket players were passing through the palm trees, arriving en masse in their crisp white uniforms.

Akal rose to join his team, while the doctor and Taviti went their separate ways to greet various other European spectators. Both of them had far warmer greetings from their friends than Akal did from his teammates, Europeans and Indians alike, most of whom had thawed enough to give him a curt nod. The inspector-general ignored him. Akal imagined that if he wasn't such a superb bowler, something the team otherwise lacked, the inspector-general would have barred him from the team. Still, the curt nods represented a vast improvement to his reception even six months ago.

The coin was tossed; the Suva Constabulary would field first. Akal was first to bowl. He loped his long-limbed stride towards the pitch. On his way there, he glanced towards where the flame-haired woman had been seated. His eyes snagged on hers for a long moment. A small, secret smile lit up her face.

"Play!" the umpire called.

Akal looked down at the pitch, rubbed the seam of the ball, and prepared for the run up. He pushed away the warm buzz that smile had given him and focused on the task at hand, making another bid for acceptance in this exile home of his.

ON MONDAY MORNING, Akal was sitting in a cramped room at the Totogo station, Suva's central police station, removed from the celebratory backslapping still going on from the previous day. Despite his own contributions to the police team win, Akal hadn't even tried to tell his own stories in the face of the ongoing antipathy towards him from his fellow officers. Instead, he was once more reviewing his notes from the Night Prowler case, the bane of his existence.

He had inherited the unsolvable case upon his arrival in Fiji a year ago, a way for the inspector-general to sideline the disgraced officer who had been foisted on him against his wishes. Akal had been sent to Fiji as a deal done between the governors of Fiji and Hong Kong to distance him from the mistakes he had made in Hong Kong and to bolster the struggling, fledgling Fijian police force. Unfortunately, Inspector-General Thurstrom, who had had no say in this transfer, wasn't interested in an officer who had already made a serious lapse in judgement; as soon as Akal arrived, Thurstrom had handed Akal the Night Prowler case and washed his hands of him. The rest of the Suva Constabulary had followed their inspector-general's example and ignored Akal unless there was some cricket to be played.

The Night Prowler—what the *Fiji Times* called him, and, to Akal's chagrin, the name that had stuck with his colleagues on the force—was a Fijian man who, naked as the day he was born, peeped in the windows of the European children in Suva. He had done nothing more than look so far, but Akal thought that this couldn't last long. Eventually he would do something more than peep. No two descriptions of the man were the same, other than to concur that he was Fijian. Traumatised children did not make the best witnesses. Even granted Akal's brief reprieve from the Night Prowler in the previous year, as he worked the case of the missing coolie woman, he was resigned to chasing the elusive Night Prowler for the rest of his career.

Akal abandoned his futile review of the case notes. Seeking comfort, he pulled the latest letter from his father out of its usual place in his pocket and smoothed it out on the table in front of him. Even without reading the words, the familiar neat script on the rough, cheap paper brought a tumble of emotions. An aching longing for home, a feeling of gratitude, tinged with shame, for his father's support during Akal's fall from grace. The enduring feeling, which lasted when the intensity of all the others faded, was a sense of peace and belonging.

Akal's eyes tracked directly to the sentences that he treasured the most.

Beta, I feel that you have honoured Vaheguru with your work on your last case. Finding justice for this poor Indian woman, when nobody else would represent her, is one of the finest actions you have ever done. I know you do not want to be in Fiji, yet if you were not there, who would have helped her daughter to know the truth?

His father's words echoing in his mind, Akal resumed his review of the case notes. His good intentions lasted for about a minute before the sense of listlessness settled back in. He decided it was definitely time for a break. Standing, Akal stretched his arms overhead to his full impressive height, hitting the ceiling. He scratched a spot in his beard at the edge of his turban, and wandered into the main reception of the station to slouch against the front counter.

Taviti was in his usual place, manning the front desk, his nose buried in a book. No matter how capable he was, Taviti was likely permanently confined to this position; his uncle was a prominent Fijian chief who had sent Taviti to Suva to represent the village socially and politically. He did not approve of Taviti's interest in policing. Akal looked at his friend and wondered, not for the first time, why he preferred the frustrations of policing over the glamor and influence of the political career his uncle had lined up for him.

"What are you reading?" Akal asked Taviti.

Taviti held up a manual on police procedure, one Akal had read years ago when he was starting as a police officer in Hong Kong.

"Learning anything?"

Taviti snorted and threw the book down on the desk. "There is not much point, is there, if I'm just going to be stuck here."

"I really thought your uncle would agree to you being

more active after the case last year. But I suppose he is worried about your safety?"

Last year, Taviti had saved Akal's life in a dramatic scene as they were wrapping up the missing persons investigation, resulting in a minor arm injury, which he had worn like a war hero. Taviti had hoped that his showing on the case would prove to his uncle that he could do more than administrative duties. He had been wrong.

"No. The opposite. He's now more convinced that I am wasting my time. I don't even think it is about keeping me safe. I think it's that he doesn't see the value in police work."

His complaint was cut short by the entry of a young man.

"*Bula*," the man greeted Taviti.

"*Bula vinaka*," Taviti responded casually, taking the bundle of envelopes and flipping through them as the mailman made his exit. Grinning, Taviti pulled one of the larger envelopes out of the stack. "Hmm . . . a report from the Levuka station. It's the first one we've gotten from that young Indian constable, Kumar. The one who got left on his own when the sub-inspector there retired. This should be interesting."

Akal chuckled, remembering how long he had agonized over his first report. Taviti opened the envelope and scanned through the report, then frowned.

"Oh. It's fine. Usual stuff. He has requested some supplies. Reports some small disputes over yams, a stolen chicken." His face brightened as he came to the end of the report. "Oh, here we are. Apparently, a shopkeeper just outside of Levuka reports that some Germans have been coming at night to buy supplies from him."

Akal raised one eyebrow. "Germans?" he said incredulously.

"Germans!" Taviti guffawed. "Can't wait to tell the fellows

about this one. Maybe Kumar thinks it's all part of their strategy. The Germans thought if they take out Fiji first, the rest of the British Empire will crumble."

"Yes, you should put it that way when you let the inspector-general know about it," Akal responded wryly.

Taviti groaned. "Why do you want to ruin it for me, Akal? Let me have a little fun first before you mention Thurstrom."

"Sorry. No fun for either of us."

"Fine. I better get through the rest of the mail and then go give him the report. Thanks for nothing."

Akal laughed and returned to his own frustrating exercise of looking for a new angle on a case that was going nowhere.

TAVITI RETURNED FROM delivering the report from Levuka with the unwelcome information that Akal was to attend the inspector-general's office forthwith. He didn't know any more than that, and when quizzed by Akal on the inspector-general's mood, his response had been, "Normal. Grumpy."

Akal made his way up the stairs slowly, footsteps loud on the concrete. He walked along the corridor lined with dirt-encrusted louvres looking out onto an unlovely laneway marred by potholes, a motley stray dog nosing about. If he closed his eyes, he could pretend he was back in Hong Kong, walking through the elegant wooden police headquarters to a meeting with the inspector-general there, who had valued him above all others. But that was before he had made a fool of himself and earned an exile to Fiji in disgrace.

Akal knocked on the inspector-general's door and waited with trepidation and some anticipation. He ran his hands over his turban to check everything was in place, tugged on his uniform shirt to make sure there weren't any creases forming, and checked his shoes were well polished, without the ever-present dust from the Suva streets marring the shine. None of this would improve Thurstrom's opinion of him, but anything less than perfection in his turnout would be pounced on.

Perhaps the inspector-general was feeling generous after Akal's outstanding performance yesterday, when he had bowled three of the civil servants out for ducks. Perhaps he had another case for Akal, something he could actually make some progress on. Probably not, though. Probably, there was going to be more bad news.

"Enter."

Akal's stomach took another lurch, and he paused to tug his shirt down once more before opening the door and entering.

The inspector-general's office was unchanged from the last time Akal had been there, with paperwork haphazardly piled everywhere. The desk that dominated the middle of the room was covered in piles of paper, and on the sideboard, the crystal whisky decanter and glasses had been pushed precariously close to the edge to allow for more piles of papers. The police force continued to lose more men to the war in Europe, and the inspector-general wanted a European sub-inspector as his right-hand man. There were none to be had. So he waded through the paperwork himself. Or didn't wade through it, as it seemed from the general disarray.

Akal approached the inspector-general, who was seated behind his desk signing papers. He didn't look up. The sun was streaming through the louvres, causing stripes of sunlight to fall across the table and across the inspector-general's red-gold shock of hair as he bent over the file, pen in hand.

"You wanted to see me, sir?" Akal asked.

Inspector-General Jonathon Thurstrom held up a hand, still not looking up. Akal waited patiently, familiar with this habit from his commanding officer. He didn't know quite what the inspector-general thought he was achieving by calling Akal in before he was ready to talk to him, but it made no difference to Akal. *He* wasn't achieving anything, anyway. He may as well stand here, rather than sit at his own desk, not achieving anything. This small disrespect paled against the other insults.

Finally, Thurstrom signed the last piece of paper in the file and looked up, blinking as he focused on Akal. Akal stiffened his spine just that little bit more.

"I've got a job for you, Singh," Thurstrom said with a smirk.

"Yes, sir?" Akal said, his heart sinking. The smirk told him everything he needed to know.

"Hugh Clancy's sister and niece are in Fiji, and they want to take a trip to Levuka, see the old capital. Clancy has asked if somebody could escort them, so of course I thought of you. You have some experience with entertaining European women, don't you, Singh?"

Akal's jaw clenched so hard that a pain shot down his neck. Most people in Fiji didn't know exactly what his mistakes in Hong Kong had been, but the inspector-general did, and he wasn't shy about his contempt. Akal had never figured out whether it was his failure as a police officer that had so offended Thurstrom, or his apparent audacity in having had a relationship with an English woman.

Thurstrom was watching for Akal's reaction with malicious glee. Akal, determined not to give him the satisfaction, forced himself to relax. He gave Thurstrom a bland look and asked, "An escort? I haven't been to Levuka myself. I don't know the way, sir."

"It's on another island, Ovalau. You just get the ladies on the ferry, keep an eye on them, and escort them to their hotel. And then bring them back when they are ready. In fact, the women wanted to go on their own, but Clancy rightly insisted that they have an escort and he didn't trust any of the rogues floating around Suva. I told him a police officer could be spared. Surely you can manage that simple task?"

"Yes, sir," Akal replied. He suspected that under normal circumstances, the inspector-general would have told the editor of the *Fiji Times* to find an escort on his own, but the chance to humiliate Akal while getting on the good side of the newspaperman had been an irresistible opportunity. Akal maintained a serene exterior, expecting his equanimity to infuriate the inspector-general more than any argument would. His concern grew when Thurstrom's smirk deepened.

"You realise that if there is even a hint of impropriety in your dealings with the two women, I will dismiss you. I can't imagine your friends in Hong Kong will still want to protect you if you make the same mistake again."

Of course Akal knew this. The inspector-general in Hong Kong had used his connections to have Akal moved to Fiji, rather than dismissed outright, but he would hardly be willing to do that again.

"Yes, sir," Akal replied stiffly.

"Excellent. While you are waiting for the ladies to do their sightseeing, you can follow up on a report I just received," the inspector-general said, barely able to contain his laughter. "Apparently, there are some Germans lurking about in Levuka. I need you to find and apprehend these Germans who seem to have lost their way to the battlefields in Europe. I expect a full report on your search."

Taviti's excellent joke had now come to land on Akal's shoulders.

"Germans, sir? Are they soldiers?" Akal asked, wondering what on earth was in this report.

"Of course not, Singh, don't be ridiculous!" Thurstrom snapped. "It's that young Kumar. He's too wet behind the ears, and letting the locals fill his head with nonsense. A more experienced officer would have known how to calm the people down instead of accepting everything he is told. Haven't you read the newspapers? Everybody is seeing Germans everywhere. I'm not sure if they all realise how far away Europe is."

"So . . . I don't need to investigate these claims, sir?"

"I don't care how you do it, just shut them down. As you can see, I've got a problem in Levuka. Ever since Johnson retired, I've been left with Kumar trying to run things on his own. He's only a third-class constable, poor lad. I've got an Australian officer coming over whom I'll place there permanently, but until then, get Kumar sorted."

And there it was. The real reason Akal was being sent to Levuka. But rather than give him an official duty that might be seen as a vote of confidence, Thurstrom was hiding it as a demeaning babysitting job—with a wild goose chase as a final insult.

AKAL'S FIRST STEP in his fool's errand was to coordinate movements with Hugh Clancy, as the inspector-general had no further details on the timing of this trip to Levuka. Assuming the newspaper editor would be at work, Akal decided to visit the *Fiji Times* office in order to make contact with him. He left the station, stepping out into the steaming heat of a Suva afternoon. The usual afternoon rain shower had passed through recently, leaving everything damp, but without enough force to actually reduce the heaviness in the air.

The *Fiji Times* operated out of a building a short walk from the police station. Everything in Suva was a short walk from the police station, Akal thought, as he absently stretched his stride to avoid one of the ubiquitous potholes. He longed for Hong Kong, for Victoria Peak towering above him and the stretch of land to the ocean. Suva was like that in miniature, with a trifling hill that gradually dropped away and meandered to the ocean. It wasn't just the scale of the geography he missed, it was the scale of society as well. Here, everyone was a few connections away from everybody else.

Akal had met an old man, early on during his interviews for the Night Prowler investigation, who seemed to have the connections of all of Suva mapped in his head. Once Akal had introduced himself, there was a pause in the conversation while the man tried to place him. His rheumy eyes moved side to side, as if reading an actual map, and eventually slowed to a stop. When he looked back up at Akal, he seemed puzzled that he couldn't place Akal on his map. Akal had not been surprised. He had had no connections here. Perhaps if he met that man again now, he would have some tenuous connections to add to the map, to Taviti and Dr. Holmes.

Akal's musing had brought him to the *Fiji Times* office

and printery, a ramshackle wooden building that looked as if it might fall over but for the buzz of activity keeping it vibrant. As Akal approached the front door, a harried-looking man pushed past him. Akal stepped inside and asked to speak with Hugh Clancy, but to no avail. It seemed Akal had just missed him, as the editor had stepped out for a meeting. The receptionist suggested he try Mr. Clancy's home, just up the street, as he was eventually planning on going home for lunch with his visiting family. Akal set off up the street, prepared for an afternoon of waiting.

In short order, he arrived at Hugh Clancy's house. It was modest compared to some of the houses of the well-to-do Europeans in the colony. The structure was the same as usual, wooden and raised on stilts, to make the most of the breeze coming off the ocean and up the hill. The small front garden was overrun by weeds; the grass was stained purple with crushed, soggy bougainvillea petals which had fallen from the thorny vines above. The bougainvillea had taken over the garden and formed a canopy, blocking much of the light from reaching the plants below. It seemed to feel it owned the front garden and vigorously defended the house from Akal's intrusion, the dangling vines catching on Akal's turban.

He brushed them away and pushed through until he reached the shallow wooden steps leading to the verandah. Akal knocked on the front door. He expected a house girl to answer, but instead the door was opened by the young woman whose smile had spurred his bowling to new heights the day before.

"Oh . . . it's you," she said. Her clear blue eyes, fringed with thick chestnut lashes, were opened wide with surprise.

Akal merely nodded, lost for words. Up close, she was lovely. Yesterday she had been wearing a hat, but today he got the full glory of her vibrant hair, which was pulled back into a low bun and looked more auburn in the shade of the verandah, no longer reflecting the flame of the sun.

"Well, good show yesterday," she said with just a hint of a smile as Akal continued to stand mute.

"Thank you, *mem*," Akal replied, willing his frozen brain to find some words for his frozen tongue to say.

"So, a police officer," the woman said, inspecting his uniform. "That's right, I remember you were playing on the police side. Whatever it is, I swear we didn't do it!" She ended with a laugh.

"Yes, er—no, of course not, *mem*." His brain thawed just enough for him to remember his purpose for coming. "I am Sergeant Akal Singh of the Fijian Constabulary, Suva Division. I am here to see Mr. Hugh Clancy."

"Oh, Uncle Hugh is not here at the moment. He is where he always is, at the newspaper office. He said he would come back for lunch, given Aunt Mary and I are here, but knowing him he'll get caught up in some story and forget. I'm Katherine Murray, his niece," she said, stepping out onto the verandah next to Akal.

Akal hastily took a couple of steps back.

"I stopped at the *Fiji Times* office. They said he was at an appointment, but then he would come here."

"Would you like to wait for him?" she asked, her demeanour now slightly more reserved than her initial greeting. Akal wondered at this. Surely she couldn't have wanted to stand next to him? "Or you could go to the newspaper office later," she continued. "What did you need him for?"

"Mem, I have been tasked with escorting yourself and your aunt to Levuka. I wanted to introduce myself, and confirm the plans."

"Well then, you need me and Aunt Mary. Not my uncle," she said, a small frown creasing her otherwise smooth brow. "Why don't you take a seat on the verandah? It's much nicer out here than it is inside, anyway. I'll get Aunt Mary and sort out some tea and we can have a chat."

Without waiting for a response from Akal, she smiled brightly, ushered him towards a chair on the verandah, and briskly strode inside. Akal stood behind one of the seats but didn't sit. He drummed his fingers on the top of the seat back, thinking about how easily Katherine had come to stand next to him. His last encounter with a European woman had ended badly. He was wary of Katherine's friendliness, no matter how appealing it might have been.

Katherine returned, the older woman from the cricket match in tow—whom Akal now knew to be her aunt, Mary Clancy. From up close, the resemblance between the two women was even more marked, with Mary looking like the older pattern card for her niece. She was probably twenty years senior to Katherine, and everything about her seemed softer, mellower. Her face remained largely unlined but appeared calmer, compared to Katherine's eyes and mouth, which were constantly looking at something new and remarking on it. Following Akal and Mary's introductions, they all took a seat and Katherine poured tea from a battered but serviceable tin teapot into mismatched cups.

"Sergeant Singh . . ." Katherine started to say to her aunt, but paused and looked at Akal for confirmation that she had his name correct. On Akal's nod, she continued, "Sergeant

Singh will be escorting us to Levuka. Uncle Hugh insisted."
She finished with a roll of her eyes.

"Rightly so," Mary said, nodding approvingly towards
Akal. "Neither of us have been to Fiji before, Sergeant Singh.
I have spent some time in Singapore but Katherine here has
never left Australia. My brother was wise to ask for an escort.
Do you know Levuka well?"

"I have never been to Levuka, *mem*," Akal said. At Katherine's surprised look, he hastily added, "But I have travelled
out to a plantation, so I know something about getting
around Fiji."

"From what I can tell, all we need to do is get on a boat
and then find the hotel. I hardly think we need help for that,
Aunty darling," Katherine said. She flashed an arch, conspiratorial grin briefly at Akal and added, "But now I hear that
there are more exciting things going on in Levuka, so maybe
going there with a police officer will be just the thing."

"What exciting things are going on?" Mary asked her
niece with an indulgent smile.

"Apparently there are Germans roaming around Levuka.
Uncle Hugh was telling me about it when I popped into the
office this morning."

"Well, that sounds highly unlikely," said Mary, looking to
Akal expectantly.

Akal tightened his lips and gave a noncommittal head
motion, neither a nod nor a shake but somewhere in
between. He should have known that such an outlandish
rumour would not stay confidential, particularly not to people
with access to the most prominent newspaperman in Suva.

"You mean there is some substance to this strange claim?"
Mary exclaimed.

"Mem, I am afraid I can't discuss it," Akal said.

"That means yes," Katherine said, bouncing slightly in her chair.

"Well, I suppose it does," Mary conceded. "Still, I maintain that it is a tall tale."

"We will just have to find out! First one to find the Germans wins a prize!" exclaimed Katherine.

"Oh, no, mem," Akal said with a forced laugh. "Nothing to worry about. It will all be safe. I will just accompany you to Levuka for some sightseeing and wait until you are ready to return, then escort you back." He prayed that the inspector-general had not told Hugh Clancy of Akal's side task to go hunting for Germans.

"Of course not, Sergeant Singh," Mary soothed. "My niece is a little excitable, but she isn't actually that foolish. We will be doing some sightseeing as you say . . ." She hesitated before continuing in a rush. "But our main reason for going to Levuka is to sort out Hugh's house. He moved to Suva years ago, but didn't ever close up his Levuka house or arrange for his belongings to be sent over. There is barely anything in this house. We have just enough cutlery for the three of us, let alone somewhere to sit. So that is our priority."

"And if we come across some Germans in the course of our wanders, we will steer clear and come straight to you with the information," Katherine said, a little too earnestly for Akal's comfort.

Before Akal could reinforce his objections to any suggestion of even noticing Germans in Levuka, there was a clomping of shoes up the stairs to the verandah.

"Oh, hello, Uncle Hugh," Katherine said, jumping up to

give her uncle her chair. "This is Sergeant Singh. He is taking us to Levuka to look for the Germans. Isn't it wonderful?"

"No, no, there will be no looking for Germans!" Akal burst out, sitting bolt upright in his seat. All three of the Europeans laughed, Katherine and her uncle loudly, Mary with a little more restraint.

"I am sorry, Sergeant Singh. My niece and my brother have a wicked sense of humour," Mary said, giving him the sympathetic, long-suffering smile of the only adult in the room.

"I promise we will be no trouble," Katherine said.

"Humph," snorted her uncle. "I wouldn't believe her if I was you, Sergeant Singh. I expect you will have your hands full."

THEY ALL REMAINED on the verandah for a few more minutes as Akal made arrangements to meet the women at the wharf in the morning for the ferry ride to Levuka. The ladies disappeared inside to organise lunch, but Mr. Clancy remained on the verandah. Once Katherine and Mary went, the smile fell from the older man's face. Uneasy, Akal stood to take his leave, but was cut off by Mr. Clancy sternly saying, "Stay a moment. I have some questions for you."

Akal nodded, but remained standing. Mr. Clancy remained seated, crossed his arms, and considered Akal through narrowed eyes.

"I was surprised that your inspector-general agreed to provide an escort for Mary and Katherine. And when I found out he was sending you, I wondered what Jonathon was up to. You realise that I hear all the stories about new people in the colony. So I know about your conduct in Hong Kong."

Akal could feel a flush climbing up from his uniform collar towards his turban, burning hotter as he noticed Mr. Clancy noting it.

"At least you have the sense to be embarrassed. Thurstrom assures me that you have learnt your lesson but I am concerned. Katherine is my only niece. She is a beautiful girl. Can I trust you with her?"

"Sir, I am not sure what you have heard," Akal responded, staring at the ground, his voice low and quiet.

Hugh Clancy's nostrils flared and he looked at Akal with a tilt to his head. Akal was reminded of a dog picking up an intriguing scent. "Why don't you tell me the story?" Mr. Clancy asked.

Akal paused for a moment, slowly resuming his seat as he scrambled to order his thoughts. He had told the story to only one other person in Fiji—Dr. Holmes, who had already felt like a friend. How much should he tell this newspaperman?

"I will not publish anything you tell me. I need to know for my niece's sake," Mr. Clancy said, as though he had read Akal's mind.

Akal nodded, and after a few more moments of silence, he started to speak.

"Two years ago, I was a sergeant in the Royal Hong Kong Police Force. One day while I was having lunch, I met a *memsahib* named Emily at the botanical gardens. I thought it was a random meeting, but I learnt later that she had made sure to bump into me.

"She was born in India and was on her way to England with her father for the first time. Her father was always busy, and she wasn't allowed to leave the hotel by herself. She was lonely, bored, and missing the food from home, from India. So she would sneak out to the botanical gardens, which were right next to her hotel. I met her there a few times and brought her some Indian snacks. I was just trying to be kind to a homesick girl.

"We would talk often—I thought she was just interested in hearing about the excitement of the policing world, so I told her about the cases I was working on. What I didn't know was that she was in a relationship with a man who had gotten her involved in a burglary ring. I knew about the vulnerable houses of wealthy families in Hong Kong, and I was inadvertently passing this information on to the burglary ring.

"When I realised what was happening, I reported it to my inspector-general, and coordinated an operation to give them false information and catch them. But the damage to my career was already done. My inspector-general intervened, so I was sent here rather than being dismissed in disgrace.

"I realise now that I shouldn't have spoken with her at all, not even once. It has ruined my life. It would have hurt my career even if there was no burglary ring involved, if I had only been discovered talking to her. I will not make the same mistake again."

When he dared to look up, Mr. Clancy's narrowed eyes had cleared and he nodded once at Akal.

"Sir, I promise I will keep the *memsahibs* safe. And I promise, I will only speak with them when necessary," Akal said earnestly, emboldened by the gesture of approval.

Mr. Clancy snorted. "Good luck with that. They'll keep pestering you. Talk to them, otherwise you will upset them. Just maintain a respectful distance. I will tell Mary about your story, so she can keep an eye on things, but I won't tell Katherine. She is young and naive and she will rail against the idea that your friendship with this young woman in Hong Kong is against the social order."

Akal gave a noncommittal nod, head moving in a figure eight, privately resolving to speak with the women as little as possible, regardless. He glanced towards the verandah steps, but once again, before he could take his leave, Mr. Clancy cut him off.

"Not so fast, Sergeant Singh. You didn't think you would get away without talking to me about these Germans, did you?"

"Sir, I don't know anything," Akal replied with a helpless shrug.

"It is a bit of a coincidence that there is a report of Germans in Levuka and now you are going to Levuka, isn't it?"

"Sir, there is a very young police officer holding the fort in Levuka until somebody more senior can be deployed. I wonder if somebody is playing a trick on a junior officer who doesn't know better. Do you truly believe that there could be Germans there?"

"You could be right," Hugh Clancy said grudgingly. "It does seem like a wild tale invented by somebody who had too much *yaqona.*"

TAVITI'S LAUGHTER ROARED through the room. He was doubled over, clutching his stomach with one arm, beating his other hand on the counter. Akal stood with his hands on his hips, shaking his head in disgust at his friend's reaction to his latest assignment and his first introduction to the ladies he was escorting. Luckily, the other police officers had exhausted their stories about the cricket match and had dispersed to their various duties, sparing Akal at least that humiliation.

"Oh, Akal, that's too funny, man, too funny," Taviti said when he finally started to regain his composure.

"I'm glad you are enjoying this," Akal said sourly.

"I tell you what, I'll help you out," Taviti said with a magnanimous nod. "I'll come with you. Help you with the ladies. And the Germans. And the third-class constable. I am a first-class constable myself. I'm sure I have a lot to teach him."

Akal snorted. "And you think the inspector-general will let you out from behind the desk? Or your uncle, the oh-so-important chief?"

"Well, it's my uncle I will be going to visit. You are going to Levuka, yes? My uncle is the chief of the village nearby. I'll tell the inspector-general that I'm going to visit my uncle. I am overdue for a visit. I'll make it part of my duty to my family. He can't object," Taviti said, an unfamiliar thread of steel in the last statement.

"Well, that's excellent," Akal said, breaking out in a grin. Instead of a despised duty to be a nursemaid to two European women and a wild goose chase after phantom Germans, maybe this would turn out to be an adventure with his friend.

Levuka Day by Day

(From Our Own Correspondent)

The cutter *Winifred* arrived from Lakeba during the week. On her voyage from that port to Levuka the vessel experienced bad weather near Vatuvara. She shipped two particularly heavy seas which washed two of the native crew and sixteen bags of copra overboard. The captain threw lifebuoys to the men, who were rescued. The cutter's bulwarks were somewhat damaged by the seas, portions of them being smashed in.

CHAPTER 2

THE FOLLOWING MORNING, IN the soft dawn light, Akal made his way from the police barracks through Suva town to Queen's Wharf. Most of Suva was still asleep, even the ubiquitous stray dogs, and the walk through town was much more peaceful than it would be in a couple of hours. Instead of dodging cyclists, horses and carts, and the occasional motor vehicle juddering down the street leaving clouds of dust in its wake, Akal was able to pay attention to the town around him.

On the ground floor, the storefronts were all closed up, curtains drawn and lights off. Some of the windows on the upper floors, where the proprietors lived above their stores, glowed softly, and Akal could hear the private sounds of households stirring. He paused under the lush canopy of the *ivi* tree at the Triangle, the angular convergence of Scott Street and Renwick Road. This was where all of Suva came to meet, sheltering in the cool shade of the majestic old tree. Akal enjoyed his last moment of solitude. From here he could already hear the clamour of humanity at the nearby wharf.

Jutting out into Suva Harbor, Queen's Wharf was sturdily constructed of thick planks of wood, with metal train tracks for loading the bigger ships. It was the main wharf for Suva and was always busy. So busy, in fact, that a newer wharf, King's Wharf, was being built farther out of Suva to accommodate the needs of the growing town.

This morning, a small crowd was gathered, waiting to load goods and passengers onto the ship to Levuka. The SS *Amra* was a steamer that did a regular rotation through the islands of Fiji, following a set route that took it from Suva to Levuka, through a number of other ports, and back again in eleven days. Akal had seen the schedule on the front page of the *Fiji Times* every day but had never been on the ship until now.

The ladies were easy to spot, an elegant contrast to the largely working-class crowd. They were wearing simple but well-made cotton blouses tucked into long skirts and straw hats tied under their chins with ribbons. They each had a small solid suitcase at their feet, which were clad in sensible boots. A middle-aged Fijian man hovered nearby, clutching a mangled cloth hat in his ink-stained hands. Katherine was scanning the crowd with interest, and waved when she spotted Akal. He nodded in return, and continued to weave his way towards them, his slight build allowing him to slip easily through the jostling crowd.

"Good morning," Akal greeted them.

"*Bula*," the ladies chorused.

"It's the only word we've learnt in the Fijian language," Katherine added. "Isn't it cheerful?"

"Shall we board?" Mary asked, turning towards the ship, its chimneys issuing large volumes of steam into the cloudless sky.

"We have one more joining us," Akal replied. "Constable

Taviti Tukana is visiting family on Ovalau, so he will be traveling with us. He should be here soon."

"Oh, excellent, somebody else to help us on our hunt," Katherine quipped, a grin revealing a dimple in her right cheek. Akal crooked an eyebrow at her but refused to fall for her jokes again. She laughed anyway.

With her thanks, Mary released the Fijian man to return to his regular duties as one of Hugh Clancy's newspaper delivery men. He left with some relief. Akal wondered what had made him so nervous. He thought it was likely to be Katherine's presence making the man flee, since that was why Akal's heart was currently pounding and his palms were damp against his uniform trousers.

As they waited for Taviti, the ladies looked around at the hustle and bustle of the busy wharf, seeming a bit braver now that Akal had arrived. It had seemed to Akal when he had first spotted Katherine and Mary that the workers had been intrigued by the interlopers in their midst, but had been keeping a respectful distance. Now that a tall, turbaned policeman was with them, even the curious glances had stopped. Luckily for Akal, Katherine's interest in the goings-on around them kept her from teasing him any further.

When Taviti arrived a few minutes later, the wharf had become busier and Akal saw he would have to shoulder his way through the mess of humanity to reach them. This wasn't particularly difficult for Taviti, given he was head and shoulders above most of the rest of the throng, who gave way to his bulk with alacrity.

"Is that Constable Tukana?" Katherine asked Akal, in a low speculative tone.

"Yes, *mem*," Akal replied reprovingly.

"He is quite imposing, isn't he?" she asked with a sly smile. Akal didn't respond.

When Taviti reached them, Akal made the introductions stiffly and they moved to board the ship. Akal and Taviti both automatically reached for Katherine's suitcase, but Akal diverted at the last moment to pick up Mary's bag instead, in what he hoped was a smooth and seamless shift in direction. Taviti gave Akal a bland, innocent look and Akal struggled to keep the scowl off his face as the women looked on.

Once they had boarded, the ticket collector directed them below deck to the dining and luggage rooms. Akal and Taviti went to stow the luggage while the ladies found a table.

"So, that's Katherine," Taviti said as they handed the bags to a porter and accepted a baggage ticket.

"Yes. That is Miss Murray," Akal replied sternly. "Must I remind you that you are a married man?"

"I'm just curious," Taviti protested. His next statement belied the innocence of the first. "She seems like a lively girl."

"You will not find out how lively she is. Come on, man," Akal groaned. "I have to protect this girl. Even from you."

"Don't worry, my friend, I won't do anything that you can be blamed for."

Taviti's grin stretched from ear to ear, with every single one of his gloriously large teeth on display. Akal was not reassured.

TAVITI ENTERED THE dining room first, having to both duck and go in sideways to fit through the door. Akal merely had to duck, his turban still barely clearing the low doorway. As soon as he crossed the threshold, Akal could feel the room close in on him, and he paused for a moment to take a deep breath.

On the journey from India to Hong Kong, it had taken him some time to become accustomed to being below deck, and he had happily spent as much time as possible on the ship's surface, gulping in the fresh air. On the journey from Hong Kong to Fiji, however, he had never become accustomed to it, but had stayed in his berth most of the time anyway, nausea and shame his constant companions.

Akal scanned the room, which was half full, with the other passengers consisting of a few men in suits and two families. Katherine and her aunt had found a table big enough for four by the window and were sitting on one side. Akal and Taviti weaved their way between the tables, the gentle rocking of the ship easily adjusted for. The Pacific Ocean was thus far living up to its name.

"*Mem*, the luggage is safely stowed away, and we have your luggage tags. Constable Tukana and I will step outside and leave you to enjoy your journey. We will find you before we arrive into Levuka in a few hours," Akal said to Mary.

Katherine had started shaking her head halfway through Akal's pronouncement and barely let him finish before bursting out, "Certainly not. You must sit with us. I wanted to ask Constable Tukana about Levuka."

"It would not be appropriate, *mem*," Akal protested.

"Nonsense. Who will even notice?" she argued.

"Perhaps we could sit at another table so we can be nearby if you have a question?" Akal said, with the sinking feeling that he was going to lose this battle.

"Oh, no, I would not feel safe if you sat at another table.

That is the whole reason you are here, isn't it, to save us from all these ruffians roaming about," she concluded with an eye roll.

All four of them looked around the room, from the children with their faces pressed up against the glass of the portholes to the businessmen reading their newspapers. Taviti's shoulders were shaking with suppressed mirth, while Akal's lips tightened.

"Please do accompany us," Mary said, adding her gentle encouragement to Katherine's insistent glare. "I would also like to hear more about Constable Tukana's home, and to ask him about our journey." She gestured towards the vacant chairs, the languid grace of her wrist disarming Akal.

He sat reluctantly, taking the seat nearest the window, with the hopes that looking at the ocean would mitigate against the nausea. As the women asked Taviti their questions, Akal gazed out to the gentle waves rippling away endlessly and let the chatter flow over him.

Once Akal's stomach had more or less settled, he tuned back into the conversation. Taviti was describing the route the ship was taking.

"We will go around one dangerous spot—Nasilai Reef. There have been a few shipwrecks there. A coolie ship called *Syria* came to grief and a lot of Indians drowned. I think close to sixty of them. But don't worry! There is a beacon there now, and this is the regular route and a clear day. We will be safe."

While everyone was focused on Taviti's story, Akal surrendered to the irresistible pull that Katherine seemed to have for him. She was leaning forward, her hands clasped in front of her on the table, her eyes bright as she listened to

Taviti. The light in her eyes dimmed when she heard about the loss of life, but she remained absorbed in the story. She was sitting opposite Akal, with the sunlight setting alight her hair, pulled back into a sensible bun. With her face still for the first time since he had met her, Akal noticed the smattering of faint freckles colouring Katherine's cheeks.

His gaze dropped down to the graceful but prominent sweep of her jaw, and up to her mouth, where he lingered for longer than he should have. Her lips curved up and when he glanced up again, she was looking out of the corners of her eyes at him. Akal flushed and snapped his gaze to Taviti who was too wrapped up in his story to have noticed Akal's momentary lapse. When Akal looked back at her a moment later, Katherine was still smiling, a quiet happy smile, but had refocused on Taviti. Akal felt a sudden constriction, and simultaneously a thrill tripping through his chest, making it hard to breathe. She was far, far out of his reach and he would keep his distance. But that smile was worth a bit of embarrassment. With half his mind off in a fantasy, Akal partially tuned back into Taviti's story.

"Once we pass Nasilai, we go on a direct course to Levuka," Taviti continued, his pleasure in introducing them to his country evident in the warm timbre of his voice. "We will pass one bigger island, Moturiki, on our way, and as we arrive into Levuka, you will be able to see Wakaya Island in the distance. I will point them out to you as we go along."

The talk then turned to why Katherine and her aunt were in Fiji. Taviti asked the questions but Akal was equally curious. Katherine, with what Akal was coming to recognise as her usual exuberance, had no qualms about telling them her

story: "I am here because my parents didn't know what to do
with me anymore. I want to be a journalist, you see, and they
want me to get married."

A *journalist*, Akal thought with some shock. A woman as
a journalist? What was Australia like that the women were
allowed to do such things? He privately agreed with her parents; marriage was the much better option.

"They even had picked a husband for me," Katherine
continued. "Somebody 'appropriate.' One of the young
politicians in my father's party. I'd hardly spent any time
with him before he proposed. I turned him down flat. I said
I wouldn't marry anybody until I'd published five articles."

At this, even Taviti looked a little scandalised. "What did
your parents do?" he asked in a hushed tone.

Katherine shrugged. "What could they do? Lock me up
at home?"

Both Akal and Taviti nodded. Katherine laughed heartily, her peals of laughter trailing off as she realised they
were being serious, at which point her aunt started to laugh
instead.

"As I've told you before, my dear, I know you think your
parents are strict, but you have far more freedom than most
girls," Mary said.

"Anyway," Katherine continued, shaking off her momentary discomfort. "I was having no luck with the newspapers
in Sydney. The most I could get was a job as a typist. I
refused to give up. So I struck a deal with my parents: they
send me to Uncle Hugh for a year to be a journalist, and
then I'll come home and get married. I'll even consider the
men they think are appropriate."

"And why are you here, *mem*?" Akal asked Mary, hoping

to divert the conversation in a different direction before Katherine could reveal any other outrageous details of her life.

"I have never been to Fiji, so I was thrilled to join Katherine. Her parents are always busy with her father's political career, so they couldn't accompany her, but they couldn't send her on her own. Hugh is always so busy. In any case, he has no idea what is appropriate for a young woman to do, so he wouldn't restrain her at all. Whereas I know what is appropriate, so I can raise an eyebrow when she does things she ought not. It won't stop her, of course, but at least it will give her pause and she won't be able to protest that she simply didn't know she shouldn't do it," Mary said with a twinkle in her eye.

Akal couldn't help but return her smile. He very much liked this kind, sensible, quietly humorous lady.

"A journalist!" Taviti marvelled, taking them back to the conversation Akal had been trying to avoid. "Mr. Clancy is allowing you to write for the newspaper?"

"Oh, of course not," huffed Katherine. "Not really. He wants me to write for the Ladies Column. Recipes and cleaning tips. Maybe, if I'm really good and patient, I might be allowed to cover a party or a wedding. What a privilege that would be."

"What would you like to report on?" Akal asked, then inwardly cursed himself. He had resolved not to engage with either of the women beyond what was necessary, but here he was asking Katherine about her intentions. The question had slipped out unconsciously because, to Akal, those seemed like eminently sensible topics for a young woman to report on, if she was to be allowed to report on anything.

That sentiment must have been evident in his tone, as Katherine proceeded to glare at him.

"Actual news, Sergeant Singh. Things that affect the colony. Politics. Crime. Events that people need to know about. Not a recipe for sponge cake or a description of lace."

"Now, Katherine," Mary said with a hint of reproachment. "Even if your uncle is the editor, you still have to prove yourself. You need to start somewhere. Do what your Uncle Hugh asks, do it well, and keep spending time with him. Hugh is very focused on the newspaper. If you show that you can write, that you are curious and determined, he will give you a chance to do more. He won't think about your mother, he will only think about what is best for the newspaper."

Katherine nodded, a look of resignation rearranging her face uncomfortably, as though she didn't quite know *how* to be resigned. It seemed to Akal that this conversation was following a well-worn route for the two women.

"Why don't you do some local recipes?" Taviti suggested. "Maybe some *kokoda*? Give the European ladies a true taste of Fiji."

"Oh, that's a wonderful idea!" exclaimed Katherine. "Don't you think so, Aunt Mary? Nobody needs another recipe for sponge cake." Without giving her aunt a chance to respond, she turned back to Taviti and pulled out a notebook and pen from the small bag beside her. "What is *kokoda*?"

Taviti leaned forward, his eyes gleaming. Akal couldn't tell if it was pride in his cuisine that lit his face up, or the mischief of giving Katherine a recipe that would make her uncle's face go red.

"First step, you go fishing. Catch some *walu*. It is the best fish for *kokoda*, nice white, firm fish. You cut it up into small, small chunks, then cover it in lemon juice. Add some chilli and onion. Then eat."

"But . . . you haven't cooked the fish," Mary said, her horror perfectly reflecting Akal's sentiments.

"It sort of cooks," Taviti responded earnestly. "In the lemon juice."

Mary shuddered. "I think I'd prefer it if it was actually cooked. On a stove."

"Oh, this is exactly what I need. I can't wait to see Uncle Hugh's face," Katherine said, clapping in delight. Her aunt merely looked at her with a reproving but amused expression. With a defiant toss of her head, Katherine declared, "I'd be doing exactly what he asked, so he won't be able to object."

"I think you will find he is perfectly able to object," replied Mary wryly.

"Probably, but what fun it will be anyway," Katherine said, not repressed in the slightest by her aunt's cautions.

"So this is what takes you to Levuka? On the hunt for a recipe to upset your uncle with?" Taviti asked with his trademark booming laugh. Akal chuckled, unable to keep a straight face when Taviti laughed. This was generally how everyone responded to Taviti's laughter, but the two women seemed to instantly sober at this question.

"No, we are going sightseeing," Katherine replied, while Mary simultaneously said, "No, we are closing up Hugh's Levuka house."

The women gave each other urgent looks, and Akal and Taviti exchanged puzzled ones. These were the same reasons that Mary had given Akal yesterday. What had thrown the ladies so much that they gave such a garbled response?

Katherine stood abruptly. In her haste she hadn't accounted for the movement of the ship, and had to hold on to the table while she adjusted to the sway.

"I'd like to take a turn about the deck," she said, looking at her aunt.

"Yes, that's an excellent idea," Mary said, finding her way out of her seat also.

As a method of shutting down this line of conversation, it was quite effective, if suspicious.

"We will escort you above," Akal said politely, though he was bemused at this sudden change of plans.

It was too noisy above deck to talk easily. Akal and Taviti trailed the two ladies at a discreet distance as they took a brief promenade about the deck. They all paused for a moment as Taviti gave them the names of the islands they were passing, and Akal braced his arms against the railing, the thrumming vibration of the steamship reverberating through his forearms.

There was no uniformity to the expanse of water; it was a patchwork of different shades, from the usual brilliant azure to darker patches which made him uneasy. Despite the serene surface, it seemed as though those darker patches were sucking the soul of the ocean into themselves, slowly devouring everything around them. The island in the distance, the one they were powering towards, was ringed by a light blue strip, with waves frothing white against it.

"That's Ovalau, the island I grew up on," Taviti said. "You can see the reef there, it forms a natural barrier to the waves. And you can see the gap which we will go through. Once we get past that reef, the ocean is very calm. It is one of the reasons why Levuka became the original capital. It was a good natural port."

"It is beautiful. What an incredible place to grow up," Katherine said, her smile brilliant as she pulled back an errant lock of hair which had escaped her bun to blow in the wind. Their time in the sun seemed to have restored the two women to their usual selves.

The rest of the journey passed pleasantly, with Taviti describing traditional Fijian life in such a romantic way that even Akal's imagination was captured by it. It left him little time to wonder what exactly the two women were hiding about their true objective in visiting Levuka.

THE SHIP APPROACHED the wharf at Levuka, confusingly also named Queen's Wharf, at noon, giving Akal, Katherine, and Mary their first glimpse of the weathered old town. Taviti pointed out landmarks to the women, Akal listening with half an ear, preferring to make his own observations. The town was nestled between a sheltered harbour at the front and a ring of tree-covered cliffs behind, curving around and to the sides to form an amphitheatre around the town. A row of stores, with their signage faded lined the waterfront, with no stirrings of life. Akal's first impression of Levuka was of a town that had lost its way, fading into obscurity. When the capital of the colony had moved to Suva some thirty years ago, so had many of the residents and so, it seemed to Akal, had the heart of the place.

The waterfront was called Beach Street, though it was scarcely a beach—just the ocean abruptly stopping when it reached Levuka. A stone sea wall bounded the land. There was none of the soft white sand Akal had seen at other Fijian beaches, no clusters of coconut palms providing shelter. Housing scattered out behind the row of stores, clustered at the bottom of the hill, becoming more sparse until finally it became too steep and then the jungle took over, climbing up the cliff.

All of the activity in Levuka was focused on the wharf. Labourers stood ready to unload the goods that were coming in from Suva and load more goods to go on to the remaining stops on the route or beyond, to be exported overseas. One European man was waiting on the wharf for his family, the children waving furiously at him through the ship's rails as soon as they saw him.

The party disembarked onto the wharf and quickly cleared the crowd, with Akal and Taviti taking charge of the women's bags as well as their own. Katherine and her aunt were staying at the Royal Hotel, just slightly set back from the waterfront, a short walk from the wharf. As they walked, Taviti provided a running commentary on all the buildings they were passing.

"Here is the original Morris Hedstrom, the first store in Fiji. And over there, the first post office."

"A town of firsts," Mary quipped.

"Yes," Taviti responded with uncharacteristic gravity. "Everything is moving to Suva now, but the firsts all happened here."

Before long, they arrived at the hotel, which had been rebuilt a couple of years previously following a fire. The two-story building had a wide verandah on the upper floor, with a latticework railing that gave the hotel an elegant touch.

The preponderance of dark timber inside made the lobby

gloomy, but the smartly dressed European man behind the polished wooden counter was anything but. He greeted the ladies by name and seemed thrilled with his new guests. His face brightened even further when he saw Taviti and he waved cheerily to him, but his eyes slid over Akal with no apparent interest.

Once the ladies had checked in, they disappeared upstairs to their rooms, followed by the hotel porter carrying their bags. Taviti handed his and Akal's bags over to the hotel manager to hold onto while they took care of things in Levuka; Taviti was going to stay at his family's home in the village, while Akal would check with the local constable to find out where he would be quartered.

They all reconvened in the hotel's dining room for a restorative cup of tea. Akal looked around the room, empty other than their party. The dark wooden chairs and tables were solid and well upholstered, in keeping with the newly built hotel. But the lack of patrons made it seem neglected regardless, the stillness in the room making it possible to observe the dust motes in the sunlight, which was slanting through the blinds of the window nearby. Akal was lost in a reverie until the clink of a teacup being placed in its saucer brought him back to the assembled company. This intermingling of an Indian man, a Fijian man, and two European ladies would never have happened in Suva, but here in this strange, lonely town, it seemed natural.

"What is first, sightseeing or clearing Mr. Clancy's house?" Taviti asked the women, curiosity evident on his face.

"The house this afternoon," Mary answered. "We need to see how big the job is before we can really make a plan."

"What will you be doing?" Katherine asked Akal.

"I must check in with the constable who is stationed here," Akal replied. "Taviti will join me, then go and visit his uncle and the rest of his family in the village."

"Oh, are you going to find out about the Germans?" Katherine asked eagerly. "I'll come with you."

"No, *mem*, this is not possible," Akal said, shaking his head vigorously. "It will not be safe."

"Why not? I'll just come and observe. What possible harm could come to me at the police station?"

Before Akal could come up with a reason Katherine might actually accept, Mary intervened. "Sergeant Singh, could you please help us find Hugh's house? Perhaps the local constable could help? We could accompany you to the police station, and then you could escort us to the house and leave us there. And then," she said, fixing a stern gaze on her niece, "we will leave you to do your job without having to worry about us."

Akal gave the older woman a grateful look as Katherine conceded with a sigh. "Fine. But I want to know all about it when you come back," she insisted.

"I will tell you everything I can," Akal promised, hoping she didn't notice the caveat in the statement. From Katherine's narrowed eyes, it was evident that she did.

THE LEVUKA POLICE station was a single-story wooden building. It was neat and well maintained, with a green lawn of perfectly mowed grass, and looked like nothing more than a very small home. It was so unimposing in its stature that Akal kept looking around for the rest of it.

"Is this it?" he asked Taviti.

"Oh, no, the cells are over there," Taviti replied, gesturing towards what looked like a row of three sheds a few yards away. Noticing Akal's puzzled look, Taviti elaborated, "Not much happens here anymore. Levuka isn't the wild town it used to be before the British took over."

"It is so . . . charming," Katherine said with a little crinkle in her nose. "Not at all how I thought a police station would look."

"Believe me, the Suva police station is much less charm, ing," Akal said wryly, thinking of the unlovely concrete building where he spent most of his days.

Leaving the ladies on a shaded bench outside the front door of the station, Akal and Taviti crowded inside. They found a young man in uniform behind the desk, concentrat, ing fiercely on the paperwork in front of him. He was at most eighteen years old; the smattering of pimples glowing red across his dark forehead and nose betrayed his age. He seemed slight, short, diminutive, hunched behind the desk. Akal cleared his throat and the young man jumped to his feet, upsetting his chair in the process.

"Hello . . . sir—sirs," he stammered, as he disappeared behind the desk to pick up his chair.

"Constable Kumar?" Akal asked. He thought back to his early days in the Hong Kong police force and couldn't remember ever being quite as anxious as the young man in front of him. It didn't bode well for his mentoring efforts.

"Yes, sir, that's me, I'm Constable Raj Kumar," the young man replied, coming out from behind the desk and nodding continuously.

"I am Sergeant Akal Singh and this is Constable Taviti Tukana. We are here with Miss Mary Clancy and her niece Katherine, who are waiting outside."

"Yes, sir. I received a message through the pigeon post that you were coming."

"The ladies are here to organise things at Hugh Clancy's house. Do you know where it is? We need to escort them there."

"Yes, yes, of course," Constable Kumar said. "I know where it is. I can take you there."

"More importantly, I hear there are Germans around here somewhere," Taviti said with a huge smile. In Akal's experience, Taviti's grins, like his laughs, were hard to resist, and most people reciprocated without thinking about it. But Taviti was not having his usual effect today. Constable Kumar was already agitated, and at the mention of Germans, his face crumpled.

"I'm so glad you are here. I did not know what to do," he said, the last sentence almost a wail.

"All right, calm down," Akal admonished. "We are here now, we will help. Just tell us what has happened."

The young policeman nodded and took a deep breath, visibly calming himself. "A few days ago, one of the local shopkeepers, Mr. Sanjay Lal, came in and made the report. He said that a group of five European men had come into the store and were buying lots of supplies. Only one of them speaks English and with a funny accent, definitely not a Britisher."

"There are plenty of Europeans who aren't Britishers. It doesn't mean they are Germans!" Akal exclaimed. In Hong Kong, with its position as a central port, he had come across all flavours of European: French, Portuguese, Spanish, and more.

"I said that to Mr. Lal. But he also pointed out that they are not staying in town. Mr. Lal said that the one who spoke

English pretended not to understand when he asked where they are staying. That does seem suspicious, doesn't it?" Kumar asked anxiously.

"It does rather. There may be a perfectly good explanation. Perhaps he really did not understand. Still, it is worth following up. They might not be Germans invading Fiji as part of the war effort," Akal said with a smirk, "but they sound like they are up to something."

"Excellent," Taviti said, rubbing his hands. "Shall I tell Katherine we are hunting Germans after all?"

The reactions across the room varied. Constable Kumar looked with confusion between the two superior officers who had appeared in his police station but didn't seem to take police matters very seriously, Taviti was delighted at the mischief, and Akal simply groaned. He was less concerned about the supposed Germans and more concerned about how he was going to keep the headstrong women safe—and his head off the inspector-general's chopping block.

THE GROUP LEFT the police station, Constable Kumar in the lead. He turned left on the dirt road outside the station to head inland. Akal walked with him, planning to have a quiet word with the young man about his real reason for being in Levuka, while Taviti kept the ladies occupied behind them. Before he got a chance, he heard Katherine speaking behind them, and turned to see her moving in the wrong direction.

"What is that building?" she asked. She had come to a stop in front of a concrete building that stood out with its Roman architecture, quite a contrast from the wooden bungalows all around it. The Romanesque feel was enhanced by a row of columns before the doorway and a strange symbol on the triangular pediment above the columns.

"That looks like a Freemasons symbol," Mary replied with a puzzled look. "Do the Freemasons have a lodge here?"

Constable Kumar nodded, hanging back from the rest of the party as they approached the building. "Nobody knows what happens in there. They say there are secret tunnels to the Royal Hotel."

"Oh, that is where we are staying!" Katherine exclaimed, clapping gleefully. "I'll definitely be popping down to the basement to look for secret tunnels. Wouldn't that make a great story for the newspaper, Aunt Mary?"

Mary chuckled and shook her head. Akal hoped fervently that this would keep Katherine sufficiently occupied that she would stop concerning herself with the question of whether there were Germans roaming about Levuka.

Curiosity satisfied, they returned to the route that Constable Kumar had been taking. Akal took his chance to speak with him, hoping there wouldn't be any more diversions, and said, voice somewhat lowered, "Inspector-General Thurstrom has asked me to temporarily step in as your senior officer."

Constable Kumar jerked to a stop and stared at Akal, hope and disbelief warring in his eyes. His expression told Akal that the inspector-general had left this information out of his message to the inexperienced constable.

"You will be staying here? In Levuka?"

"Not permanently. I understand a European officer will be arriving from Australia to take over from the previous one, so I will just help you while I am here in Levuka."

Tension drained from Constable Kumar in a long exhale.

"Thank you, Sergeant Singh. I am very glad to have you here, even if just for a while."

"We will talk more about how to go on after we drop the *memsahibs* to the house," Akal said, giving the young man a chance to recover his equilibrium. They kept walking, Constable Kumar sighing as though he had been holding his breath for some time.

A few yards on, the hush of the town was broken by the sound of childish voices reciting the times tables. It was only the second evidence of activity Akal had witnessed in Levuka. What did people do in this sleepy town, Akal wondered.

From behind them, Akal heard Taviti tell the women, "And here is the first public school in Fiji. This is where I went to school."

The school in question was a substantial two-story wooden building set into the foot of the hill, with the cliffs behind it and a lush green lawn surrounding it. The most striking thing about the schoolhouse was a tower built into the middle of the building at the front. The upper floor was graced with verandahs on either side of the tower, with iron lacework fringing the edge of the roof. It seemed a beautiful place to learn. Akal wondered if Taviti had been happy to sit inside and recite his times tables in this lovely building, or if even then he had been a restless child, looking wistfully out the window, wishing he was running outside instead.

They continued their journey through town, the slope of the road growing steeper as they went. A short way up the hill, Constable Kumar stopped in front of a large house. It was the usual wooden bungalow, its wide verandah facing the ocean. The front stilts of the house were long and the back stilts very short, giving the impression that the house had been built into the hill.

Constable Kumar swung open the crisply white wooden fence and started down the path to the front steps. The front garden was immaculate, the edges of the path ruthlessly trimmed, all the garden beds carefully laid out. Akal wondered that this vacant house was being cared for so diligently, when the house in Suva that Mr. Clancy actually lived in was falling down around his ears.

A young Indian man appeared from around the corner of the house, carrying a hoe. He started and gave an inarticulate shout when he saw them. Constable Kumar waved at him and called out "Samir." He seemed to calm when he recognised Constable Kumar and waved back with a brilliant smile.

The front door opened and an older Indian woman stepped onto the verandah, wiping her hands on a tea towel and looking around anxiously until she saw the young man was safe. Only then did she greet Constable Kumar.

"*Namaste*, Aunty *ji*," Constable Kumar said, running up the steps to the older lady.

"*Namaste, beta*," she responded. Continuing in Hindi, she asked, "Who are these people?"

"These two *memsahibs* are relatives of Clancy *sahib*. And the two police officers have come from Suva. They are here to help me look for the Germans, you know, the ones that Sanjay Lal reported."

The woman seemed uninterested in the police officers, but warily eyed Katherine and Mary, who responded by smiling encouragingly.

"Why are they here?" she asked, nodding at the two European women with a weak smile.

Constable Kumar looked confused, seeming to misunderstand her question, and at this point Akal stepped in, joining Kumar on the verandah.

"*Namaste*, Aunty *ji*," he said, echoing Kumar's greeting. "I am Sergeant Akal Singh of the Fijian Constabulary, Suva Division. This is Miss Mary Clancy and her niece Katherine." Each of the women grew alert and waved when their names were mentioned, the only words they understood in the exchange. When Akal explained their purpose in coming to Levuka, the older lady's face fell.

"*Acha, acha, koee baat nahin*, never mind. It had to happen someday. I don't know what will happen to me and my son when we lose this job. He is a bit slow, you see. The farmers won't give him work."

Seeing the distress on the housekeeper's face, Mary had come up the verandah steps also.

"Is everything all right, Sergeant Singh?" she asked.

"Yes, it seems this is the housekeeper and her son, who look after the house and gardens," Akal said, looking to Constable Kumar for confirmation, disapprobation at Constable Kumar's handling of the introductions evident on his face. On Constable Kumar's sheepish nod, Akal continued, "She is a little upset they will lose their jobs when the house is closed up for good."

"Oh, please reassure her that Hugh will make sure she is taken care of. I will make sure he does. It is obvious what a good job they have been doing."

As Akal relayed the message, the housekeeper's anxiety faded away, and she clasped her hands together and bowed her head to Mary. "Thank you, *mem*," she said in halting English. "I help you." She gestured towards the house.

"Oh, that would be wonderful. I won't know where anything is, so having somebody who's familiar with the house would be so helpful."

The housekeeper's eyes had grown wide at this onslaught of words, so Akal translated. After some back and forth, he established that the housekeeper had enough English that they could get by with some patience and perseverance. The housekeeper agreed that she and her son would escort the ladies back to the hotel before sunset, so Akal was satisfied that he had executed his chaperone duties for the moment. With some baleful glares from Katherine, who would clearly rather be joining them than sorting out cutlery and crockery, the three police officers departed to hunt for Germans.

UNLIKE THE REST of the Levuka businesses, Sanjay Lal's store was somewhat out of town. Constable Kumar, Taviti, and Akal walked north, back along Beach Street, past the hotel, and out of Levuka, along the curving coastline. Farther along the shore, looming above them was an enormous boulder jutting out of the cliff. There were fissures in the rock where it seemed that the outer layer had been damaged, revealing different coloured rocks underneath. The fissures didn't follow any natural pattern that Akal could discern.

"Gun Rock," Taviti said, nodding towards the monolith. "The Britishers fired cannons on it from their ships, before Fiji became a colony. They wanted to show us the power of their weapons. You can still see where the cannons struck the rock."

"Ah, yes, the mighty British weaponry," Akal said. "We know something about this in India as well."

As they rounded the curve, they came to another shallow bay spread out ahead of them. At the far end of the bay was a large grove of coconut trees clustered near the ocean, with a modest house set up the hill behind them. Halfway along the bay was another building, a single-story wooden structure backing into the jungle. Even from this distance, Akal could read LAL'S GOODS above the doorway.

"That's it, then?" Akal asked.

"Yes, sir," Constable Kumar replied.

"Does anyone else live nearby?"

"My uncle's village is in the next bay along," Taviti answered. "But we don't buy very much from the stores. We grow and make everything we need. Is Mr. Lal selling something special that people would come all this way from Levuka?"

Constable Kumar shook his head but didn't say any more. Akal and Taviti exchanged glances and Akal shrugged. This was a mystery they didn't need to solve. They just needed to clear up this German thing and then get back to their escort duties.

From afar, the store had seemed dark, and as they approached, Akal saw why: the curtains, old enough that the patterns had faded, were drawn, blocking the two windows on either side of the door. Constable Kumar led them in, with Akal ducking his head to clear the doorway.

It was very dark inside, the only light coming in from the doorway and pinpricks of light from the tiny holes in the curtains. As Akal blinked to adjust to the gloom, the room came into focus; it was in complete disarray, all the items knocked off the shelves that lined the walls. Flour and rice had burst out of the tops of their bags and spilt across the floor, crunching beneath Akal's feet and coating his shoes.

"What has happened here!" Taviti exclaimed from behind Akal.

"I don't know, sir," replied Constable Kumar, sounding alarmed. "It's not normally like this."

"There isn't normally flour on the floor?" Akal asked wryly. The younger man flushed.

"A robbery?" Taviti suggested.

"Perhaps. But why take the time to throw everything on the floor if it is simply a robbery? Why not just take what you want and go?" Akal frowned. "We need to find Mr. Lal."

"He lives in the back," Constable Kumar responded. He headed towards a door in the wall opposite the entryway and rapped on it, calling out for Mr. Lal. There was no response. Constable Kumar flung the door open and Akal and Taviti ran into a kitchen.

There was a man on the floor, slumped against the shelves beneath the chipped wooden countertop, his blood staining the curtains that were covering the otherwise open shelves.

"Mr. Lal!" Constable Kumar gasped.

"Step back," Akal ordered, kneeling at Sanjay Lal's side.

Searching through his memory, Akal dredged up what he could from the minimal medical training he had received and what he had seen Dr. Holmes do before. He checked the man's neck, slippery with blood, for a pulse, but couldn't find one. His chest wasn't moving. He wasn't breathing.

"Kumar, go get a doctor. Taviti, check the rest of the house."

Akal heard Kumar's footsteps pounding back through

the front room, then fading down the hill, as Taviti moved through the rest of the rooms. Akal put his hand under the prone man's head and lifted it up to inspect his face. Sanjay Lal's eyes were open but unseeing. His skin was discoloured, tinged purple. He was still warm to the touch, but by testing against his own cheek, Akal discovered that Mr. Lal's skin was not as warm as a living person's.

There were two long cuts across his face, diagonally slashing across each of his cheeks, one of them dangerously close to his left eye. Farther down, his shirt was torn and more slashes were evident on his chest and arms, with rivulets of blood finding their way through and around his chest and arm hair. As soon as Akal removed his hand, Sanjay Lal's head lolled back down, his chin resting once more on his chest.

Taviti returned to the room and reported, "There is nobody else here. How is he?"

"I think he's dead," Akal replied. He stood and wiped the blood off his hands with a nearby tea towel. Removing the blood was a relief, like taking a small step away from the horror, just a little bit of symbolic distance. But the iron-rich smell of the blood still filled the room, and Akal's work was clearly only beginning. Setting the tea towel aside, he squatted down again and took a more measured look at the victim.

Sanjay Lal looked to be in his thirties and appeared to have lived an indulgent life. His face was puffy with excess, his stomach prominent. The collared shirt he was wearing, which had been rent with the same lashes as his face, was well made of a finely woven cotton. On his right hand, on the little finger, he wore a gold ring. Gingerly finding a clean spot on the man's arm, Akal lifted the dead man's heavy right hand to look at the ring. When he lifted the hand from the floor, he realised that it had been covering something. A pattern, drawn in the man's blood. Akal squinted at it. It looked like a lightning bolt with a tail.

"What do you think that might be?" Akal asked Taviti.

Taviti squatted down to take a closer look. "No idea. I haven't seen anything like it."

Akal inspected the dead man's right hand once more. The blood on the index finger was smudged and caked into the fingernail, unlike the other fingers. It seemed that the dying man had drawn this pattern in his own blood. Akal delicately lowered Sanjay Lal's hand, then retrieved his notebook and pen from his pocket and started to make a careful sketch of the pattern.

Taviti stood and said, "I will go take a closer look at the bedroom."

Akal nodded absently as he focused on the sketch. Once he was satisfied that he had captured it exactly, Akal tucked his notebook away and pushed himself up to standing. He walked back into the front room and surveyed the ransacked store again. Everything had been swept off the shelves; not a single item remained in its place. Jars of nails and other small pieces of hardware had been knocked to the ground, surrounded by glittering pieces of broken glass. Amongst the flour and the rice were jars of spices which had fallen to the floor, their stoppers loose, seeds and colourful powders spilling out.

Despite his best efforts, Akal had stood in some of the spices. The pungent cumin and cinnamon mingled with the kerosene to give the room a comforting, familiar smell.

Akal's childhood home in Punjab had had a similar smell, the smell of his mother's cooking, their kitchen dimly lit with a single kerosene lamp. The memory of home sat uneasily with the more recent memory of the horrifying scene in the kitchen next door.

The spilt contents of the store had created a moat of goods by the walls—although, despite the chaos that appeared at first glance, not a substantial one. Based on the sparsity of the products on the ground, it seemed that Lal's Goods was not a flourishing business. Not in keeping with the well-dressed body in the kitchen.

By one wall, there was a counter, clear except for a pile of newspapers and a ball of string, ready to wrap up packages. Akal stepped behind the counter and looked underneath, where there were some drawers and shelves. One of the shelves contained a utilitarian metal box with a handle. Akal tested the latch and found it locked. He opened the drawers, methodically feeling to the top and back of each drawer. No key. Same result with the shelves. Akal sighed and stretched out his neck, steeling himself for the unpleasant task of searching Sanjay Lal's body.

He brought the box with him to the kitchen, wanting to get this over with as quickly as he could and minimize how much he disturbed the body. Luckily, a ring of keys was in the obvious spot, the first place he looked: Lal's right-hand trouser pocket. Akal tested the smallest key in the lock, and to his relief, it opened easily—but revealed little. There was only a small smattering of coins and papers in the various compartments, more evidence that the business was struggling.

He took a deep breath and lifted himself back up to his

feet to assess the room. Other than the body and the blood surrounding it, the kitchen had not suffered the same fate as the store.

To his immediate right was the cupboard that Sanjay Lal was slumped against. Somebody had sewn the curtains that had been added to cover the shelves, a common practice in Fiji, where cabinetry tended to be rudimentary. Given the neat stitches, Akal assumed it wasn't the dead man who had set to with needle and thread. Whoever it was, their work was now being soaked in Sanjay Lal's blood, slowly overtaking the light floral pattern.

Light was coming into the room from a glassless window above the countertop. The hinged wooden shutter was propped open using a small post. On the wall across from Akal, next to the back door, some open wooden shelves contained a small assortment of pots and pans, with plates and glasses neatly arrayed next to them. A small table was set near the back door, with two chairs. Everything in this room was of good quality and well constructed.

Taviti emerged from an internal door to his left. "Come have a look at the bedroom," he said, nodding to the room he had just come from. "It's a mess, like the store."

Akal followed Taviti through to find another room in disarray. It was dominated by a sturdy wooden bed, big enough for two. The pillow had been thrown to the floor and the sheets had been pulled off the bed with enough force to have ripped them. A wardrobe stood by a chest of drawers, both ransacked: the wardrobe doors were open, clothes yanked aside, some hanging precariously, some on the floor. The drawers hung open, their contents rummaged through and left bunched together and hanging over the edges.

One item stood out to Akal. Amongst the debris on the floor was a jewellery box. It didn't belong in the dusty, dark room, full of masculine things and the unmistakable smell of unwashed socks. Akal's eye was drawn to it straight away, despite it being partially hidden under the other items that had been swept off the dresser. Something on the side of the box glittered through the rest of the detritus, and its lid lay open, showing a pale-pink velvet interior. There was nothing in it.

Picking it up from the floor, Akal closed the lid and traced his fingers across the delicate gold patterns inlaid into the wood on the top, then turned the box about, looking at it from various angles. The bottom was fairly plain, but had rows of tiny holes in the shape of a diamond. He opened the lid again and pulled the velvet insert out to see if there was a second layer which might have some jewellery in it.

It came away easily to reveal what looked like the bottom of the box. But it clearly wasn't. The box was much bigger on the outside than the inside, and it was light in Akal's hands. There was no way the bottom was a solid slab of wood. There must have been a compartment at the bottom— but no obvious way of accessing it.

Akal continued to turn the box over in his hands, looking for a latch to open the bottom, until he heard a knocking at the back door and Constable Kumar's voice calling out. He replaced the insert and closed the box again, tucking it under his arm. He would take a better look at it later. For now, he had to make sure Mr. Sanjay Lal was taken care of.

Germans in Levuka

PUBLIC MEETING PROTEST

The public meeting held in response to a numerously signed requisition was held at the Town Hall, Levuka. The object of the meeting was to petition his Excellency the Governor that effective steps be taken with a view to ensuring the safety and security of the people of this Colony and to curtail the movements of alien enemy subjects in our midst, thereby affording protection of the loyal inhabitants of Levuka.

The Mayor outlined the danger it was to have German residents, naturalised or otherwise, at large, and emphasised the importance for the Government to take drastic measures to put them in a place of safety . . .

CHAPTER 3

DR. STEPHEN TAYLOR, A short, rotund man, was red faced and huffing from the journey from Levuka. He gave Sanjay Lal a cursory examination before declaring him dead under the expectant eyes of the three police officers.

"You made me leave my patient and marched me out of town double-time for a dead man?" Dr. Taylor grumbled, glaring at Constable Kumar as he wiped his hands on a tea towel. "What did you think I could do? Resurrect him?"

Akal found the doctor's thick New Zealand accent rendered everything he said a touch comical, even though the man shooting daggers from his eyes at Akal, Taviti, and Constable Kumar was not intending humour. He suppressed an absurd desire to try and imitate the accent, surely a reaction to the stresses of the afternoon.

"What killed him, please, Dr. Taylor?" Akal asked.

The doctor looked at him disbelievingly. "What do you think killed him? He's been whipped, for God's sake."

"It doesn't seem like such a severe beating to have killed him," Akal replied, giving Dr. Taylor a quizzical look. "There is not that much blood."

"Are you a doctor? No? Well, then, why don't you leave the medical decisions to me?" the doctor said, bristling.

Akal drew his shoulders back and straightened to his most formidable height, looking down his nose at the shorter man with some disdain. Dr. Taylor wilted under his withering gaze. "And his blue lips?" Akal snapped.

The doctor bent down again to look at Sanjay Lal's face. "No, it's nothing. It happens sometimes with corpses."

Akal raised one eyebrow. That was not an explanation. It sounded like this doctor didn't quite know what he was talking about. He resolved to ask Dr. Holmes about it next time he saw him.

"I need to get back to my patients," Dr. Taylor said, rubbing his hands as though to wipe them clean of the situation, despite the fact that he had not touched the body again. He turned to Constable Kumar. "Bring the body down to the hospital and the family can come and make arrangements for his funeral."

"He doesn't have any family," Constable Kumar said with a frown. "But I will inform Vijay Prasad, his very good friend. I'm sure he will take care of it."

They improvised a stretcher, wrapping the body up in a sheet. Taviti took the head, Akal the feet, and Constable Kumar guided them, transporting Sanjay Lal back past Gun Rock and to Levuka for the last time.

VIJAY PRASAD'S FARM was the other house they had seen in the bay north of Levuka. After a quick stop back at the police station to drop off the jewellery box, they retraced their steps north, past Gun Rock, past Lal's Goods, reaching the coconut grove before turning left and proceeding up the hill to the house. As he guided them, Constable Kumar gave them some background on the man they were going to interview.

Mr. Prasad was a well-respected pillar of the community, an educated, religious man, Constable Kumar told them earnestly. He was an early arrival to Fiji, having completed his five years of indenture ten years ago. Since then, he had been so successful with his farm here on Ovalau that he had been able to marry, buy a second plot of land to plant sugar cane on Vanua Levu, where land was more readily available, and employ his wife's brother to work the new farm.

"His friendship with the victim?" Akal probed.

"They knew each other in India," Constable Kumar replied. "So few of my parents' generation have that sort of connection, somebody from their home village who is here with them. I know my father wishes he had a friend like that living here. When he signed up for the *girmit*, the indenture, he signed up with a friend. They were on the ship together, but when they got here, they were sent to different plantations. His friend died before they could ever see each other again."

Constable Kumar seemed so matter-of-fact, so unmoved by his father's tragedy. Akal supposed that it was something he had grown up around, just part of the story of his family. It wasn't an unusual story in Fiji. Friends, whether from home or *jahaji bhai*—friendships forged during the difficult ship journey from India—lost to the plantations.

"What about you? Do you wish for that connection to India as well?" Taviti asked, curious as always about this race of people who were being brought to his home and were changing the face of it. This question broke the solemn silence that had descended after Constable Kumar's account, and they all visibly loosened.

"I was born here. I grew up here. All my friends are here.

My parents talk about growing up with their cousins. My aunts and uncles are back in India, so I have never met my cousins. I suppose my friends are like my cousins," Constable Kumar said.

This was something Akal could relate to. His parents had both come from small families, and none of their siblings had survived to adulthood. He didn't have any cousins. But his childhood friend, Heminder, had been his constant companion. Both horse mad, they had spent all their time in Heminder's wealthy father's stables.

It was Heminder's father who had helped Akal secure the policing position in Hong Kong, when Akal's father had become ill and the responsibility to support the family had fallen to Akal. This job, better paid than any he could have found in India as a young man without education or experience, kept a roof over his family's heads, but had sent him far away from all of them. Akal didn't know if he envied Constable Kumar his life full of family and friends or pitied him for his narrow view of the world. Perhaps a little of both.

They had arrived at Vijay Prasad's farm. Facing the house from the dirt track, Akal couldn't help but be impressed. Most of the other farmhouses in Fiji looked faded and insubstantial, as though the first stiff wind might blow them over. This house was freshly painted and at least half again the size of any other he had seen, solidly rooted in the ground and announcing its presence proudly. The garden around it was neat and a large patch of marigolds flourished at the front, looking to Akal like nothing less than orange heads of sunshine.

As Constable Kumar was the local, Akal asked him to find the Prasads and make the introductions. The young man agreed, swallowing nervously. After knocking on the front door yielded no results, he guided them to the other side of the house in search of the family.

Around the back, there was a lean-to housing the wood fire for cooking. This was a familiar sight. What Akal was surprised to see was a second structure which looked like a large cupboard. The doors were open, revealing three statues of Hindu gods with flowers scattered around them, and a stick of incense almost burnt through, a trail of ash hanging off the end.

"I see you were not exaggerating when you said he was religious," Akal observed.

"What are these statues?" Taviti asked, approaching the cupboard.

"They are the Hindu gods Ganesha, Lakshmi, and Krishna," Constable Kumar replied.

"Do you have something like this at the police barracks?" Taviti asked Akal.

"I'm not a Hindu," Akal reminded him with some exasperation. "I am Sikh. We believe in only one god. Let's go find the Prasads. I doubt they would appreciate us gawking at their shrine."

Constable Kumar led them farther away from the house, towards the neat fields climbing up the hill behind. The fields sported a variety of crops, certainly more than enough for two people. Vijay Prasad must have been growing extra to sell. Constable Kumar had indicated that Mr. Prasad was an enterprising man. His main income was from copra, dried coconut flesh, but clearly Vijay Prasad was not a man to rely on one source of income, or to sit on his hands when other opportunities existed.

Shading his eyes, Akal looked up the neat rows of tomato plants and saw a man and a woman at a field of young plants. The man was crouched down, lifting the leaves of a plant to inspect it, while the woman stood, one hand at her lower back, and the other on the man's shoulder. She noticed the police officers first and alerted her husband, who then raised a hand to wave at them, and gestured with an open palm for them to wait there. He stood and assisted his wife down the hill. As they came closer, her pregnancy, seemingly in its earlier stages, became more apparent.

Vijay Prasad was a tall man, broad shouldered and powerful. From the history Constable Kumar had given them, he should have been in his early thirties, but his age was hard to tell with the battering his body had taken. The left side of his face sported a cluster of scars, but it was clear from the right side that he had once been a handsome man. Now his skin was leathery from long years of work in the sun and he was starting to run to fat. Presumably his life had gotten easier in recent years.

"Mr. Prasad, this is Sergeant Akal Singh and Constable Taviti Tukana," Constable Kumar said quickly, pointing at the wrong man each time as he said the names. He realised his mistake and with a panicked look started to correct himself. Vijay Prasad nodded at each officer each time they were introduced.

"Should I be worried about so many police officers coming to my house?" Mr. Prasad asked, stemming the flow of words coming from the young constable.

Akal paused for a moment. The awareness that he would have to tell this man that his friend had died had been lurking in the back of his mind, growing more present the closer they came to the farm. Now he felt it in his whole body, muscles tensing to flee, stomach lurching. He swallowed, cleared his throat, and started to speak.

"We do have some bad news about your friend Mr. Sanjay Lal," Akal said. At the last minute, he lost his nerve and delayed the inevitable. "Should we return to your house first, make sure your wife is comfortable?"

Mr. Prasad nodded slowly, wariness in his narrowed eyes. "Yes, perhaps that would be best."

Mrs. Prasad was looking on, head swivelling from one person to the next, clearly not understanding the conversation that was occurring in English. Mr. Prasad explained the situation to her in a language that Akal didn't know—not Hindi, but one of the myriad languages of India. She nodded and started back towards the house, without making eye contact.

"Come," Mr. Prasad said, ushering them back to the house, past his wife who was now busy at the outdoor stove. "She will bring us some tea."

It was Akal's first time inside the house of an ex-indentured servant. Mr. Prasad brought them to a room at the front of the house which had a small dining table and four chairs. The room had a hard-packed dirt floor and the windows did not have glass but had wooden shutters that were open to let light and air in. Everything inside the house was humble but sturdy.

Once they had seated themselves at the dining table, Vijay Prasad leaned forward, his arms on the table.

"What has happened with Sanjay? Is he in trouble?"

"No, sir. I am very sorry to tell you he is dead," Akal said, the words coming out in a rush.

Mr. Prasad paled. "Did you say dead?" he asked. On Akal's nod, he slumped back in his chair, his arms dropping from the table to fall in his lap.

"I'm very sorry for your loss. I know this must be a shock," Akal said, remembering the vague, soothing phrases he had heard his sergeant say the first time he had been present at such a scene as a constable.

"How did this happen?" Mr. Prasad asked. "He wasn't sick."

"It appears as though he was attacked. Can you think of anyone who would have wanted to hurt Mr. Lal?"

"Attacked? Attacked?" Mr. Prasad said with a rising tone, standing to pace around the room. "Who would attack him?"

"Did anyone have a grudge against him? Had he upset anyone recently?" Taviti asked.

Mr. Prasad shook his head in immediate denial, and then shrugged.

"Not recently. Though there is one man who has been upset with him for a long time—ever since Sanjay arrived a few years ago. Another store owner, Arvind Chand," he said, reluctantly, as though he didn't want to betray his dead friend.

"Why was Mr. Chand hostile towards Mr. Lal?" Akal asked, as he retrieved his notebook from his front pocket and made a note of the name.

"Something about some business dealings when Sanjay was first setting up his store. Arvind thought Sanjay was dishonest. He's . . . he was always quick with a scheme," Vijay said, the dry humour in his voice tinged with sadness.

"And you were friends? You don't seem like the kind of man to appreciate a scheme," Akal pointed out.

Vijay Prasad smiled sadly. "You are correct, Sergeant Singh. We are very different people. In India, we were not friends. But in Fiji, you cling to familiar things."

Akal looked over at Constable Kumar, who seemed surprised to hear this. Clearly the history between the two men was not well known, and the information Constable Kumar had provided was based on assumptions about their longstanding friendship.

"Thank you, we will follow up with Mr. Chand," Akal said to Mr. Prasad.

"I don't think he could possibly have been part of this," Mr. Prasad said with a frown. "He is a businessman, not a thug. Arvind wouldn't hurt anybody."

"Anybody else Mr. Lal had had dealings with lately?" Akal asked. A man who was quick with a scheme probably had more than one enemy.

"Well, there were the Germans," Mr. Prasad said, spinning around to look at Akal with some animation.

Akal started. Germans again. Could there actually be Germans?

"Who are these Germans?" Taviti asked, catching some of Mr. Prasad's excitement.

"They are European sailors. They came to Sanjay's store a few days ago, wanted a long list of supplies. Sanjay didn't have most of what they wanted. He doesn't keep a lot of stock on hand. So he sold them what he had and told them to come back for the rest. But he was trying to make his money two ways. He was selling the sailors their supplies, yes, but he had also reported them to the police. He was hoping for some reward money. Maybe they realised he had double-crossed them."

"Reward money? Nobody in the government knew anything about these sailors. You said European sailors—are they even German? Even if they are, there is no reward money on offer," Akal said, frowning.

"No, but that didn't stop Sanjay," Vijay said with a wry smile. "He thought maybe the administration would give him one anyway. And even if they didn't, he thought he would look like a hero, and this would help him with his business, help him make contacts with influential people. He was wanting to move to Suva and thought that this was his way to get there."

"Can you describe these men?"

"No, I didn't meet them," Vijay replied. He paused to think, and then continued with a speculative expression. "You know what I think, Sergeant Singh? These men were clearly doing something suspicious because they never went into town, they avoided everybody. We keep hearing about the war and how bad Germans are. I think Sanjay had no idea whether they were German or not. I think he just thought they were doing something wrong and he might get some reward, but he would get more attention if he said they were German. What do you think of this idea?"

"So they didn't speak with anybody else?"

Mr. Prasad responded to Akal with a slow, considered nod of his head. "As far as I know, they only ever spoke with Sanjay. Nobody else has mentioned seeing or talking to them. Still, they must have found out that he reported them somehow. Nobody else has a reason to kill Sanjay."

"Even though he was always quick with a scheme? None of those schemes hurt anyone else in town?"

Mr. Prasad looked out of the window, deep in thought,

and eventually came back to Akal. "No, nothing like this. Nothing involving the police. These Germans, I think it must be them."

"I see," Akal said impassively. It sounded far-fetched, like a story concocted after too much gin. "Do you know where we can find them?"

Mr. Prasad sighed. "No, I don't know. They are sailors, they had a boat. They may have left Ovalau already."

Mrs. Prasad returned at this moment with a tray with cups of spiced, sweet tea, filling the room with the comforting scent of warm milk mixed with the warmth of ginger. Taviti accepted his cup with interest, the Indian-style ginger tea being a new experience for him. Even for Akal it was a rare treat, not something he made for himself. They blew on their tea, took tentative sips, and bowed their heads in appreciation to the standing woman. She smiled shyly and left the room, presumably returning to the outdoor kitchen.

"Thank you for answering our questions," Akal said, after they finished their tea.

"You will look for the Germans? And please let me know what happens," Mr. Prasad asked with an anxious tone. "I am the closest thing to family Sanjay had here in Levuka."

"We will investigate thoroughly," Akal replied, as he folded up his notepad and put it back in his pocket. This vague reassurance seemed to satisfy Mr. Prasad, which Akal was relieved to see. He didn't have anything more concrete to offer, given his best lead at the moment was some phantom German sailors.

THE SUN WAS setting behind the cliffs, throwing the eastern side of the island into a cooling shade, as they left

Vijay Prasad's farm. Akal's thoughts were chasing each other through his brain, flipping between how to find the Germans and debating whether they were even real. They still hadn't spoken to anyone who had actually seen them, though there didn't seem to be any compelling reason for Sanjay Lal to make them up and then tell his friend and the police about them.

"We need to send a report back to Suva on the Germans and on the murder," Akal said. "I understand the pigeon post is the fastest way?"

The cables had not been laid out to Levuka to connect telegraphs, let alone telephone. There was talk of laying the cables under the ocean to allow this, but with Levuka's fading glory, it had not been a priority. Hugh Clancy had been the first to introduce homing pigeons to carry messages between Suva and Levuka. At the time, the capital had already moved to Suva, but Mr. Clancy had initially kept the *Fiji Times* in Levuka and started a new paper, the *Suva Times*. In order to keep the news flowing between the old capital and the new, he had installed a pigeon post. It was the fastest way to get information back and forth; it took the pigeons about half an hour to fly unerringly to the corresponding stations with messages attached to their feet. Now a public service had been established.

"Yes, of course. We can use the pigeon post," Constable Kumar replied. "But not until the morning. John, the boy who takes care of the pigeons, will be home by now. The service won't be operating."

"Right. First thing, then," Akal said. It wouldn't make much difference; there was not too much more they could do tonight. "And where is your police barracks?"

Constable Kumar gave him a blank look. "No, no police barracks here."

"Where do you stay, then?" Akal asked.

"I live with my parents. Sub-Inspector Johnson rented a house across the road from the station, and visiting officers would stay with him, but when he left, it was rented to somebody else. You are the first to come from the Suva station since he left. Maybe you could stay at the hotel?" Constable Kumar ventured with a helpless shrug.

"The inspector-general didn't organise anything for you?" Taviti asked Akal.

Akal let his silence be the answer. Taviti roared with laughter, while Constable Kumar stood staring between them.

"No, of course he didn't, that makes complete sense," Taviti said when he stopped laughing.

"I suppose I will stay in the station. Perhaps one of the cells," Akal said with dismay.

"No, no, don't stay there," Taviti said, as Constable Kumar shook his head in horror. "Why don't you come and stay at the village? My family will take care of you."

"Are you sure they won't mind? I would very much like to meet your family," Akal replied with some relief. He had never been to a traditional Fijian village before.

"I'll go check with my uncle. He will agree, but there are correct ways of doing things that we all must follow."

They decided that Akal would let Katherine and Mary know what had happened and why he and Taviti would not be available to escort them the next day, while Taviti went to the village to let his family know that Akal would be staying. They agreed to meet back at the station.

Akal and Constable Kumar stopped at the station on their way to the hotel so Akal could retrieve the jewellery box. He wanted to get a female perspective on the box, to see if either Katherine or Mary had seen anything like it before. They arrived at the hotel to find that the ladies were still out, presumably still working at Hugh Clancy's house. The two men sat in the parlour to wait, Akal with a gin and tonic and Constable Kumar with a glass of water.

"We have the place to ourselves again," Akal observed, taking a long, satisfying sip of his drink.

"Yes. There are fewer and fewer visitors to Levuka, since Suva became the capital."

"It must be boring for a young man?"

"No, no. I much prefer it. I didn't like Suva," Kumar replied emphatically.

"Oh, you spent time in Suva?"

"Yes. I went there for my training, but I was glad to come home when it was over. Suva is too loud, too dirty, too dusty. Here, the dogs won't bite you and the people won't bite you either. There . . ." He trailed off with a meaningful shrug.

Akal inclined his head thoughtfully. He remembered stepping off the boat in Hong Kong and plunging into the chaotic, malodorous cacophony that was one of the busiest ports in the world. He had loved it. But somehow Suva didn't have the same vibrancy—just the noise and grime. He could understand why Constable Kumar might prefer the peace of Levuka.

"What did you think of what Mr. Vijay Prasad had to say about our victim?" Akal asked, moving the conversation back to a more professional tone. "He seemed to suggest that Sanjay Lal is not well liked."

Constable Kumar nodded. "Yes, this is true. Nobody went to his store unless they had to, like when the other stores ran out of things. Mr. Prasad was his only friend, really, and nobody understood why he'd put up with him. They were so different. Mr. Prasad is a good man, talks to everyone, helps everyone, works hard. Mr. Lal, he just thought he was too good for Levuka. He thought he could be the big man just by being here. He would have been better off in Suva."

A victim the town had no liking for. Akal was not convinced by Vijay Prasad's insistence that the European sailors must be responsible. He resolved to look at the locals first, rather than chasing after what could be the figment of an ambitious man's lurid imagination.

The hotel doors swung open, and a wilted-looking Mary and Katherine drooped into the parlour. Akal and Constable Kumar jumped to stand and pull out chairs for them; Katherine perked up when she saw Akal, then ushered Mary over so she could gratefully sink into the padded seat of a vacant chair.

"Did you find the Germans?" Katherine asked, still standing, an avid gleam in her eye.

"Do tell us all, Sergeant Singh, but do you think I could have a cup of tea first?" Mary said plaintively.

"Of course, *mem*. Constable Kumar, could you ask for some tea for the ladies?"

"Yes, sir. And then may I have leave to go home?"

"Oh, no, stay and have a drink, Constable Kumar," Katherine insisted.

Constable Kumar declined, blushing furiously, and left to organise the requested drinks, disappearing through the door to the lobby at a rapid clip.

"Did we scare him off?" Katherine asked with a coy smile from across the table.

Akal didn't think this needed a response. The energetic young lady rather scared him, let alone poor young Constable Kumar.

Over cups of tea, Akal filled them in on the events of the afternoon. "Constable Tukana, Constable Kumar, and I were following up on a report Constable Kumar had received a few days ago. In the course of this, we discovered a man had been attacked and killed. Taviti and I will continue to work on this case tomorrow. Unfortunately, we will have limited time to escort you."

Katherine's jaw had been gradually dropping through the story and at the end she snapped it shut and shook her head in disbelief. "Is that how you tell a story? Oh, no, no, no, Sergeant Singh, this simply won't do. Details, my good man, details!"

Akal looked at her with incredulity. He knew she wasn't a shy, retiring type, but this reaction was beyond what he had expected. How was he going to keep this woman out of trouble?

"*Mem*, this a police matter," he said, trying to keep the panic out of his tone. "I cannot discuss the details. You must understand."

Akal looked to Mary for some support, but she merely nodded encouragingly. Where Katherine was sitting at the edge of her seat and leaning forward, her aunt was sitting serenely with her hands folded in her lap, somehow implacable in her demeanour and clearly expecting more of a story from Akal. Perhaps it was good that they both wanted the same thing. Between the two of them, he didn't know whom he least wanted to cross.

"If you aren't going to fulfil your duty to us tomorrow, you had better give us more to tell Uncle Hugh, otherwise he will be off complaining to the governor," Katherine added, smirking.

Akal sighed and refilled his glass with water from the pitcher on the table. He was starting to understand Katherine. She wouldn't really complain to her uncle. But if he didn't tell her the story, she would persist and find out for herself, which at best would fuel more speculation and at worst could put her in danger. He would feed her just enough information to keep her satisfied.

Akal started from the beginning. Initially he was very matter-of-fact and clinical, but at some point, spurred by Katherine's shining eyes, his inner storyteller took over. Lowering his voice in the tense moment of finding the body and pausing before revealing that Vijay Prasad had accused some German sailors, Akal became lost in the tale.

He told them everything, forgetting to gloss over the bloody details. The two ladies listened, rapt. When Katherine started to interrupt with a question, her aunt stilled her with a hand on her forearm. But she couldn't restrain her for long. As soon as Akal wound down, Katherine burst out with her question. "So there really are Germans here in Levuka? I knew it! Are they from the navy?"

"It remains unconfirmed. Mr. Prasad hasn't actually seen these alleged German sailors. It seems very unlikely that they would be Germans. Why would they be all the way here in Fiji?"

"Of course there are German ships in the Pacific!" she exclaimed. "I read about them in the papers in Sydney. Going around sinking any ships they come across, generally being disruptive. Didn't you know about this?"

Akal frowned, unsure if the volatile young woman was teasing him. His skepticism must have shown on his face because she continued earnestly, "No, really, it was in the *Sydney Morning Herald* a few weeks ago. An American ship was scuttled in the Pacific. Wasn't it reported over here?"

"No, I'm not aware of it," Akal replied, starting to wonder if this could be real. Too many people were saying there were Germans about.

"Surely if it was happening in the Pacific the police would have heard about it," Mary said, injecting a sense of reason into the conversation.

"Perhaps not," Akal said. "We get our news second-hand from Sydney. They may not have thought it relevant, depending on where it happened."

"Well, anyway, are you going to look for them?" Katherine asked impatiently.

Akal looked around the room, searching for salvation.

"Thank you for telling us such a fascinating tale, Sergeant Singh," said Mary diplomatically, giving Katherine the patented look she had that seemed to pull her niece back into line.

Katherine reluctantly sank back into her seat. "Yes, that was much more satisfying. Thank you, Sergeant Singh," she said in a more subdued tone.

"I found another mystery at Mr. Lal's house, which I am hoping you can help with," Akal said, placing Sanjay Lal's jewellery box on the table with a flourish. Hopefully this would distract Katherine away from her fascination with the supposed Germans.

Katherine immediately picked up the box and started tapping the bottom. "The man who was killed, what happened to his wife?" she asked.

"I do not believe he was married," Akal responded.

"Oh, really? I assumed he must be. This jewellery box is certainly something I would expect to be owned by a woman. Not a single man, certainly," Katherine said, passing the box to her aunt for her assessment.

Akal sat up a little straighter. This was precisely the kind of analysis he had been hoping for when he'd chosen to bring the jewellery box from the police station.

"I agree," Mary said after inspecting the box. "Was there any jewellery in it?"

"No."

"Maybe it was a robbery after all," Katherine said, intrigue in her voice.

"Perhaps. I will consider it," Akal replied, remaining non-committal. He was walking a fine line here, between asking for their help and keeping the women at arm's distance. He had already stepped over the line once. He needed to remain vigilant against doing it again.

"So, you will be searching for the Germans tomorrow?" Katherine asked eagerly, returning once more to the topic she was so intrigued by. Akal inwardly groaned. He should have known he couldn't distract her for long.

"We still don't know that there are any Germans, despite what you read in your Sydney newspaper," Akal corrected automatically. "I will have to contact Suva to let them know of these developments. We will see what we do after that."

"Oh, will you use the pigeon post? May I join you? I would love to see that! Uncle Hugh is ever so proud of his pigeons," Katherine said.

"Yes, of course," Akal said, relieved that there was

something he could easily say yes to. Surely there could be no danger in this activity. "I will return tomorrow morning to send the message. I will stop by here to collect you?"

"Yes, please, Sergeant Singh. We will both attend," Mary replied. "After that, we need to visit the cemetery. We must pay our respects to Hugh's late wife, Clara."

"Yes, *mem*," Akal said, trying to keep the frustration out of his voice. He had a murder to investigate, but instead, he was going to trail all over the island after two women who actually seemed perfectly capable of taking care of themselves.

Some of his reluctance must have shown on his face, because Mary cleared her throat and suggested, "Perhaps the local constable could take us. I'm sure it will be more efficient, given he knows the area."

"No, *mem*, you are my responsibility. If I left you with the young constable and something happened, I would be very ashamed. We will go after the pigeon post tomorrow. I will ask Constable Kumar to guide us."

Arrangements thus made, Akal prepared to take his leave of the ladies. He stood and glanced at Katherine, who was still intently inspecting the puzzle box. She finally looked up when her aunt said her name.

"I think this jewellery box has a secret compartment."

Akal sat back down.

"See here, I think this is a false floor at the bottom of the main compartment," Katherine said, opening the box and turning it around on the table to show Akal and Mary. She traced her finger along the outside of the box, a couple of inches from the bottom. "The floor is here, so there is all this space underneath. It isn't that heavy, so I don't think it's solid wood. When I tap it, it sounds hollow. And when I shake it, I can hear something in there." She picked up the box and demonstrated.

"Oh, how intriguing," Mary exclaimed.

"Yes, it is very interesting," Akal said, impressed at her deductions. He had noticed most of these details himself but had not taken the step of tapping or shaking it. "I don't know if it is relevant to the murder, but it is certainly worth exploring. Thank you for pointing this out." He reached out his hand for the box, but Katherine held onto it.

"Do you think I could keep it for the night?" Katherine asked. "I can try to open it. I'm very good at puzzles."

Akal was tempted. He had a feeling it was important, but he didn't have time to spend on it himself. If Katherine was able to open the box, what would it reveal? And what would the impulsive Katherine do with it?

"Don't worry, Sergeant Singh. When I shake it, I think what I am hearing is paper and nothing else. I don't think there are any diamonds in there," Katherine said with a laugh, as though she could read his mind.

"It is the victim's property, so I should secure it at the police station," he replied, his tone betraying that he wished he could leave it with her. "Perhaps I could bring it to you tomorrow and you could take another look?"

Katherine nodded and reluctantly handed the jewellery box over, and she and Mary bade Akal a good night before retreating upstairs. In turn, Akal finally—albeit somewhat unenthusiastically—exited the lobby to return to the station and prepare for the journey to the village and whatever hospitality he would receive there. Given Taviti's presence, he was hoping for a warm welcome, but not necessarily the trappings of civilisation the ladies were enjoying at the Royal Hotel.

IT WAS WELL and truly dark by the time Taviti returned from the village. Akal had been cooling his heels at the station after taking his leave from Katherine and Mary. He had had plenty of time to replay the conversation with the ladies and curse his lapse of judgement. What had happened to his plan of giving Katherine the minimum of information? Had he learnt nothing from Hong Kong?

At some point, the effects of the long day overrode his internal recriminations. He hadn't realised that he'd nodded off in the chair until he heard Taviti calling his name. Disoriented, Akal blinked and shook his head to clear the sleep from his brain. He swung his feet down from the desk and stood up, leaning his hands on the desk and stretching his back.

Taviti was looking at him with a mixture of sympathy and amusement. "Are you awake yet, Akal?"

Akal's nod was somewhat belied by his enormous yawn.

"My uncle is looking forward to meeting you. Let's go. Now you have a choice. Would you like the coastal route, back past Mr. Prasad's farm again, which is easier and slower, or the inland route, which has a bit of hill to climb but is much faster?"

"Faster, please," Akal said, as eager to get his first glimpse of Taviti's home as he was to get a good night's rest.

They started walking north along Beach Street again, but instead of following the coastline around Gun Rock, Taviti veered inland. He stopped at the base of a flight of solid concrete stairs that seemed to go forever.

"Are we going up these steps?" Akal asked in horror.

"Of course. This is Mission Hill. I told you there was a bit of a climb," Taviti responded, nonplussed by Akal's concern. "Don't worry, the steps are very sturdy. The Royal Engineers built them. And there are only ninety-nine steps. Or is it one hundred and ninety-nine? Something like that. Not too many, anyway."

Akal questioned Taviti's grasp of maths. One hundred and ninety-nine steps seemed quite a lot more than ninety-nine. And it seemed like a lot either way. He gritted his teeth and started to follow his friend on the long climb skyward.

Halfway up, he paused to catch his breath, under the guise of taking in the view. He called out to Taviti, who stopped and turned around, laughing when he saw how far Akal had fallen behind. Irritated, Akal looked back, more to ignore Taviti than for the vista. As his breath evened out, his irritation faded.

Levuka spread out below him under the moonlit sky. The houses here towards the upper slope of the hill were large and graceful, built with stilts into the side of the hill, with plentiful windows to enjoy the view. They were spread out up here, and clustered closer and closer together the farther down the slope he looked. The town was only visible in shadows, the faint glow of lamps in the windows the only sign of life. Beyond the town, the ocean rippled black and silver.

When Akal finally heaved himself to the top of the hill, he found Taviti lounging on the top step.

"One hundred and eighty-five," Akal wheezed.

"One hundred and eighty-five?"

"Steps. One hundred and eighty-five steps. Not ninety-nine. Quite a lot more than ninety-nine."

Taviti's teeth gleamed in the moonlight as he gave Akal a vaguely apologetic shrug. "Don't worry, it is all downhill from here." Taviti walked away from the steps, towards the forest, looking for the path. He passed over the same area, back and forth a few times, until Akal started to worry.

"Here it is," he said finally, pointing at what seemed to Akal to be just more jungle.

Squinting, Akal could see the faintest suggestion of a thinning in the grass—a path wending its way between the trees. "That's the path?"

"All the path we needed when we were kids," Taviti replied with a grin. "Don't worry, bosso, I won't get lost."

"It isn't you I'm worried about," Akal muttered, as he ducked under some vines to follow Taviti into the darkness of the jungle.

The route to the village didn't follow any discernible track, but Taviti seemed to find a way that didn't require any untoward efforts now that they were at the top of the hill. Very little moonlight filtered through the dense canopy of the jungle. Akal was moving by instinct. There was little point looking at the ground; he couldn't see anything anyway. He focused on Taviti's back ahead of him.

Taviti was an excellent guide, stopping regularly to check on Akal. On occasions where there was a hazard to be avoided, he would stop, point out the obstacle, and ensure Akal was watching him before proceeding.

After walking along the top of the ridge for about ten minutes, Taviti stopped and turned to face Akal.

"The village is down the hill, so we will go slower now. Don't want you going down the hill on your bum!"

"I can't believe you already did this journey twice today," Akal marvelled. "Once is enough for me."

"It is not difficult for me. I grew up here, I walked this way every day in my childhood." In the dark, Akal couldn't see Taviti's expression, but he could tell from his tone that Taviti was nonplussed. It was the same reaction Taviti had had when he realised that Akal couldn't swim. Taviti was always so at one with his environment, it seemed inconceivable to him that Akal didn't have the same connection.

They resumed the walk downhill. The thick layer of leaves beneath their feet was wet and slippery, and Akal found himself watching where Taviti held on to trees as he descended. Eventually, the jungle thinned, and thinned further, until they could walk side by side.

The village was quiet when Akal and Taviti arrived. Akal couldn't discern very much in the darkness, other than the locations of the buildings. The houses were just triangular shapes grouped together in clusters, with open spaces between them. Taviti strode confidently to one of the clusters of houses, Akal following behind him. There was light in the doors of the houses that they passed, and inside Akal could hear the sounds of children laughing.

As soon as they walked inside the door, they were greeted with a chorus of calls, all in Fijian, but sounding welcoming, as far as Akal could tell. "Welcome to my family's home," Taviti said proudly.

The house was one large room, dimly lit by kerosene lamps dotted about. There were quite a few people in there, sitting in smaller groups, working on various projects, but before Akal could get a good look at all the activity going on, a small sturdy child came waddling towards Taviti and latched onto his leg. Taviti detached the boy and casually tucked him against his chest. The little boy leaned his soft curls back against Taviti's chest, his dark eyes studying Akal with curiosity but not a hint of fear.

In the meantime, Taviti had been swarmed by the rest of the children in the house, who were jumping around his legs, chattering and laughing. Taviti teased one boy, or at least Akal assumed that's what he was doing, by the peals of laughter from the other children and the exaggerated huff that the boy went into, until Taviti ruffled his hair. Taviti's complete and immediate affinity for these children struck Akal in his solar plexus, like a blow from an invisible, velvet-covered fist, sinking deep into him, making it hard to breathe. Seeing Taviti in his place—for now Akal could see that Suva was not Taviti's place at all—brought home for Akal a painful reminder of something he was usually able to ignore: how very far he was from his own place.

The children kept darting glances at Akal and saying things to Taviti that Akal knew must have been questions about him. One of the questions had Taviti roaring with laughter and all the children giggling with him. Akal threw a reproachful glance at his friend.

"Sorry, Sergeant Singh," Taviti said with a bow of exaggerated respect. "They assumed I was your boss, I guess because my uncle is the chief. Don't worry, I set them straight."

"Of course you did," Akal said wryly, wondering what Taviti had actually told them. Taviti's grin was not reassuring.

One of the men of the family wandered over to Taviti and greeted him with a friendly thump on his shoulder. Taviti handed the child over in a movement that required no conscious thought on either side.

"Akal, this is my brother Peni. He is my uncle's right-hand man."

Akal and Peni nodded at each other, Akal murmuring "Hello" and the other man responding with something Akal couldn't make out.

"His English is not that great," Taviti explained. "He'll understand you, but he can't speak it well. It's how I was before I went to Suva."

Peni nodded again, supporting Taviti's assertion that he could understand what was being said, and took the child back over to a woman at the far side of the room, who tucked him down next to her and resumed her work.

Now that the initial excitement of Taviti's arrival had mellowed, Akal could look around the interior of the house. The walls and high triangular roof were framed with wood and filled with reeds and leaves, tightly packed together and precisely held into place in a lattice pattern. The floor was covered in mats made of strips of dried leaves woven together; they felt smooth and supple under Akal's feet. A couple of women in the corner were weaving another large mat, using tan and black strips to make geometric patterns across the mat.

"*Ibe*," Taviti said, seeing where Akal's gaze had rested. "They are making the *ibe* for a present for a wedding. It is the gift women give."

Another cluster of women seemed to be winding leaves into balls around their hands, while a group of men sat separately in a circle, smoothing long leaves with instruments that looked like they were made from mollusc shells.

"Come and sit, try some *yaqona*. Looks like they are making a fresh bowl," Taviti said. They joined the group of men on the floor. At the head of the circle sat a man mixing a brown liquid that looked like tea with a dash of milk in a large bowl with legs, which was called a *tanoa*, according to the running commentary Taviti was providing Akal to explain what was happening. Peni passed Akal and Taviti empty cups—*bilo*—made from the half shell of a coconut.

Once the man mixing the *yaqona* was satisfied, the first man to his right passed him his *bilo* and received it back full of the brown liquid. The man said *"Bula"* to the circle and drank down his entire cup in a series of gulps. The whole circle then slowly clapped in sync three or four times before the whole process was repeated by the next man in the circle.

The circle of men talked and continued their work on the leaves while this went on, pausing when their turn came. When Akal's turn arrived, he looked down at the cup of *yaqona* with interest. Up close he could see the powdered root swirling through the cloudy water. After calling out *"Bula"* to the circle, he downed his cup. When the *yaqona* hit his tongue, he had to resist the urge to spit it out. It tasted bitter and earthy. Not foul, but not enjoyable. He grimly continued to swallow it down. A nudge from Taviti's elbow reminded him to clap.

"What do you think? How do you feel?" Taviti asked eagerly as he accepted his own *bilo* of *yaqona*.

"Well, yes, it is interesting," Akal said, through tingling lips. "Is it normal for my face to feel numb?"

"Yes, that's good. A few more bowls and you will be very relaxed."

Akal silently groaned. He didn't think he could stomach

a single drop more. Luckily, he got a reprieve. A man ducked his head inside the side door of the house and beckoned to Taviti.

"Let's go. The chief is ready for us," Taviti said.

They followed the other man to another, much larger hut.

"This is the *bure* where all the ceremonies are held. The man leading us, he is one of the chief's main advisers. He will perform the introduction and the chief will formally accept you into the village," Taviti explained as they walked up the path to the door of the hut. "Just do what I do."

They entered a room that was much like the one they had just left, but quite a bit larger. Akal couldn't tell if it was truly that much larger, or if it just felt that way because it was completely empty except for the man sitting on a stool in the middle of the room. The chief sat with his hands on his knees, a stern look on his face. In the flickering light of the lone kerosene lamp, he cast a long shadow along the *ibe*-covered floor and up the thatched wall.

The chief watched without any change of expression as they entered the room and found their places, the adviser moving to the left of the room while Taviti guided Akal to the right. They sat cross-legged on the floor. From a sack he had been carrying, the adviser removed a small pile of roots, gnarled and wound together, and placed them on the floor in front of the chief. He started to speak in what appeared to be a ritual, speaking quickly and without pause.

Akal couldn't understand any of what was said, other than when the chief would respond with the word "*naka*." Akal had heard Fijians saying this as a shortened version of "*vinaka*," or thank you. Despite the simplicity of the ceremony, there was a palpable sense of solemnity and reverence towards the chief.

Eventually, the adviser stopped talking, and the mood in the room shifted, lightened. It seemed they were done. The adviser gathered the roots up and put them back in the sack, handing them to the chief as Taviti and Akal stepped back outside the *bure*.

"What were those roots?" Akal asked.

"That was your *sevusevu*, your gift to the chief. It was *yaqona*, the root that makes the *kava* that we drink."

"My gift? But I didn't—" Akal started to say in a worried tone, but Taviti shook his head and waved off his concerns.

"I took care of it for you. I had brought it from Suva for my family to try. It is a bit different from what we grow here. Not to worry, Akal."

The chief joined them outside the *bure*.

"Taviti!" he boomed, his broad smile a stark contrast to the serious demeanour he had had inside.

"Uncle!" Taviti boomed back. The men gave each other meaty back slaps, which were vigorous enough to make Akal wince just hearing them.

"Uncle, this is Sergeant Akal Singh. Sergeant Singh, this is Ratu Teleni, the chief of this village of Tabenu."

Ratu Teleni gave Akal a long, appraising look, while Akal tried to make his inspection a little more subtle. Taviti's uncle appeared to be somewhere in his forties, with grey starting to appear at his temples. Unlike Taviti and his closely cropped hair, the chief wore his hair in an impeccably cut high dome over and around his head. At around five foot ten, he was short compared to both Akal and Taviti, but exuded a quiet, assured power.

"Sergeant Singh, welcome. Is this your first time coming to Ovalau? What do you think of our home?"

"It is very beautiful," Akal replied, startled to realise that while he had abstractly recognised this fact, he had not yet had a chance to truly appreciate it.

The chief nodded with a satisfied smile. "Most beautiful island in Fiji. And the best village."

"Don't let them hear you say that in Suva, Uncle," Taviti said in mock horror.

"That's why I have you there, Taviti. You will cause less trouble with that sort of thing than I will. More trouble with the ladies, though!"

Ratu Teleni roared at his own joke, but Taviti's laugh was more muted and he glanced at Akal nervously. It dawned on Akal that if this was Taviti's home village, his wife and children should be here. But Taviti had not mentioned them once on the trip over from Suva. Nor had he cited them as part of his desire to visit home. Taviti's family life had never really made sense to Akal, with Taviti permanently in Suva and his wife and children back in the village. Now the situation made even less sense. Where was Taviti's family?

Hastily changing the topic, Taviti said, "Uncle, Akal needs to find these Germans we keep hearing about because . . . well, because they are German, and the British Empire is at war with the Germans. But also, because we think they killed a shopkeeper from Levuka."

Ratu Teleni was taken aback at the mention of the murder. Akal briefly explained the scene they had found at Lal's Goods to the chief, and the accusation by Vijay Prasad. By the end of Akal's description, the chief looked more thoughtful than surprised.

"There have been some European men—men we haven't seen before—on the island in the last few days. Not in Levuka—in the jungle and some of the other beaches. These could be your Germans. We will show you tomorrow where we've spotted them."

"Thank you, Ratu Teleni. I would like to go look for these Germans tomorrow morning," Akal said.

"Of course. But in the meantime, come and join us for some *talanoa*."

At Akal's blank look, Taviti explained, "Tell stories. You know, talk as men do."

BACK AT TAVITI'S family's home, dinner was being served. A different mat had been laid over a section of the floor to represent the dining area. Food was brought in from the door at the back of the room, where the outdoor kitchen must have been. It was a simple meal of a fish soup, the fish boiled in coconut milk, and boiled *dalo*, a starchy root crop which itself was bland but worked well with the soup. Taviti's family put away astonishing quantities of the *dalo*. The soup, on the other hand, was being eaten like a garnish, making relatively little soup stretch to feed the whole family.

After eating, Akal and Taviti sat with the men for a while as they told their increasingly improbable stories about hunting and fishing and playing pranks, with a running translation from Taviti. They were the sort of stories which probably had a seed of truth but had grown wilder and more fabulous with each repetition. Akal could tell from the body language of the assembled group exactly when the climax of each story was coming, the faces of the listeners tense in anticipation of whooping and hollering and clapping, as that was indeed what each heroic deed deserved.

Finally, Akal and Taviti took their leave, by mutual, unspoken consent. The chief excused them and they escaped, though not without being teased. It was difficult being teased in another language. Akal could tell that they were trying to be friendly, but instead of being able to laugh with them, he had to wait for the translation. In the moments until he understood, he had the unsettling sensation that they were laughing at him.

"Your uncle speaks English very well," Akal said as they walked to the nearby building, part of the cluster of buildings that formed the family home, where they would be sleeping.

"Yes, he was one of the first students at the Levuka Public School. Then he went away to New Zealand to go to university. He studied history. He wanted me to go to his university and study law, but I didn't want to go away. Anyway, I wasn't that good at school."

"Let me guess," Akal said. "You always wanted to be outside?"

Taviti chuckled. "You know me too well, my friend."

"And then you joined the police force and they stuck you behind a desk."

Taviti shrugged, a small movement, but no movement really seemed small on his powerful frame. "I'm out from behind the desk for now, thanks to you."

"Oh, yes, just keep following in my footsteps and you will go far."

Even in the dark, Taviti's grin could illuminate the village.

"Now, did you say that Peni is your brother?" Akal asked.

"You never mentioned your brother before." The question had been nagging at the back of his mind since Taviti had introduced him to Peni.

"He's my father's second brother's son. We grew up together like brothers. So he's my brother, my cousin brother. That is how it is in Fiji. I know it is strange for the *kaivalagi*."

"Oh, no, not strange for me. That is how it is in India as well. If I had older male cousins I would call them *Anna*. It is also what I would call an older brother if I had one."

"Not so different after all."

Akal found this thought comforting. Though Taviti's family had been kind in their smiles and gestures, it had been difficult not being able to communicate. More than that, it had been difficult feeling like an exotic creature. In Hong Kong and in Suva, Indians were commonplace. But for this community, to have an Indian in their home was a new experience. Akal's muscles loosened as he settled into his surroundings a little more, this small similarity in their familial bonds grounding him in a way no formal welcome could have.

They walked in silence, Akal gathering up his courage to ask Taviti something personal. "One more question, Taviti. Did you say this hut we are staying at, this *bure*, is Peni's home?" Akal asked as they approached the hut in question.

"Yes."

"As a guest, I will stay anywhere. But why are *you* staying there?"

"To keep you out of trouble," Taviti said, laughing nervously.

"Where is your wife, Taviti? Why are you not staying

with her?" Akal asked. His genuine concern seemed to cut through Taviti's evasiveness.

"She and the children are at her parents' village on Bau," Taviti responded without inflection, keeping his eyes on the ground in front of them.

"When will they be back? Will I have a chance to meet them?"

"They aren't coming back."

"It is a shame we didn't have more notice about this trip. You could have let them know and maybe they could have come home."

More firmly, Taviti insisted, "They aren't coming back, Akal."

Akal looked at him sharply, concerned. Taviti sighed. They both stopped walking.

"My wife is the daughter of the chief of Bau. She is a fierce, serious woman. From the first time I met her, I couldn't look away. And I know it was the same for her. But you know me, Akal, I'm not serious. I could turn everything into a joke, even when she was trying to talk to me about things she cared about. After a while, she stopped trying. And then she left, went back to Bau, and took the children with her. So I went to Suva. I haven't seen my children for three years."

They resumed walking in silence. There had to be more to this story, but Akal didn't ask any more questions. Taviti had reluctantly trusted him with this much of his pain while Akal still hadn't told him why he had been sent to Fiji—even though he suspected Taviti already knew most of the tale. Why should Taviti tell him more, when Akal couldn't find the courage to tell his own shameful story?

The Ladies Column

The Double Antimacassar

One of the latest ideas in home adornment is the double antimacassar. Everyone knows the difficulty of keeping the single antimacassar in its place on the front of the chair. If two are made as here shown, one acts as a counter-balance to the other. These articles look very pretty in coloured satin, bordered with a frill of plain material or wide lace. Measure your chair, then cut the material to the right size. The floral design here seen is quite artistic, and should be copied in coloured embroidery. Two lengths of ribbon connect the antimacassars, sufficiently long to form into a tasteful bow at top.

CHAPTER 4

CO . . . CO . . . RI . . . CO . . . ROOO . . .

Startled into wakefulness, Akal lay for a moment trying to place where he was, and what that awful sound was.

Co . . . co . . . ri . . . co . . . rooo . . .

It sounded like a geriatric rooster still trying to crow, but what should have been a trumpeting announcement of the dawn instead seemed like it could end in the rooster's demise.

Co . . . co . . . ri . . . co . . . rooo . . .

Akal groaned and threw his arms over his eyes. Taviti and Peni and his family continued to sleep peacefully, soft snuffles and snores all around Akal. This *bure*, like all the others, was one room, so everyone slept in the same space on their own sleeping mats. It was tight quarters, and it felt strange to sleep in a room with so many people he didn't know, but as he had drifted to sleep last night, Akal had felt safe and comfortable.

Co . . . co . . . ri . . . co . . . rooo . . .

In a fit of pique, Akal shoved the thin piece of cloth he had used as a covering aside and sat up on his mat. Rubbing his hand over his face, he sighed. This damn rooster was making sure he didn't get any more of the sleep that he desperately wanted. Akal glared at the next mat where Taviti peacefully snored.

Akal dressed and rewound his turban in the gloom of the hut, the only light filtering in around the edges of the door and covered windows. He then quietly made his way past the slumbering family and emerged into the peaceful village.

Co . . . co . . . ri . . . co . . . rooo . . .

The mostly peaceful village, Akal mentally amended.

Having arrived after dark, he had not seen much of the village yesterday. Now he took the opportunity to get his bearings. The village was situated on a flat area of land, with the hill they had walked down last night behind it and a short, sandy slope down to the ocean at the front. It was bordered at one side by a river, which was fed from a water source farther up the hill behind them, cascading down through the dense jungle in a series of small waterfalls.

The ceremonial *bure* where Akal's welcome ceremony had been completed with the chief was in the middle of the village with a large square of land around it; the rest of the buildings were organised around that square. The *bures* seemed to consist almost entirely of their large thatched triangular roofs, the walls paling into insignificance underneath the glory of the roofs on top of them. In the soft morning light, the village seemed washed clean. It was immaculate, everything exactly in its place, not a hint of rubbish anywhere.

Akal walked over to the bank of the river and leaned against one of the coconut palms growing there. He looked out over the water, unfocussed, lulled by the sound of the waterfalls rushing down the hill.

"Good morning, Sergeant Singh."

Akal started out of his reverie to greet the chief. Ratu Teleni leaned against his own coconut palm, the two men and the two trees framing the sun which was just starting to make an appearance over the horizon. They were both quiet, and Akal resumed his contemplation of the water. Some time later, Akal couldn't have said if it was five minutes or fifty, a young woman approached with two plates of fruit and offered one to the chief. She then shyly offered Akal the second plate. Akal accepted with a smile and thanked her with one of the few Fijian words he knew, *vinaka*. This earned him a smile that lit up her face as her wariness faded. She gave him a coquettish glance over her shoulder as she departed. Akal looked over at the chief nervously, but luckily he was focused on his breakfast.

Akal turned his attention to the plate of fruit with great anticipation. The fruit he had eaten in Fiji had beaten out any he'd tried anywhere else. The plate in front of him had slices of papaya, red and slippery; a tiny, plump banana; and a small whole mango which had already been peeled to reveal bright orange flesh, the juice bleeding to form a puddle on the plate.

He started with the mango and its vibrant aroma of honeyed sunshine, knowing from experience that while sweet, the mango also had a tartness which would be too prominent if he ate it after the simpler sweetness of the papaya and the sugary banana. Akal put down the plate and leaned forward to take the first bite of the mango, which caused the inevitable stream of juice to threaten to run down towards his chin. He caught the stream of juice with the fingers of his other hand before it could make it into his beard. Akal couldn't afford a sticky beard today when he wasn't sure what facilities he had for his ablutions. Scraping the flesh from the seed with his teeth, he made short work of the delicious fruit.

"Well done. You know how to eat a mango properly," Ratu Teleni said, nodding approvingly.

"Thank you, sir," Akal said, a little embarrassed to have been observed with mango juice on his face by this prominent man. "We had a mango tree at my home in the Punjab. I grew up eating them every day in the summer. Though I think the mangoes here are sweeter still."

The chief seemed pleased by this praise of the local produce. They both returned their attention to their respective plates. Akal tried the papaya next, handling it gently to avoid it falling to pieces. It yielded its succulence with just the push of his tongue. The nectar flooded his mouth and the delicate aroma made its way up his throat and to his nostrils, sending Akal into a sugary daze. He sighed contentedly, leaning back against his tree. Somewhere in the distance, the cock continued to sound its tortured crow, but with a belly full of fruit, it no longer disturbed Akal's peace.

"I hear you saved my nephew's life."

Akal shook his head to clear the drowsy haze and turned to look at Ratu Teleni. The chief's gaze seemed to hold a challenge.

"I would say he saved mine," Akal replied, being deliberately vague as he did not know what Taviti had told his family.

"What I would like to know is: why was he somewhere where lives were in danger at all?" the chief asked, his stern tones resonant with authority. "I had assurances from your inspector-general that Taviti would be kept safe."

"He accompanied me to interview a witness, and the situation got out of control. Neither he nor I could have predicted this. Taviti wishes to serve his community as a police officer—he wants to learn. I help him where I can."

"His service should be to his *vanua*, to his village, as my heir. He is my older brother's son, the eldest son of the eldest brother. I have no younger brothers, so the role of chief goes to him when I die. I wanted him in Suva for some time, to make connections, learn how the Britishers work, so he can represent our interests. He should be working in the government building. Instead he has joined the police force. It is a distraction."

Taviti had never told Akal that he was his uncle's heir. It seemed a significant omission.

"I wonder, sir," Akal said slowly, "if perhaps he doesn't find the diplomatic duties challenging enough. He is exceptionally good at handling people. I wonder if he is looking at the policing duties as a different way to challenge his abilities."

"Is he exceptionally good at handling people?" Ratu Teleni asked. "If he was, then surely his wife and children would still be here."

Akal nodded, conceding the point. Taviti's revelations last night about his marriage had been news to Akal, but it seemed that it was not a hidden secret in the village. He wondered how Taviti felt knowing that everyone knew about the state of his marriage. It must have been easier to be in Suva, far away from the speculation.

"So far, the inspector-general has not managed to control Taviti particularly well. Taviti respects you, he looks up to you. I would thank you, Sergeant Singh, to stop teaching him policing. Instead, I expect you to steer him towards fulfilling his duties to me and his village, his larger destiny."

Akal made no reply and the chief didn't appear to require one. He seemed to believe that his wishes would be accepted as an order, regardless of the fact that he had no authority over Akal. Both men were silent and resumed gazing at the river until Taviti arrived, clad in one of the *sulus* that the local men preferred when they weren't working. Akal eyed the simple piece of patterned cotton tied around Taviti's waist with envy. He was already sweating in his uniform.

"Good morning," Taviti said, scratching his stomach and then yawning as he stretched. "Oh, good, breakfast."

"Good morning, nephew. Here, take my spot. I will send someone to you with some breakfast."

"*Vinaka.*" Taviti thanked his uncle and leaned against the tree he had vacated. "So, what first?"

"First we need to go back to Levuka and send a report to Suva on what has happened here. Then we go looking for our Germans. But before all of that, you need to put on some real clothes."

"Don't worry, Akal, my *sulu* is tied tight. Won't fall in the middle of the search," Taviti replied with mock seriousness.

"Maybe not, but I don't think the Germans will take us very seriously with your chest on show."

"What is wrong with my chest?" Taviti asked, puffing said chest out and looking down.

Before Akal could reply with the many things wrong with Taviti wandering around without a top on, the same young lady from earlier arrived with Taviti's breakfast and handed the plate to him, without taking her eyes off Akal. Taviti said something to her in their native language, and the young woman blushed and giggled, then beat a hasty retreat, presumably before Taviti could tease her any more.

"You have made a friend," Taviti said, raising his eyebrows at Akal as he tucked into his breakfast.

"How could I have made friends with her? I didn't say anything to her!" Akal protested.

"Well, just be careful. She is my cousin, and the chief's favourite niece. Unless maybe you want to marry her?"

Akal glared at Taviti. "I was really enjoying breakfast with Ratu Teleni before you arrived. But if you are going to be annoying, I will go find the Germans myself."

"No, no, I will stop teasing you," Taviti said, inhaling his papaya a little faster. "I have a lot to learn about interviewing witnesses. I would like to join you."

"All right. Well, I'll go wash up a little and then meet you back here."

"Careful my cousin doesn't catch you on your own."

TAVITI HAD DRESSED and rejoined Akal and they were just about to head into Levuka to send their pigeon post message to Suva when a teenage boy, one of Taviti's many cousins, came running into the village, shouting.

Taviti shouldered his way through the crowd that seemed to spring up from nowhere to surround the boy. He barked orders at the lot of them, and they quietened down.

The boy, winded, was bent double, panting. He straightened up when Taviti put a hand on his shoulder and asked him something. Taking a deep breath, the boy started to talk, and seemed to calm as he answered Taviti's questions, while

Taviti seemed to tense. He looked at Akal with urgency, and Akal pushed his way past the gathered onlookers to join Taviti. "What's happened?"

"We have to go. A group of warriors were out this morning and they think they've captured our Germans."

They departed immediately, following the teenager to plunge into the jungle. There was a short walk on flat land before the incline grew steep. Akal alternated between looking at the path, where the roots conspired to trip him, and looking up to avoid the branches which snatched at him. He could hear his harsh breath and knew his face was turning red. Ahead of him, Taviti seemed entirely unaffected, bouncing slightly on his feet as he walked. Akal gritted his teeth and pushed on.

As he laboured up the hill, Akal pondered the implausibility of the expedition they were on. In Suva, they had laughed at the idea that there were Germans anywhere in Fiji. But now multiple men had reported seeing them, and one of those men was now dead. If there weren't actually any Germans, there was certainly something strange going on in Levuka.

The path finally levelled out and Akal was able to catch his breath. He leaned against a tree, taking a moment to look around. There were no coconut palms in this part of the forest, and the ground was rich dirt, with no sand. His deep breaths filled his nostrils with the smell of the earth and the leaves they had crushed beneath their feet, of green and brown, heavy and damp.

"Are we close?" he called after Taviti, who had picked up speed and was moving out of sight.

"Still a little way to go," Taviti replied over his shoulder, momentarily slowing down. "You need to run up more hills, Akal."

Despite the fact that Akal was looking at Taviti's back, he could hear the laughter in his voice. He groaned and started moving again, jogging to catch up to Taviti.

"Would the people from your uncle's village use this path?"

"Not the part we have been on. There is an easier way to get to the beach we are going to, but this way is faster."

Indeed, the next part of the track, sloping downwards now, was wider and more established. This close to the ocean, the ground was a blend of sand and dirt and the trees were a curious mix of coconut palms and the lush trees of the jungle. All three of them picked up speed as the going got easier and as the end of the path was approaching.

They broke into a run when they heard the shouting.

The last few hundred yards of the path blurred by. More light filtered through the thinning foliage, so Akal's eyes had a chance to adjust. He was not completely blinded when he, Taviti, and Taviti's cousin skidded to a halt at the beach, though he still held his hand up to his forehead and blinked to focus. They had emerged at a cove, jungle-covered cliffs on either side, with a path out to the open sea between.

Directly ahead of them, a remarkable scene was playing out on the beach. Six European men were surrounded by a group of Fijian warriors armed with spears. The Europeans stood back-to-back in a tight circle with their hands in the air as the spears jabbed dangerously close to their necks. They had clearly been taken by surprise as they all had pistols in holsters on their belts, but none of them had drawn their weapons. One of the Fijians was reaching through and systematically disarming them, while another tied their hands. A few feet away, a cache of goods lay on the white sand—coiled ropes, wooden crates of tinned food, and other odds and ends.

When they noticed the interlopers, a few of the warriors switched their attention to Akal and Taviti, spears bristling and then dipping when they realised who it was. Peni broke off and came to talk to them. He and Taviti engaged in a brief, intense conversation, which Taviti then summarised for Akal.

"The fishermen saw the camp and a turtle carcass this morning as they were going out to fish, but didn't see the Europeans. They must have caught a turtle and eaten it last night. This is *tabu*. Only the chief may eat turtle. The fishermen came back and told my uncle, who sent the warriors out to capture whoever it was. The camp was still empty when the warriors arrived, so they hid in the jungle. When the Europeans returned to their camp, the warriors surprised and captured them."

Akal had held his tongue while Taviti told this outlandish story, but as soon as Taviti stopped talking, Akal burst out, "This much fuss over a turtle? Is it truly that serious?"

"How serious do those spears look to you?" Taviti asked.

"You make a good point. Very well, thank Peni for us. Could you ask him to lend us a few men to help take them back to the station?"

"No, you don't understand. Peni is taking them back to my uncle to answer for their crime. He sent word back to us when he realised they may be our Germans, but he only did that as a courtesy, in case we wanted to wait at the village rather than go into Levuka. He wasn't expecting us to come here," Taviti said.

"No, no, we need to take them back to Levuka. They may have murdered a man. No taboo can possibly be more important than that. Tell your cousin that he must release the Europeans to us."

"He can't do that. He doesn't answer to me or you. Only the chief. We will have to talk to my uncle."

Akal blinked at Taviti in momentary surprise. Their friendship had always been irreverent, but there had always been an underlying understanding of the chain of command. Akal was accustomed to Taviti following his lead. But here, Taviti assumed an unconscious air of leadership that was unfamiliar, at least from Akal's perspective, but seemed entirely natural. Nonetheless, Akal shook his head, preparing to argue with his friend, but a commotion by the water pulled their attention over.

"Hello! Hello!" one of the Europeans was calling out in English, angering his captors, who shouted at him and gestured menacingly with their spears.

"Can you make sure they don't hurt him?" Akal urged Taviti. Taviti relayed this to his cousin, who barked some rapid-fire commands to his warriors. When things calmed down, Akal tried a different angle with Taviti: "Could we at least talk with them before they go to the village?"

After some conversation between Taviti and his cousin, Peni reluctantly nodded.

"We had better keep it quick, Akal," Taviti warned.

They approached the group cautiously. Peni went ahead and gave instructions to the warriors, who moved back a little, but maintained an alert posture. The man who had spoken earlier stepped forward. Towering above his compatriots, fair and broad shouldered, he cut a dashing figure.

With high cheekbones and a straight, narrow nose, his features were sharp and aristocratic. He wore the mantle of leadership easily, his movements assured and calm despite the weapons pointed at him.

"Gentlemen, I'm very glad to see you," the European man said, shaking Akal and Taviti's hands briskly. "My shipmates and I are in a bit of trouble here. You seem to know these fellows. Could you help us?"

"I am Sergeant Akal Singh, of the Fijian Constabulary, Suva Division. This is Constable Taviti Tukana," Akal replied, nonplussed. This was not the usual reaction Europeans had to non-European police officers. He could not remember the last European man to shake his hand. He supposed that perhaps the spears were a good incentive for the unexpected levels of friendliness. "Who am I speaking with?"

"Ah, excellent, British policemen! Now we will get this resolved. Well met, Sergeant Singh, Constable Tukana. I am Johannes Larsen, captain of the *Petropolis*, a merchant ship hailing from the port of Oslo. These men are my crew. Do you know why your friends have taken us captive?"

Akal privately tucked away the name Oslo, to investigate where this actually was when he had a moment. The mention of the *Petropolis* being a merchant ship was telling—Larsen clearly did not want to be taken for military. Looking around at the rest of the sailors, alert and tense, it was difficult to tell whether they were at military readiness, or merely well disciplined.

"Apparently you have angered the local Fijian chief and you must make reparations," Akal replied.

"How can this be? We haven't even met the chief. We

have been staying well outside of town. We only went ashore twice to get supplies, which we last did yesterday, and we were about to go back to our ship. If you can get them to release us, I guarantee we will leave and never return to these shores." Some disdain filtered through this last statement, incongruous against Larsen's otherwise bluff charm.

"The supplies, you bought them from Mr. Sanjay Lal?" Akal asked. Upon receiving a blank look from the captain, Akal clarified, "The store outside of town?"

The confusion cleared from Larsen's face and he nodded. "Yes, the Indian man. Has he made some sort of complaint to the chief? Is that why they have captured us?"

"No, that is not the case. The chief has some other issue to discuss with you that I don't fully understand. However, you should know that Mr. Lal has died under suspicious circumstances. You and your crew are the last people to see him alive. Even if I convince the chief to release you, I'm afraid you won't be departing any time soon."

"Dead!" Captain Larsen exclaimed, his head jerking back in surprise. The news briefly broke the façade of charm he had been projecting. "We just saw him yesterday. He was alive when we left," he hastened to add. "He seemed perfectly happy. We left him with plenty of gold, twice what we should have paid."

"We will investigate his death. But for now, you will have to go to the village. I will make sure you are treated fairly there."

As Akal walked back to Taviti and Peni, the European man continued to protest their innocence, until the warriors encircled the group and he fell quiet.

"Let's get to the village and talk to the chief," Akal said to Taviti. "I'd like to get our European guests safely in the holding cells."

"No chance of that. We have to go through the formalities. My uncle will want to consult with his advisers. That will take some time."

"We are the law, Taviti. Ratu Teleni can't just do whatever he wants."

"Are you sure about that?" Taviti replied, a smirk hovering around his lips. Akal followed his gaze to the ferocious warriors, spears at the ready.

"You will have to advise me on how to proceed," Akal said, heaving a frustrated sigh, making the request sound churlish. Hearing his own peevishness, Akal tried to adopt a more genial tone. None of this was Taviti's fault, after all. "I don't want to offend them and have one of those spears pointed at me."

"We should go back to the village with Peni, make sure the Germans are locked up and safe. Then I will find out about getting an audience with the chief."

THE WARRIORS TOOK their prisoners back to the village the longer way, going around the hill instead of over it. A few younger men had also arrived at the beach, excited to witness the capture of these Europeans, and they were tasked with gathering up the items at the camp and bringing them back to the village.

The Europeans were fractious and dragged their heels, talking to each other in their own language, and looking around in a way that made Akal think that they were planning a bid for freedom. The warriors kept a close eye on them, spears at the ready, giving them no opportunity for escape.

Akal and Taviti followed along behind. Akal sighed and broached a topic that he had no real desire to discuss, but felt he had to, now that they were in the throes of an investigation. "Your uncle has asked, or rather told, me not to help you learn any more about policing. It seems he expects you to be learning how to be his successor instead."

Taviti's lips tightened, setting his face into unfamiliar tense lines. "Are you planning on obeying him?" Taviti asked. Generally everything Taviti said, no matter how prosaic, sounded like it could be a joke. There was none of that thread of humour this time.

"It does sound like you have more important things to do," Akal replied with a questioning lilt.

"My uncle has his crusades. He wants to restore the chiefs as the main power in Fiji. He doesn't want the Britishers to have control," Taviti said, shaking his head, a frown deepening the tense lines on his face. "If only Peni was first in line. He thinks much more like my uncle. Me, I believe in looking forward, not back."

"Have you told your uncle this?"

"Not exactly like that," Taviti said with a sigh. "I will."

"Good. In the meantime, please don't tell him I'm pulling you into situations where I need to save your life."

"Sure thing, Sergeant Singh. I definitely won't tell him that you begged me to come chase Germans with you!"

Akal looked at him with horror and Taviti gave a shout of laughter, his good humour not repressible for long.

"So, what first, Teacher Akal?"

Akal sincerely hoped this nickname would not stick.

"I want to take a look at the items from the sailors' camp. It looked like Sanjay Lal had been whipped, so we need to find that whip. Then let's talk to Captain Larsen, see what he has to say for himself. After that, we need to get back to Levuka and get that message sent over to Suva, let the inspector-general know what has happened. And we need to see what is happening with Miss Katherine and her aunt."

"A relaxed morning, then."

Upon arrival at the village, Akal and Taviti went their separate ways, Taviti to organise an audience with the chief and Akal to look for the whip amongst the sailors' possessions. Their goods had been dumped into a storage hut and the men locked into a separate hut. When the curious boys had gathered up the goods to transport back to the village, Taviti had impressed on them that the items could not be scavenged. It looked as though his instructions had been respected, as the goods seemed to be intact.

There was only space for one person to be inside comfortably, so a guard held the door of the windowless hut open to let some light in while Akal squatted down next to the goods, his back against the wall.

The heavy ropes had uncoiled and were now a tangled mess. Akal lifted them carefully, separating each coarse length and methodically moving them to the side. No whip hidden within the ropes. He emptied one crate of all the tinned goods, at which point the floor of the hut looked a lot like the debris-strewn floor of Sanjay Lal's store. No whip. He emptied the second crate full of other assorted items, largely tools. Still no whip. Disheartened, he was putting all of the items back into the crate when Taviti arrived.

"As expected, Ratu Teleni is calling a council of his advisers and the heads of all the families," he announced.

"When can I meet with him?" Akal asked.

"We won't know anything until after the council, this afternoon. He will talk to you then. Did you find the whip?" Taviti asked hastily, forestalling any further conversation on pushing his uncle for an audience earlier.

"No," Akal responded, still considering whether he should insist Taviti try again. He suspected his friend had done all he could. "But is this everything they bought? It doesn't seem like enough. They were here for a few days trying to secure supplies. I don't quite understand what our European friends are doing here in Fiji, or who they are. Let's go ask them."

They walked over to where the Europeans were being held, which looked a lot like the hut that their goods were stored in. There were no windows for them to escape out of, and the single door was guarded by a young warrior. Taviti spoke with the guard briefly, and he nodded and opened the door for them.

"Captain Larsen," Akal called through the door. "This is Sergeant Akal Singh. Please come out so we can talk to you."

One of the men stood and emerged from the hut, dishevelled but still maintaining his upright bearing.

"Aha, the gentlemen who are going to help us get out of this nasty little hovel," Larsen said. "I am very glad to see you."

"I'm afraid that your accommodation is out of my hands," Akal replied.

"Never mind. I hope we won't be in there for long. Have you found out why we are being held?" Larsen said, some urgency creeping into his tone.

"Did you kill and eat a turtle on the beach where you were captured?" Taviti asked.

"Yes, a few days ago. It was the first good meal my men and I had had for weeks."

"The flesh of the turtle is only for the chief."

Larsen laughed, initially heartily but gradually trailing off as nobody joined him. "You are joking?"

Taviti shook his head.

"It cannot possibly be a serious crime!"

"This is an ancient law. And my uncle, the chief, is very serious about the ancient laws. He doesn't want to lose our culture. So I think he will make an example of you. There will be a meeting with the village council today to decide what the punishment will be."

"Punishment? What kind of punishment? Can't we make some kind of reparation?"

"I don't know. My uncle makes the final decision, but there are more moderate voices on the council."

"What about the British? Do they not have any control here? I thought this was a British colony," Larsen said, switching his attention to Akal, clearly hoping to find a more sympathetic hearing from him.

"I will inform my inspector-general. I am sure he will involve the governor if matters become more serious after the village council," Akal replied evenly. He didn't know precisely what the administration's response would be, but he imagined they would be interested in European sailors being subjected to Fijian cultural laws.

"But I don't know that my uncle will pay much attention to anything the Britishers say," Taviti cautioned. "It might simply be too late by the time they get here and get involved."

"Well, this is quite the sticky situation we find ourselves in. I trust you gentlemen will do all you can to help us?" the captain asked, somehow making it seem like a magnanimous gesture on his part to allow them to help him. "Even if the chief is your uncle," he added to Taviti.

Akal and Taviti both nodded. "Of course, once you have resolved your differences with Ratu Teleni, I will be taking you into custody for questioning regarding the death of Sanjay Lal," Akal reminded him.

The captain looked both puzzled and amused. "So you said before. I am not too concerned. You look like excellent policemen, and you will come to agree that this is absurd. Beyond absurd! Why would we kill him? We had a simple transaction: he sold us goods. We paid him. That is all."

That was hardly all, Akal thought. Who were these men? Captain Larsen had not yet made a good accounting for himself.

"Perhaps we should start at the beginning. What are you doing in Fiji?" Akal asked, keeping his question as broad as possible.

"My ship, the *Petropolis*, ran into a bit of trouble. Some weather pushed us onto a reef about two weeks ago. She is salvageable, but we lost supplies when we ran aground. Luckily, our longboat wasn't damaged, so I refitted her to venture out and find some inhabited islands to source supplies for the repairs. From where we were, Levuka was a good option, big enough that we wouldn't have too many problems buying supplies. I've left most of the crew with the ship and brought just a few men with me."

"The supplies—is that what you had with you when you were captured?"

"Some of them. We had already done one trip to the boat with half of them. We had left the rest there on the beach with one man to guard, and we were coming back for the rest when we were captured."

"So why did you go to Lal's store? It is a little out of the way, isn't it?" Akal asked. "There are stores down on Beach Street, right in town, which seem to have more supplies."

"Ah, well, yes, we realised later that perhaps another store would be better stocked. But five days ago, we arrived at the other side of the island. The way we came around the coastline, his store was the first we saw. We asked if he could supply what we needed: some foodstuffs, some items we need for repairs. We gave him a list. He said he would look into it and to come again the next day. When we returned the next day, he had most of the goods. He helped us get them to our boat. He also said he could get us the rest of what we needed and told us how much it would cost. Of course, he was overcharging us, but we just needed our provisions to repair our ship. Finally, yesterday we came back to pay him and take the goods. We had nothing more to do with him. Why on Earth would we kill him?"

Akal rapidly assessed the situation. Would they admit to knowledge of Lal's double-cross? He didn't think so. But their reaction would be interesting nonetheless. It was worth a try. He twitched an eyebrow at Taviti, hoping this would silently communicate to him to follow Akal's lead.

"Perhaps you found out that he had told the police that there were Germans trying to buy goods from him?" Akal said slowly, stressing the word German.

Larsen froze momentarily, consternation flashing across his face before he launched into a vehement denial.

"German? We aren't German. We are Norwegian. I told you; we are from Oslo. I have a merchant ship, nothing to do with the war. No, no, no, this is all a mistake."

Akal was not convinced. Naturally Larsen would not want to be identified as German, the enemy of the British. But it was too easy to simply say they were from some other European country. And there was something about that momentary lapse in Larsen's otherwise unshakably confident demeanour that had Akal's senses on high alert. His skepticism must have been visible on his face.

"Look here, I have a letter from my father—you can see it's written in Norwegian," Larsen said, pulling an envelope from an inside pocket of his jacket and brandishing it at Akal.

Akal's hand automatically went to the letter from his own father, well thumbed in his own pocket. He looked blankly at the envelope the captain was holding out insistently. "I can't read Norwegian."

"Well, is there anybody on this ridiculous island who might?" the European man snapped.

"I will check," Akal said, taking the letter.

"In any case, regarding the shopkeeper," Captain Larsen continued, "I didn't know he had contacted the police with this absurd idea that we are Germans. How would we know? We haven't spoken with anyone else. Only him. He isn't likely to have told us himself, is he?"

This Akal believed. Behind the bluff humour and charm, frustration and conviction rang through every word. The captain was looking at him intently, his hands spread open in an appeal for reason.

"When you spoke with Mr. Lal over these few days, how did he seem? Was he worried about anything?" Akal asked.

"How would I know? I didn't know the man. If anything, he seemed excited to have our big order."

Given the scarcity of goods in the store, evident despite the destruction that had been wrought, Akal thought the last statement was probably true.

"And where is your boat?" Akal asked.

Captain Larsen looked at him through narrowed eyes for a moment, then seemed to come to a decision. "Well, I don't know how to give you directions. But I could take you there if you like."

"No, no. My uncle will not allow this," Taviti responded immediately.

"You didn't even ask," the captain said, a challenge clear in his voice.

Taviti looked at Akal, who gave him a small nod. With a huff, Taviti went and had a brief conversation with the warrior who was guarding the European men, while Akal and Larsen looked on. He returned with a look of triumph.

"No need for you to take us to your boat, Captain. My cousins know where it is. They will take Sergeant Singh and me there this afternoon. We'll make sure it is all safe and sound for you."

"Well, excellent, thank you," Larsen said. Only the faint tightening of his lips betrayed his disappointment.

"We will continue to investigate Sanjay Lal's death," Akal said. "In any case, nothing can be done unless Ratu Teleni releases you."

WHEN AKAL AND Taviti entered the small police station back in Levuka, Constable Kumar jumped out of his seat behind the desk and saluted them.

"Good morning, Constable Kumar," Akal said, returning the salute. Taviti looked at him with raised eyebrows, confused about the formality, but followed suit with an equally formal greeting. Akal's formality was an attempt to hide his amusement. He did not want to embarrass the anxious young man, who had not had the benefit of training at a large police station. They would have to show him how to go on.

But first they had to fill him in on the developments of the morning. Akal summarised the capture of the Norwegian sailors, who seemed to have been the "Germans" that Sanjay Lal and Vijay Prasad had been talking about. Constable Kumar listened intently, his eyes growing wider as the story developed. In fact, Akal thought he looked dismayed, perhaps even anxious. He supposed this was a lot for a young man who was just starting his career. The best way to help Constable Kumar to gain confidence was to work through this case with him, however it turned out.

Their first stop was the Royal Hotel to collect Katherine and Mary, so they could join them on their second stop, the pigeon post. The ladies were ready for the day and waiting at a small table outside, in the shade of the verandah. On the floor next to Katherine was a basket with a bouquet of flowers peeping from the top, ready to be laid at Hugh Clancy's wife's grave. Akal recognised the flowers as Fiji's ubiquitous bright red hibiscus and velvety white and yellow frangipani, the latter filling the air with their intense sweet perfume.

"Good morning, gentlemen," Katherine sang out as they approached.

"Good morning!" Taviti boomed back, while Akal responded more gently and Constable Kumar merely nodded.

"Ready to go," Katherine said, lightly springing down the stairs to meet them. Her aunt followed more slowly behind, escorted by Taviti. As they walked down Beach Street, Katherine maneuvered herself to be beside Akal, who was at the front with Constable Kumar. Constable Kumar immediately sped up, presumably due to his fear of being caught in any conversation with the young woman. Akal looked at the younger man with envy.

"So, what is your first step in the murder investigation?" she asked, an avid gleam in her eyes.

Akal paused for a moment, then decided to answer, given she might be able to help him. He once more told the story of the capture of the European men that morning, which she listened to with sporadic, scandalised gasps. He ended with their explanation of their disputed nationality: "They say they are Norwegian. As proof, the captain has given me a letter, which he says is from his father, written in Norwegian. Do you know the language?"

"No, I don't know anyone who would know Norwegian. But I do know German. I should be able to tell you if it is German, if that will help?"

Akal nodded and handed her the letter, which was in his pocket next to his own letter from his father. She pulled the letter out of the envelope and scanned it.

"Well, I can tell you it isn't German. So maybe they *are* Norwegian? That's disappointing," she said with a pout. "Norwegians aren't very controversial."

"I'm happy with less controversy. I think we've got quite enough at the moment as it is," Akal replied with a rueful smile. Katherine's laughter shimmered over him.

"So the Germans were fictional after all. What a shame. I

remembered some more about the stories in the newspaper back at home. They were writing about a German aristocrat named Count Felix von Luckner, who has been sinking ships all over the Atlantic, and they think he might be in the Pacific now. He's supposed to be tall and handsome and very charming. They have dubbed him the Sea Devil for all of his exploits. I was really hoping to meet him!"

Akal frowned. Tall, handsome, very charming. That sounded rather a lot like Captain Larsen. Perhaps the German question was not fully resolved after all—though it would not do to let on to Katherine. He made some interested noises, and then diverted Katherine with questions about Sydney for the rest of the walk.

The pigeon loft was nearby, at the water's edge, facing the sea. It was a solidly built wooden structure, on stilts to keep the birds high off the ground. The front of the loft did not have a wall but was instead covered in mesh. From this open front, Akal could see an array of the cooing messengers cozy in their nests. A wooden stepladder leaned against the side of the loft. Akal eyed the whole construction warily. The steps seemed solid enough, but they led to a door so small he'd have to bend himself in half to get inside.

There was a young man sitting in the shade of a coconut tree nearby; Kumar identified him as John, who ran the Levuka pigeon loft. When John stood, the top of his head wasn't even close to Akal's shoulder. Now here was someone who could fit easily through the door of the pigeon loft. Akal wondered if this was a primary criterion for the job.

"What is your message?" asked John, looking down at his notepad and not making eye contact with any of the three police officers.

"I will write it. It is sensitive information," Akal said.

"No. I must write it. You will make it too big." The response was immediate and almost panicked, the young man shaking his head repeatedly.

"It is all right," Constable Kumar explained to Akal. "John doesn't talk to anyone, just the pigeons. He won't even remember what is on the message, will you, John?"

"No," John replied, still shaking his head but more gently now, his agitation seeming to ease with Constable Kumar's understanding. "I must write the message because you will make it too big."

There was some negotiation on the wording of the message. Akal wrote out his full version on his notepad, then John wrote a version that dropped all the words he deemed unnecessary.

Local Indian shopkeeper murdered. European sailors have been accused. Deny being German, seem to be Norwegian. Are being held by local village for theft of turtle.

After being reassured by Taviti, who saw these messages in his deskbound role, that this abbreviated version would be understood, John transcribed it onto special paper— extremely thin and light—that he had for this purpose. He rolled the paper up into a tiny cylinder, ready for insertion into one of the sealed tubes which were attached by cuffs to the pigeons' legs.

John then climbed up into the loft to choose a pigeon to fly this message over to Suva. Akal watched as John opened the mesh with a pigeon in hand, slipped the message into its tube, and boosted the bird into the air. They all watched as the bird fluttered, seeming disoriented for a minute, before righting itself and proceeding directly over the ocean.

"Well, there it goes," Katherine said with wonder. "It is truly astonishing that such a little bird can fly all that way and deliver such a powerful message."

"In half an hour all of Fiji will be convinced that the war has arrived in Levuka," Taviti said. "To be honest, I never thought we would actually find any Germans here."

"I don't think we should assume anything," Akal said with a frown. "I do feel that there is something suspicious about the captain, but nothing concrete. And Miss Katherine has confirmed that a letter the captain claims is from his father is written in a language other than German. Who knows, maybe they are a Norwegian merchant ship as they claim."

"Where are Norwegian people from?" asked Constable Kumar.

Akal and Taviti looked at each other blankly.

"Norway, which is a country in Europe," Katherine replied, before either of the two senior officers had to admit their ignorance. "They are not part of the war. They certainly aren't supporting Germany."

"Anyway, it doesn't matter," Akal said briskly. "If they are Germans, they are hardly going to admit it. We will get them released, get them back to Suva, and let the inspector-general deal with them." He twitched an eyebrow at Taviti, and they laughed silently while the others weren't looking. Thurstrom had sent Akal out here on a wild goose chase in his ongoing efforts to humiliate him. Now it looked like the goose was going to come back to bite the inspector-general.

However, before they could get on with investigating the situation with the Germans, or the Norwegians or whatever they actually were, Akal had to get his duties as Katherine and Mary's escort squared away. He was champing at the bit but knew that if he didn't take care of this, which was originally why he was sent to Levuka, the inspector-general would relish the opportunity to reprimand him. He had to manage both.

"Constable Kumar, the ladies wish to visit the grave of Mr. Hugh Clancy's wife. Do you know where this would be? We need to escort them."

"Yes, sir," Constable Kumar replied. "The Draiba Cemetery. It is a short walk."

"Are you ready to go now?" Akal asked the ladies.

"Actually, isn't the police station nearby?" Katherine said, with an eager, hopeful air. "Before we go to the cemetery, could I take another look at the puzzle box? I have an idea on how to open it."

At the station, Akal retrieved the box, which he had locked in a desk drawer, and handed it to Katherine. Katherine sat at the front desk of the station as the rest of the group crowded around her. Flipping the box over, she ran her finger across the tiny holes on the bottom of the box, then reached under the flowers in her basket to retrieve a small tin. She opened the lid and carefully shook some pins out onto the table. Not carefully enough. Akal slammed his hand down on the table to block the pins from rolling onto the floor. Katherine smiled her thanks up at him, and Akal forgot where he was for a moment.

Picking up the nearest pin, Katherine inserted it into one hole, then another. She frowned, and repeated the process more slowly.

"Hmm . . . There is definitely something to this. I can feel a difference when I put the pin into some holes. Some of them I feel like I hit wood, while the others have some give at the bottom."

"So, you think this is how to open the secret compartment?" Akal asked, leaning in to get a closer look. He didn't realise how close he was until he felt the puff of her breath on his cheek when she responded.

"I think so. I must have to do it in some order. Or perhaps a pattern," Katherine said absently, as she continued to try different holes with her pin.

Akal stood upright with a sense of regret and glanced around. He caught Mary's knowing gaze and flushed, looking away quickly. Luckily, everyone else was too engrossed with the mystery of the jewellery box to have noticed his momentary lapse.

Something Katherine had said tripped a memory for Akal. He withdrew his notebook from his pocket and flipped to the last page.

"Something like this?" he asked, showing her the symbol the dying man had drawn in his blood.

Katherine seized the notebook and traced the lightning bolt-like shape with her finger. "Yes, this could work," she said, her eyes shining excitedly up at Akal. "Where did you find this?"

"Erm . . . in the victim's house," he replied vaguely, wanting to spare her the gory details.

"But was it near the jewellery box?" she asked with some urgency.

"No, but . . . it seemed to be very important to the victim," he said. Taviti started to speak but stopped when he noticed Akal's glower.

Katherine frowned at him, then shook her head impatiently and said, "Let me see what I can do."

For the next few minutes, the group clustered about the desk barely drew a breath. Brow furrowed with concentration, Katherine didn't notice the scrutiny. She tried the pattern one way, shaking her head absently after inserting a few pins. Turning the box clockwise, she tried again. On the third turn, Katherine's brow smoothed and she smiled. She completed the pattern, and with a click, a drawer slid open.

Silence reigned in the room for a moment, until Mary murmured, "Oh, very well done, my dear."

Trance broken, the rest of the group added their congratulations, Katherine beaming at the praise. Attention then turned to the contents of the drawer: a battered envelope, with a stamp peeling at the edges. Etched in faded ink was a woman's name, with an address in India.

Akal opened the envelope and slid out the letter. The coarse paper was covered in cramped letters on both sides; he couldn't read it and didn't recognise the dialect. Handing the letter to Constable Kumar, he asked, "Can you read this?"

Constable Kumar scanned the page and shook his head. "No, sir. The Indians here, we are all from different parts of India. Generally we get by with Hindi and English. This must be somebody's home dialect."

"How many languages are there in India?" Taviti asked, his usual humour giving way to genuine curiosity.

"Who knows," Akal replied, waving his hand in dismissal. "Too many to count. I suppose Mr. Lal could have read them. Surely Mr. Prasad could read them, given they knew each other from India, but I can't rule him out as a suspect yet, so I can hardly hand evidence over to him. Assuming he can even read. Are there any other options, Constable?"

"There is a teacher, Master Thakur. He has set up a school for the Indian children. He might be able to help."

"Hmm . . . I'm not sure if that is a good idea," Akal said, forehead wrinkling under his turban as he considered this. "For all we know, he could be the one who attacked Mr. Lal."

"Oh, no, Master Thakur was at a meeting with the parents of the schoolchildren yesterday afternoon. They were trying to figure out how to raise more money for books and such. They were there for many hours."

"Still, he is a civilian," Taviti pointed out.

"Yes, sir," Kumar said, seeming less certain now that there were two officers raising doubts. "But . . . Sub-Inspector Johnson worked with him previously when he needed help with Indian translations."

"Well, then perhaps we can get his help," Akal said, his forehead smoothing out. "Let's at least meet him this afternoon."

Constable Kumar brightened as his suggestion met with approval.

"Do you recognise the woman's name, Kumar?" Akal asked as he handed the constable both the envelope and the letter.

Constable Kumar pursed his lips as he inspected the documents.

"No, sir, I don't know her."

"Well, it certainly doesn't seem to be Sanjay Lal's letter. It is addressed to a woman. I suppose he could have written it to a woman and then never sent it. But it is too beaten and battered; it seems like it has been through the postal service. I wonder why he had it. We will try the teacher this afternoon. Maybe when we know what it says, things will be clearer. Meanwhile, we should get you to the cemetery," Akal said to Mary.

They looked at Katherine, who was still seated and still inspecting the jewellery box. Finally registering the gap in the conversation, she looked up, her eyes refocusing on the people all looking at her with curiosity.

"I think there is another compartment. See, the sides *also* seem to be hollow," Katherine said, tapping the sides of the box.

"I'm afraid we do have to go. We want to get the flowers on Clara's grave before they wilt, and we still have to get back to sorting the house out," Mary said, gently placing a hand on her niece's shoulder.

Katherine seemed to recognise the sense in what Mary was saying and nodded ruefully. "Can I look at it again later?" she asked Akal.

"Of course. By then we might have the letter translated and know whether this is even relevant," Akal said. His instinct was that it would turn out to be important, given the care taken to hide it, and that in his dying moments, Sanjay Lal had given them the information to open the secret compartment.

THE WALK TO the cemetery, which was to the south of Levuka, took twenty minutes. They quickly left the town behind them and walked along the coastline, the ocean glittering to their left and the ever-present hills looming to their right.

Constable Kumar led the way, Akal accompanying him, while Taviti walked behind them with Katherine and Mary. The latter group seemed to be enjoying themselves. Akal gritted his teeth every time a fresh round of laughter drifted forward, Katherine's lilting tones threading around Taviti's booming guffaws. Constable Kumar threw curious glances in Akal's direction but refrained from saying anything, probably because he didn't know what to say.

When they arrived at the cemetery, the rest of the group looked expectantly at Constable Kumar.

"Oh, I am so sorry, I do not know how to find a grave," Constable Kumar stammered. "I only knew the way here."

They all looked across the scattered graves. As with all things in Ovalau, the cemetery spanned up a hill, though a more gentle one than Akal had had to surmount recently. In fact, the land rippled inwards and then back outwards here, so it seemed as though the graves were on two slopes facing each other. It was a modest burial ground, neither tiny nor so enormous that finding an individual grave would be impossible.

"We can take a quarter of the cemetery each," Akal suggested. "Look for the grave of . . ." He gave Katherine an enquiring look.

"Her name was Clara. Clara Clancy," Katherine said quietly, her generally irrepressible demeanour subdued. Mary patted her niece's arm and the two women shared a sad smile. Akal turned and got Constable Kumar and Taviti moving, directing them towards the other side of the cemetery, to give the women a moment of privacy.

Akal allocated himself the upper slope of the hill they were standing on, with Katherine and Mary taking the lower portion. He took his leave from the women and started up the shallow steps that had been cut into the dirt. When he reached the top, he left the steps and moved towards the gravestones. Akal glanced down the hill and saw Katherine looking up towards him, shading her eyes with her hand as she stood next to Mary, who was bending down to peer at a gravestone. Akal raised his hand in greeting, wondering whether she needed something, whether he should walk back down to them. Katherine waved in response before moving on to the next gravestone and bending down to examine the letters engraved there. It seemed she didn't need him after all.

Akal made his way to the first gravestone in his section. The top of the hill flattened out and there were twenty or so graves scattered across the plateau. He wound his way through the gravestones, checking each one for the name Clara Clancy. The gravestones varied from upright head-stones to simple crosses to plaques embedded in the ground to concrete slabs covering the graves. Many of them were grey with time, their inscriptions worn away by wind and rain, the monuments listing to the side from their long years in the ground, while the new graves were still upright, bright and untarnished.

There was no order to the cemetery. Graves seemed to have been added haphazardly, newer graves intermingled with older. The cemetery was only slightly overgrown, giving the sense that it was regularly maintained but overdue for a once-over.

This was Akal's first time walking through a cemetery. He was fascinated. Sikhs generally cremated their dead, and they certainly didn't have headstones. So for him, a cemetery seemed an abstract concept. It was hard to understand that beneath his feet were the bodies of people who had lived, who had worked and eaten meals and laughed and bled somewhere near here, on this same island, probably in Levuka. Why would anyone want to be buried in the ground, trapped, he wondered, rather than be scattered as ashes in the water, free?

Akal reached the furthest end of the plateau without finding Clara Clancy's grave. There, the land sloped downwards so sharply that there were no graves except at the bottom, near the path to Levuka. Coconut palms grew out of the side of the hill, their trunks growing horizontally out of the ground towards the ocean, then taking a turn upwards, towards the sky. Akal turned his own face to the sun, closing his eyes and feeling the warmth on his skin, the changing of light as clouds drifted past. A light breeze brought the salt of the ocean to tingle his nose and tangle in his luxurious nostril hairs.

Akal opened his eyes and turned back to the task at hand, to examine the last few graves on the plateau, the three graves towards the edge. If they were alive, these people would have the best view in the cemetery. Perhaps their spirits could still enjoy it. The first gravestone he looked at was older, and he couldn't discern the inscription. Akal hoped this meant it was too old to be where Clara Clancy was interred, otherwise they might never find her. The next one was newer.

Phillip John Hughes
Born in Manchester 18 June 1870
Died in Levuka 1 April 1904

Aged 33 years
So he giveth his beloved sleep

Engraved underneath this, a more recent inscription, stark against the weathered stone:

Sarah Margaret Hughes
Born in Manchester 14 September 1875
Died in Levuka 4 September 1914
Aged 38 years
Beloved wife and mother

Akal wondered what had brought Phillip and Sarah Hughes from England to Fiji. Prospects of fortune in this far-flung colony? And what had taken Phillip Hughes so young? How had Sarah Hughes taken care of their children after her husband had passed? Where were these orphaned children now that they had lost their mother last year? Even if they were grown enough to take care of themselves, what grief to lose their parents so young. Questions he had no reason to ask, really, other than the aura of mystery, the sense that there was a multitude of stories that had already been lived, that were being played out as ghostly emanations around him—if only he could see them.

Kneeling down in front of the final grave on the plateau, Akal pulled away a tall piece of grass that was obscuring the inscription. *In loving memory of Clara Clancy, beloved wife.* Akal stood and walked to the other side of the plateau, looking down over the slope where Katherine and her aunt were still searching. Katherine was just straightening up from looking at a gravestone; Akal caught her eye and waved her over. She directed her aunt's attention to Akal and the two women walked up the shallow dirt steps to reach him.

When they arrived, Akal wordlessly knelt again and pulled the offending piece of grass aside so they could read the inscription. Katherine nodded at Akal, while Mary's eyes filled with tears. Akal stood up and stepped away to give the women some privacy. Katherine took his position and yanked the weed out by its roots, throwing it over the edge and down the slope. She looked up at Mary.

"It is only Aunt Clara, no other name mentioned. Maybe we were wrong?"

This was said in hushed tones, but in the quiet, still air of the cemetery her voice carried. Akal hastily increased his distance from the grave, walking back towards the dirt steps. As he walked, he wondered what other name Katherine had hoped to find.

When he reached the entrance to the cemetery and looked up to see how the women were doing, he saw they were looking at the graves around Mrs. Clancy's. They didn't seem to find what they were looking for, both women shaking their heads at each grave. They returned to Mrs. Clancy's grave and, pulling aprons and gloves out of the basket Katherine had been carrying, started to weed and tidy around the grave. The final step was to lay the flowers they had brought reverently at the gravestone.

During all this activity, Constable Kumar and Taviti had joined Akal. They stood quietly, nobody really in the mood to talk. Constable Kumar scuffed the tip of his shoe against a clump of grass until he became aware of Akal's glare. Then even that fidgeting stopped and they all stood in their own silent contemplations.

When Mary and Katherine had completed their work, they joined the men and the group departed, more sombre than when they had arrived. As they walked away, Akal glanced back up the hill. The flowers laid at Mrs. Clancy's grave were the only bright spot, red and white against the green of the lawn and the grey of the gravestones.

As they rounded a curve, the mood lifted.

"Where to next, bosso?" Taviti asked Akal. This informality prompted a look of horror from Constable Kumar.

"We need to escort the ladies to Mr. Clancy's house and then meet with the teacher to see if he can translate that letter."

"Well, why don't we switch it around and we can come to meet the teacher with you? I wouldn't want to be responsible for delaying you when you are trying to find a murderer," Katherine said, eyes large in her face in an attempt to look innocent.

"Oh, no, this I really can't allow," Akal said firmly, as Taviti and Mary shook their heads. "This is a police investigation. Opening a puzzle box is one thing—following us around as we speak with the public is another. Anything could happen, you could be hurt."

Looking around at the disapproving expressions of Taviti and Mary, and the implacable resolve on Akal's face, Katherine sighed.

"Perhaps you would like to attend the *lovo* that my uncle is organising for tonight?" Taviti asked, by way of consolation.

Katherine's crestfallen face brightened. "What is a *lovo*?" she asked.

"It is how we cook for a special occasion, such as Sergeant Singh coming to visit," Taviti explained. "We make an oven underground—it is very different than the oven you use. I think you will find it interesting. Maybe you can write something for the newspaper."

"Oh, of course, Constable Tukana, you are brilliant!" Katherine exclaimed. "We would love to come," she said, and belatedly looked at her aunt for agreement. Luckily, Mary appeared equally intrigued and nodded.

"Excellent. I will find you in the evening to escort you to the village," Taviti said. "My uncle will be very pleased to have such lovely guests."

Indian Immigration

Summary of Commission Report

. . . As we consider that the removal of defects would be the most satisfactory result of our inquiries both for emigrants and for the colonies to which they emigrate we think it desirable to recapitulate briefly the more important general remedies which we have recommended in the preceding paragraphs. They are as follows: . . .

7. Facilities for occupying land on a satisfactorily secure tenure should be provided.

8. The registration of marriages should be facilitated.

9. The special needs of Indian children in the matter of primary education should receive consideration.

CHAPTER 5

AKAL AND TAVITI MADE their way back to the police station, where they found John waiting on the bench outside. Without a word, the young man handed them a piece of paper and stumped back towards the pigeon post hutch. Akal and Taviti watched him go, looked at each other, and shrugged.

Akal read the note out loud. "Take the Europeans into police custody for murder. Try to confirm identity. Treat as prisoners of war in case they are Germans. Bring to Suva immediately."

Taviti looked grim. "My uncle will not just hand them over because the inspector-general said so."

"We will have to explain at the village council tonight."

"*I* will have to explain. You don't have standing."

"Very well, a test for the diplomatic skills you have been learning in Suva."

Taviti rolled his eyes as Akal grinned.

"So, do we do as we are told? Are we assuming the European sailors murdered Mr. Lal?" asked Taviti.

"We cannot assume anything—we must prove it. In any case, we can't return to Suva until we get them away from the village. I'll keep working the murder until then. But you should go talk to your uncle."

At this point, Constable Kumar returned from lunch, looking sleepy.

"What did your mother feed you?" Akal asked, faking a hearty laugh to hide his pang of nostalgia.

"*Roti* and *bhindi*," the young constable responded, blinking slowly, his eyelids weighted down with the post-lunch haze. Now Akal was even more envious. Okra was his favourite, and his own mother's *bhindi* was famous in his village.

"Well, if you can stay awake long enough, could you take us to see the teacher?" Akal said. He tried to moderate his snappish tone with a conciliatory smile. It was hardly the young man's fault that Akal was missing his mother's cooking.

Constable Kumar nodded sheepishly and started to walk towards the beach.

"Isn't that the school behind us here?" Akal asked, nodding to the school that Taviti had pointed out the day before. It was a two-story wooden structure painted a crisp white, with the entrance dominated by a bell tower. The arched windows gave it a touch of elegance compared to the buildings around it. They had passed the school a few times as they walked around town, but he had yet to see any children there.

"No, sir," Constable Kumar replied. "That is the Levuka Public School. It is only open to European children and some high-ranking Fijian students. This is why Master Thakur set up his school for the Indian children."

Akal looked at Taviti. "Did you say you went to school there?"

Taviti nodded. "Yes. I was admitted because I am part of the chiefly family. So all my cousins came, but not all the children from my village could." He frowned. "I never asked if they wanted to."

Constable Kumar led them to the Indian school, which turned out to be nothing but a group of children sitting cross-legged on the ground beneath a tree, creating a ring around a man who was also seated in a cross-legged position and reading aloud from a book. He asked a question in Hindi, and the children chorused an answer.

Akal's hand instinctively found the folded square of paper in his pocket, his father's letter, as the sound of their piping, enthusiastic young voices transported him back to India, back to his father's classroom. The memory was rendered in sepia tones, hazy with yearning. He would sit cross-legged on the floor of the schoolroom with the other children from the village, while his father guided them from the blackboard at the front of the room. His father's school in the village in the Punjab had not been as grand as the Levuka Public School, but at least lessons were not conducted under a tree.

On seeing the police officers approach, the teacher signalled an older child to take his place reading from the book, and walked over to where Akal, Taviti, and Constable Kumar waited under the shade of a neighbouring tree. The children were naturally curious and craning around to see what was going on, until a gentle but firm word from their teacher had their eyes forward and focused again.

"*Namaste*, Constable Kumar. Who are your colleagues?" the young man asked. The teacher looked to be in his mid-twenties, about Akal's age. He was a compact man with a slight build, not much taller than his students. His words were accompanied by an assessing gaze.

"Master Thakur, *namaste*. Please meet Sergeant Akal Singh and Constable Taviti Tukana. They are here from Suva."

The teacher nodded to each of them in turn, his innate courtesy once again reminding Akal of his father. "I am pleased to meet you, Sergeant Singh, Constable Tukana."

"As am I, Master Teacher. Apologies for taking you away from your students," Akal said.

"It is a good opportunity to have Samba practice teaching the class," Master Thakur replied, glancing over at his protégé and nodding approvingly.

"My father was a teacher, and he often did the same thing, asking me to step in when he needed a break."

"And yet here you are, a police officer," the teacher said in an enquiring tone.

"I was a little too restless to be a teacher," Akal said ruefully. "Whenever my father stepped away for a moment, I would always think of something more interesting for the other students to do, rather than whatever my father had assigned."

"Perhaps that is not such a bad thing," Master Thakur suggested. "Sometimes capturing a student's interest is more important than letters and numbers."

"It is fortunate that my father can't hear you saying that," Akal said with a chuckle. "He is retired now, but he maintained his standards right until the end of his career."

"That is part of why I came here, to be able to teach as I wanted," Master Thakur responded earnestly. "When the British Indian Association of Fiji advertised for teachers and offered to pay my way out here and help me set up the school, I jumped at the opportunity."

"Well, I think they have some way to go on helping set up the school," Akal said wryly, inclining his head towards the makeshift school, which largely consisted of the shade of a tree.

The teacher laughed. "I am working on it. I have found a location, and the parents will help me build it. It is just a matter of timing now, when the fathers can get away from their fields."

"I wish you the best of luck with it. I am glad to see that at least some of the Indian children in Fiji are receiving an education. I met some on a plantation who had nothing at all."

"Correct, Sergeant Singh. In India, had they been able to go to school, these children would be much more advanced in their studies. But here, depending on the plantation, they often don't start to learn until their parents are out of indenture and have had some time to establish themselves. I keep the fees as low as I can, just enough to keep a roof over my own head, but it isn't easy for those just out of indenture."

Akal pondered this. In his previous case, he had witnessed firsthand the degradation of the indentured servants on the plantations, the appalling accommodation, the hard labour. He had spoken with children who described watching their parents being beaten. He had uncovered systemic abuse of the Indian women. In his mind, the saving grace was that if they could survive the five years of indenture, then there was opportunity here in Fiji that wasn't available in India for the class of people who would sign up for the indenture. But it seemed that this idea was naive also. There may have been opportunity, but it still required a lot of hard work.

"In any case, Sergeant Singh, I'm sure you didn't come to

talk to me about the state of education for Indians in Fiji. How can I help you?"

"We are investigating the murder of Sanjay Lal," Akal said.

"I'm very glad to hear it. It is quite frightening to think that he was savagely attacked in his own home. I have heard some stories that the perpetrators are a group of European men. Is this correct?"

"We are still investigating, sir, nothing conclusive yet," Akal replied smoothly. He had suspected that the rumours would already be flying, but he still wished it wasn't so. "Where were you yesterday afternoon?"

The teacher looked at him quizzically. "At a meeting with the students' parents."

Akal was not surprised that Constable Kumar had known the teacher's whereabouts so accurately. In his village back in India, everybody would have known when his father was having a similar meeting. "What was your relationship with Mr. Lal?"

The teacher's confused expression deepened, but he obligingly answered, "I didn't know him. I could probably recognise him on the street, but I don't think I've ever had a conversation with him. He doesn't have children and he didn't seem to be interested in the school, so our paths didn't really cross."

Constable Kumar was nodding in the background as the teacher was talking. Between this information and the confirmed alibi, Akal concluded that it seemed very unlikely that the teacher was involved in this crime.

"Thank you. We are here to ask for your help with the investigation. I believe Sub-Inspector Thompson has asked you to help with some translations in the past?" On Master Thakur's nod, Akal continued, "I assume he had impressed on you the need for discretion. If I ask for your help, you must not mention anything that we speak about to anybody. This is part of a murder investigation—it is highly sensitive."

"Of course," the teacher said solemnly.

"We have found a letter at Mr. Lal's house, but none of us can read the dialect. Do you recognise it?" Akal handed over the letter from the puzzle box.

Master Thakur scanned the page, eyes inching from side to side so slowly that Akal could track his progress. He waited with bated breath until the man responded with an ambiguous waggle of his head.

"The language may be Magahi, from the south of Bihar."

"That is where Mr. Lal was from," Kumar said.

"It is not one I know well, but I know enough. For now, I can at least tell you that they are to a mother from her son."

Akal pondered this for a moment, trying to make this new piece of information fit in the incomplete puzzle. Why would Sanjay Lal have hidden a letter to his own mother? It didn't make sense.

"How long do you think it would take to translate the entire letter?" Akal asked.

"If I can concentrate, it won't take too long. My lessons are nearly done for the day. If you wait for about fifteen minutes while I conclude the class with the children, I can work on it straight away for you."

"That would be greatly appreciated," Akal said. "I will wait here."

The teacher returned to his pupils under the other tree and took the reading back over from his apprentice. Akal

suggested that there was no point in all three of them waiting for the teacher, so the two constables could return to the
police station, where Taviti would mentor Kumar on the more
day-to-day aspects of running the station. The two men set
off and Akal settled in to wait. He found a good spot by the
trunk of the tree, brushed some twigs and rocks away, and
sat down, the tree trunk solid behind his back. Akal watched
the outdoor schoolroom for a moment; so different, yet
so similar to his own childhood school. He pulled out his
father's letter once more and started to read.

"Sergeant Singh?"

Master Thakur's querying voice jolted Akal out of the
doze he had fallen into. He hastily folded up his father's letter and placed it back in his pocket. From his other pocket,
he withdrew the letter that had been hidden in the jewellery
box and handed it to Master Thakur, who had taken a seat,
cross-legged, opposite Akal.

"This might take me a little while," the teacher said
absently, already focused on the letter as he pulled a pad and
paper from his battered satchel.

"That is fine, I am happy to wait," replied Akal, settling
back against the tree once more. He watched Master Thakur
for a little while as the man muttered to himself and then
jotted down notes in his pad, completely absorbed in his
task. This quickly became boring, and Akal instead started
to think through the case, trying to figure out what it was
that made him uneasy about simply assigning the guilt to the
Europeans. He hadn't come up with any satisfactory answers
when the teacher finished.

"I wasn't able to translate all of it, but enough to make
sense of the letter," he said, handing Akal his notepad. "It

seems to be a letter from a son to his mother, but there are no names mentioned."

Akal scanned the translation, his eyes snagging on the word police.

"Is this correct? The son is apologising to his mother that the police are still bothering her? And he thinks they will give up looking for him eventually?"

"Yes, that part of the translation I am quite sure about."

"But no clues as to the identity of the writer?" Akal asked. When the teacher confirmed with a shake of his head, Akal continued, "Did you recognise the name on the envelope, the recipient, Seema Tripathi?"

The teacher once more shook his head.

"This has been very helpful, Master Thakur, thank you. And please remember, not a word to anybody."

"I was happy to help. I think we will all be much relieved when this murderer is caught."

The two men made their farewells and went their separate ways. As Akal walked to the police station, he pondered the mystery of the letter. Was it Sanjay Lal's letter? Had he been the one to have been wanted by the police? But no, the date on the letter was from eight years ago, and Mr. Lal had only been in Fiji for a few years. So whose letter was it, and why did Sanjay Lal have it hidden in his jewellery box?

THE AFTERNOON WAS wearing on by the time Taviti and Akal returned to the village, leaving Constable Kumar behind to man the police station, a familiar duty he gratefully retreated to. Taviti's cousin Peni was waiting for them in the central clearing, and when he saw them, he sprang up from the log he'd been lounging on and loped over to meet them. The cousins greeted each other enthusiastically and Peni gave Akal a shy grin. His smile was so reminiscent of Taviti's, equally jaw splitting with the same excess of toothiness, that Akal couldn't help but automatically reciprocate.

"Peni knows where the boat is, but it isn't too easy to get to. He'll take us there now. Are you ready?"

"I suppose I have to be. I'd rather it be easy, though."

"Of course," Taviti said with faux sympathy. "Next time we'll ask the criminals if they can leave their boat somewhere more easily accessible."

The first leg of the journey was to return to the beach where they had captured the sailors that morning. Thankfully, they went the longer but easier way, which was more or less flat, the trees well spaced apart and easily navigated. Once they arrived, Peni walked over to a spot at the treeline at the east of the cove. He disappeared behind a tree, and then poked his head back out, gesturing for them to come over. Together, they plunged into a dark, dense forest that immediately started to slope upwards. The more challenging part of the journey had commenced.

Ten minutes later, they emerged from the forest. Akal tried to surreptitiously catch his breath as Peni and Taviti discussed their next obstacle with much gesticulating. They needed to navigate down a steep, rocky, tree-covered slope of about thirty feet to get down to the bank of a narrow inlet, which was cutting into the island from the east. Peni pointed to a spot at the bottom of the slope, where the boat was, per Taviti's translation. All Akal could see were leaves and branches. After a few moments, his brain caught up with his eyes and started to sort through what he was seeing. The wind gently moved the treetops, and Akal started to see glimpses of the mast of a boat, its sails rolled and tied up.

Once again, Peni took the lead, showing them which trees to hold onto as they skidded their way downhill. Their progress was steady, if slow, until about two-thirds of the way down Akal lost his footing on some loose rocks, sending them skittering down past Peni. Landing heavily on his left side, Akal slipped a little down the hill, rocks grinding against his hip as he slid. He could feel it to his bones. His death grip on the branch that he was using for support, which Peni had used before him, slowed his fall. He instinctively scrambled with his feet until he found some solid rocks to brace against and came to a stop.

Taviti was shouting down at him in English, Peni shouting up at him in Fijian. Akal rested in place for a moment, but the muscles in his arms were burning so he couldn't stay there long. "I'm all right, Taviti. Just stay where you are," Akal called out.

"Are you sure? I can come down and help you."

"No. Just give me a minute."

Taviti relayed this message to Peni, as Akal, with his arms screaming, pulled his way up until he was seated by the tree he was holding onto. Panting, he rested there, nauseated, head swimming. Peni had come back up the hill towards him and waited anxiously for him to recover. When Akal's breath finally evened, he nodded to Peni, whose face slackened with relief. He started pointing out to Akal how he could safely get down, going around the loose rocks. Gritting his teeth, Akal pulled himself to standing, and resumed his journey down the hill.

The bottom of the hill was only marginally less precarious.

There was no clear place to stand, with the water seeming deep to the very edge of the land. Trees grew to the waterline and their branches overhung the water, leaves dipping in and out as the wavelets rippled their way inland. There they found the boat, tied to a tree and well hidden amongst the branches.

"This must be it," Taviti said. "Nobody from around here has a boat like that. I wonder where the actual ship is."

"Captain Larsen said it had run aground and they have been sailing in the longboat for days, so it must be a fair way away. It seems quite risky to have left the rest of his men on a wrecked ship, but I suppose he might not have had many options."

It was a long, open boat, with a single mast. Given there had been six sailors in it, Akal assumed it was stable enough for all of them to be aboard, but to be cautious they agreed that Taviti would go first, Akal would follow, and Peni would stay on land. Taviti took a large stride and landed heavily on the boat, causing it to rock alarmingly. Once it had settled, Taviti stepped over the boards which spanned the width of the boat to form benches. Then Akal took a similarly large stride to board. He landed with less disturbance, due in no part to his skill, but likely simply because he was lighter than Taviti. In fact, he was less graceful, his injured hip smarting at the requirement to be nimble.

Now aboard, they started searching through the crates in the boat. Several of the crates were securely lashed down. Akal tested the knots on one of them and couldn't budge it, unsurprising given it had been expertly tied by a sailor. One set of crates, towards the front of the boat where Akal was, had not yet been tied down. Akal gestured for Taviti to come back towards him, which Taviti did very carefully.

"These must be the first round of supplies that the captain mentioned. No wonder they had to do it in two rounds. You really couldn't carry much down that hill. Help me search them."

Akal lifted the lid off one crate, while Taviti lifted the lid off another. At the top of Akal's crate, he found a coiled whip, stained black with dried blood. Next to it, a small sack lay on its side, a few gold sovereigns spilling out; the sunlight glinted off the coins' surface, showing a man on horseback slaying a dragon. Akal lifted the whip in one hand and a gold sovereign in the other to show Taviti.

"I think our Norwegian friends have some explaining to do."

The men quickly dismissed the possibility of sailing the boat to a more hospitable harbour, given that none of them had any sailing experience, particularly not with this type of boat. They took the whip and the bag of coins and secured the loose crates to the best of their abilities, and Peni agreed to set a guard on the boat once they returned to the village. Akal happily agreed that Taviti and Peni should carry the whip and coins, given they were more familiar with the terrain and less likely to fall. He shuddered as Peni casually looped the whip over his shoulder, a shower of dried blood flaking off as he moved.

The journey back up the hill was more strenuous than the way down, but much less treacherous. Retracing their steps, they walked back through the forest and reached the beach, where Akal called for a rest. He and Taviti sat side by side on the sand, looking out over the water.

"Did you notice anything strange on the boat?"

"No. What are you thinking?"

"Did you see blood on anything else, other than the whip?"

Taviti shook his head.

"Why didn't anything else in the crate have blood on it? No bloody handprints. Surely with the amount of blood on Mr. Lal, they would have got some on themselves and it would have gotten everywhere."

"Maybe they washed the blood off themselves, and off the crates. How else would these things have gotten here?"

"They could have washed themselves," Akal agreed doubtfully. "But inside the crate where the whip was—how was that so clean? Unless the whip went in there when the blood was already dry."

"Akal, man, what are you doing? Are you just looking for complications? Aren't things hard enough already?"

"I don't know, Taviti. Something just isn't adding up."

"Well, we can think about it some more when we get back to the village. Unless you need more time to rest after your little fall?" Taviti asked with fake solicitude as he rose to stand, offering Akal a hand to get up.

"Little fall?" Akal said, batting Taviti's hand away and wincing as he heard how high pitched his voice was. He lowered it back down to a manly timbre to continue. "That could have happened to anyone. And did you see how well I caught myself and recovered?"

"Oh, yes. You could teach a course on how to fall down a hill. We should suggest it to the inspector-general."

Akal declined to reply to this absurdity, instead pushing himself up to standing. He stumbled a little bit as he put weight on his injured hip. Luckily Taviti was too busy laughing at his own joke to notice.

Akal followed Taviti and Peni into the forest as they made their way back to the village. A few minutes into their journey inside the forest, he once more lost his sense of direction and had to rely on Taviti completely. Frustrated, Akal concentrated fiercely on his surroundings, looking for landmarks in the dense foliage. He frowned as he saw a twisted tree that he could have sworn he had seen ten minutes before. He stopped by the tree and called out to Taviti, "Are you taking me in circles?"

Taviti turned halfway with a grin. "Getting lost?"

Akal glared at him. Taviti laughed and kept walking. Akal huffed, then hurried to catch up with him.

When they arrived at the village, they saw Ratu Teleni talking to a group of men clustered outside the *bure* that served as the village meeting house.

"That looks like the men who would have attended the village council," Taviti said with some concern. "Let me find out what is happening." He jogged over to the group and conferred with his uncle. As he walked back to Akal, his face was creased with a severe frown. Akal had never seen his friend so angry.

"They have conducted the meeting without me. Ratu Teleni says for us to wait in the meeting house and he will tell us the outcome."

Without waiting for Akal's response, Taviti marched to the *bure* and disappeared inside. Akal waited for a moment, giving Taviti a chance to cool down, before he followed him. He found Taviti standing by a stool, holding up a wide piece of cloth between his outstretched arms and staring intently at it, still in a way Akal hardly ever saw.

"*Masi*," Taviti explained when Akal approached. "The

women of the village make it. They pound out bark to make
the cloth and then add the design. My mother's *masi* is
particularly beautiful." The cloth was covered in geometric
patterns in shades of black and brown. The resulting design
had a hypnotic quality to it.

"It is lovely," Akal said. "Will I meet your mother, so I can
pass on my compliments?"

Taviti was quiet for a long moment. Akal knew he had
asked something difficult. Taviti was rarely quiet.

"My parents both died in an accident when I was twelve.
My uncle raised me."

Akal nodded gravely, lay his hand on his friend's shoulder, then returned his attention to the pattern on the bark
cloth. A moment later, so did Taviti.

The moment was pregnant with the sense that their
friendship was changing. They had met when Akal had
stepped off the ship from Hong Kong over a year ago and
had found Taviti waiting to greet him. They had fallen
almost immediately into an irreverent camaraderie, but
perhaps one without true depth. Akal was starting to learn
Taviti's true stories here in his family home. The chances
they would ever visit Akal's family home were negligible. He
would have to find a way to tell Taviti his true stories anyway.

Their contemplation of the *masi* and their own internal
musings were interrupted by the arrival of Ratu Teleni.

"Nephew," the older man said, giving Taviti a conciliatory
pat on the back.

"Ratu Teleni," Taviti responded stiffly. "I have informed
Sergeant Singh that the council has already met while we
were away investigating Mr. Lal's murder. Can you please tell
us what the outcome was?"

Taviti's uncle regarded him for another moment, then sighed when Taviti remained stiff and upright.

"We agreed that the Europeans must be punished severely for their grave offence. A flogging."

Taviti nodded, seeming unsurprised by this pronouncement, while Akal fleetingly recalled the slashes on Sanjay Lal's skin. "No, you cannot do this—no flogging," Akal said urgently. "We are to treat them as prisoners of war. Imprisonment, yes, but no corporal punishment."

Ratu Teleni gave Akal an amused glance, so reminiscent of his nephew that Akal almost grinned back before remembering the content of the conversation. "What precisely does the police force want with these men?" the chief asked.

"We have been instructed to charge them with the murder of Mr. Sanjay Lal and take them to Suva. If they are indeed Germans, they will be treated as prisoners of war."

"Prisoners of war." The chief snorted. "What should I care about the war in Europe?"

"When Chief Cakobau ceded Fiji to Great Britain, Fiji became part of the British Empire. Therefore, if the Empire is at war, Fiji is at war. If the Empire is bound by the conventions on treatment of prisoners of war, then you are similarly bound," Akal said quietly, imbuing as much respect as he could into the statement.

Taviti gave Akal a look over his shoulder that wordlessly expressed his doubts about the likely success of this line of reasoning. The chief merely chuckled.

"Are there any reparations that the sailors can make?" Taviti asked, much to Akal's relief. This was Taviti's culture. He could navigate it in a way Akal would never be able.

"Not the sailors. But if the government wants these men, then perhaps there is a way to avoid any difficulties," the chief said without hesitation. "There is a man, Apolosi Nawai. He is currently in jail, sentenced to hard labour. He has done nothing wrong. His conviction was politically motivated. Arrange for him to be released."

The rapidity and completeness of the response was telling. Akal inwardly groaned. Politics.

"We can't do that," Akal said, wearily shaking his head. "We are the police. We enforce the law, we don't make it. The inspector-general will not be able to grant this—it would need to come from the governor."

"Inspector-general, governor, it makes no difference to me who grants it. But those are the only terms under which I will consider releasing these men into your custody," the chief replied calmly. "We will meet again in the afternoon two days from now to decide what to do about them. You have until then."

AKAL AND TAVITI walked in silence to the hut where the Europeans were imprisoned. Taviti's silence seemed a separate, seething presence, walking with them. Akal looked at his friend out of the corners of his eyes, not wanting to intrude on his anger. The muscles in Taviti's jaw bunched and writhed as he clenched and ground his teeth. Finally he let go, cursing explosively as he slammed his right fist into his left palm with a force that made Akal wince.

"He knew I wouldn't agree with this, so he cut me out. I will be chief after him. How will I learn if he keeps me out of big decisions like this?" Taviti said, his words tumbling on top of each other.

Akal did not reply. Even if Taviti had given him time to answer, he had no response to give.

"This is a mistake. We need to work with the administration, not lay down threats that make us look lawless. I'm going to talk to him."

Taviti spun on his heel, ready to march back to the *bure*. Akal just managed to grab his arm and halt his reckless run towards a confrontation.

"Wait, Taviti. Just hold on for a minute."

Taviti bared his teeth at Akal. In that moment, Akal glimpsed the fierce warrior hidden behind the laughter and affability. Akal let go of his arm, not wanting to antagonize his friend any further, but the intervention seemed to have brought Taviti to his senses. He paced towards the river and stared out over the water for a few long minutes. When he finally turned back to Akal, the dreadful tension had calmed.

"Who is this Apolosi Nawai?" Akal asked, as it seemed that Taviti was ready to talk again.

"A man who shares my uncle's views on the British. They both believe the British are holding us Fijians back, taking advantage of us. He has set up a company, the Viti Kabani, which is representing Fijian farmers, getting better prices for their crops. Making sure that our people actually profit from our lands, not just let the Europeans make the profits."

Akal frowned. "That sounds fair. So why would he be in jail?"

"Apolosi Nawai is disrupting the order that the British have imposed. That scares them. He's telling our people not to give free labour to the British officials, or to some of the chiefs—the ones the British have falsely appointed, even though they have no ancestral claim to the title. Some of our people have been boycotting trade with the British. Apolosi Nawai is causing them problems. So they came up with some charges—said he had embezzled funds from the company he set up, the Viti Kabani. Eighteen months imprisonment with hard labour."

"You don't agree with this Apolosi Nawai? Or with your uncle?" Akal asked. With what little information he had, it seemed to Akal that this man might have had the right idea. He instantly regretted mentioning Ratu Teleni, as Taviti's face hardened.

"I do. I support Apolosi Nawai. I want to see him released. But what my uncle is doing here, holding these sailors hostage—this I do not agree with."

"Of course. Politics. I hate politics," Akal said with an exaggerated sigh, hoping to lighten the mood. It didn't work. As Taviti continued to glower, Akal decided that if he couldn't jolly him out of his anger, perhaps he could use it.

"Let's go talk to Captain Larsen," Akal said. "But I want to try something."

Akal explained his plan. He saw the moment he caught Taviti's interest, as his jaw relaxed and his eyes lit with anticipation. He grinned and nodded as Akal finished outlining his scheme.

"No, you need to still be a bit fierce!" Akal admonished.

"Don't worry, Akal, I've got it," Taviti said, reassembling his face into tense lines.

They walked over to the hut where the Europeans were being held. Once they were there, the guard took one look at Taviti's face and opened the door straight away. Taviti called for the captain, who emerged looking a little more rumpled than previously, but still erect and upright in his bearing.

"I must insist that my men be allowed to leave this godforsaken hut," he snapped, glaring at Akal and Taviti in turn.

Taviti barked a command at the guard, who raised what sounded like a tentative objection. The tone of Taviti's response was very clear. The guard opened the hut with alacrity and the other men stumbled, blinking, out into the light, to stretch and groan and put their faces up to the sun.

"What has the chief decided?" the captain demanded of Taviti.

Taviti grimaced and relayed the punishment that his uncle had dictated, as well as the conditions for their release into police custody. He ended with, "I do not agree with my uncle's actions. I do not think you should have such a harsh punishment over a law you had no way of knowing about. But I have no power to change his decision."

"Will your government agree to his demands?" Larsen asked Akal.

"I am sorry," Akal said, shaking his head. "I heard back from the inspector-general this morning. The governor was going to intervene when he believed you were Germans, as you would need to be treated as prisoners of war. However, now that we have established that you are from a Norwegian merchant ship, he has said that his hands are tied. He cannot interfere with the chief's sovereignty over his own land."

"That is outrageous! I can promise that if I or my men are harmed, the Norwegian government will respond."

"The Norwegian government? Are you sure there is no chance that it is the German government we should be concerned about? Perhaps over the fate of a certain Count von Luckner?"

The captain's blank face was telling. There was none of the confusion Akal would have expected to see if the name meant nothing. But it seemed the captain was not willing to relinquish his fiction yet.

"No, I tell you once again, we are Norwegian. And our government is protective of its citizens."

"Very well. Will the Norwegian government be willing to cause any diplomatic issues with the British over their citizens who also happen to be murderers?" Akal asked, responding to the threat with some bluster of his own.

"I told you, we had nothing to do with the death of the shopkeeper," Larsen retorted.

"And yet we found a bloody whip on your boat."

The captain jerked his head from Akal to Taviti and back again, in shock. "Impossible. That is not possible. We had no whip, let alone a bloody one."

"Is that right?" Akal said, pulling a gold sovereign out of his pocket, inspecting it and then polishing it against his trouser leg. "Then how did it come to be in your boat?"

"Somebody must have put it there," Larsen said, his voice faltering as he seemed to recognise the weakness of that argument. He was staring at the gold sovereign. "That coin . . . Where did you get it from?"

"Oh, this," Akal said, showing the captain the coin in his palm, the king's head showing face up. "Yes, there was a bag of these coins on your boat. Let me guess, somebody must have put it there?"

"Yes, they must have! We gave all our British sovereigns to the Indian shopkeeper."

"So you think somebody made the difficult journey to where your boat is tied up and left these items to make you look guilty?"

"Exactly. That must be it."

"Who?"

"How would I know? You are the police. Isn't it your job to find out?"

"It is our job to find evidence that points us to the guilty party. Not find ways to exonerate you. So even if you survive the chief's punishment, you will be arrested for the murder of Sanjay Lal."

"Survive? Of course we will survive. My crew are strong, we can handle a flogging," Captain Larsen said, uncertainty evident in the troubled frown creasing his forehead.

"It won't be good," Taviti replied grimly. "People have died."

Akal hoped that Taviti was exaggerating for effect as part of their plan, but he had a sinking feeling that he wasn't.

AS THE SUN set behind them, the young men of the village, including Taviti, dug up a patch of freshly turned earth. Steam started to escape as they dug, and they deftly hopped out of the way to avoid being scalded. After the bulk of the soil was removed, the remaining dirt was scraped away, revealing limp banana leaves, forming a protective layer. These were also pulled away, revealing parcels neatly wrapped in more banana leaves, free from dirt.

"Is that the food?" Katherine asked of the world in general, as she continued to scribble furiously in her notebook. Akal, Katherine, and Mary were standing well back from the

heat of the earth oven that Taviti had called a *lovo*, observing
the spectacle of the traditional cooking method. By the time
Taviti had returned from collecting them in town, they had
missed the initial drama of the hole being dug and fire being
lit, which had happened a few hours ago. Luckily, Akal had
stayed back to observe and had already filled Katherine in
on what he'd seen.

"I suppose it is. I wonder what they have cooked," Katherine continued when she had no response from Akal or
her aunt. The young men had started to pick up the parcels, juggling each one until they could place it into one of
the large bowls that the women of the village were holding
nearby.

"Your guess is as good as ours, dear," Mary replied.

"I need to find out," Katherine said. "Wouldn't this make
the perfect recipe for the Ladies Column? I'd love to see the
Suva socialites digging holes in their backyard to cook a
lovo." Akal laughed at the mischievous smile she shot up
at him, then regretted it when she immediately seized this
opportunity—having softened him up—to ask, "What happened at the village council today?"

Akal groaned. "Police business. I really can't tell you this
time."

"Even though I'm still working on the second section of
the puzzle box?"

"Even then."

Katherine's eyes narrowed when she registered how serious his voice was, but then Mary spoke, commenting, "It
seems that they have retrieved all the food."

Akal was relieved by the interruption, as it gave him the
chance to break eye contact; he turned to see that the women

had started to carry the large bowls of food towards the mats which had been laid out for the evening's feast.

"I had better go watch the food being unwrapped. Come on, Aunt Mary."

Katherine tugged her aunt towards the mats. Akal was about to follow them when Taviti jogged towards him.

"Hot work," Akal observed, as Taviti flicked the perspiration from his forehead with his hand. "No handkerchief?"

Taviti made a face. "Nasty things."

"So, did you have a chance to talk to your uncle before you went back to town?"

"Yes, but it made no difference. My uncle is adamant that Apolosi Nawai is being imprisoned on false charges. He sees this as his opportunity to do something, the only leverage he has had all this time. He isn't going to change his mind—release Nawai or the European sailors take their punishment."

Akal nodded and asked, "Did you get a message to the inspector-general?"

"No. The pigeon post was shut up and I couldn't find John. We will have to send it first thing tomorrow."

"Well, that gives me a chance to change Ratu Teleni's mind tonight."

"You can try, but if I couldn't do it . . ." Taviti trailed off with an eloquent shrug.

Akal looked over at the feast being laid out on the mats in the middle of the village. From what he could tell, there were whole fish steamed with coconut milk, a roasted chicken, and masses of the ubiquitous *dalo*, all of which had been wrapped in banana leaves before going into the *lovo*. The smells of fire and earth from the *lovo* pit mingled with the aroma of the food being unwrapped, which should not have been appetising, but somehow was. Akal felt his stomach growl.

"I suppose we eat and be merry tonight. Start again fresh in the morning."

THE MEAL WAS like nothing Akal had tasted before. There was no spice added to anything. Taviti had provided salt for the three guests, as there wasn't even any added to the food. To Akal, whose palate was accustomed to the cumin and coriander and chilli of the food he had grown up with, this seemed strange. He tried the fish first and found it tender and moist, the coconut milk sweet. The subtle thread of smoke and earth teased at the edge of Akal's senses, blending with the fish and coconut without overpowering it, tying the food to the land on which they were sitting. The *dalo*, which Akal had only previously tasted boiled, had a more crumbly texture when roasted in the *lovo*, and was also enhanced with subtle smokiness.

Akal looked up from his meal to see that Taviti was avidly watching all of them. He saluted Taviti with the piece of *dalo* in his hand and nodded approvingly. Taviti settled back with a satisfied smile.

"This is wonderful, Constable Tukana," Mary said. "Please thank all the people who prepared this meal. I doubt many outsiders have this experience, so we feel very privileged."

Taviti blushed and nodded, murmuring something indistinct in response. It was the first time Akal had ever seen Taviti being shy about anything.

After everyone else had received their food, the prisoners

were brought out of their hut to eat the leftovers. Akal watched as they filed across the village and sat down on a log in a shadowy spot at the edge of the clearing. Supervised by two guards, but not restrained, the men ate heartily. They were talking quietly to each other, low indistinct murmurs floating across the clearing.

Listening as Taviti peppered Katherine and Mary with questions about Sydney, Akal kept absently glancing over to the sailors. Everything seemed calm. The guards were also relaxed, keeping an eye on their charges but chatting to each other as they did so. As they finished their dinner, a tension seemed to fall over the group. The captain said something, and his crew stopped eating. One of the men looked around furtively and replied quietly to his captain. Akal continued to observe through narrowed eyes, no longer paying any attention to Taviti.

The men resumed eating and chatting, but there was a new alertness to them. When the same man did another scan of his surroundings, Akal's sense of unease reached a critical point. He stood to walk over to the prisoners. But he had acted too late. Akal had only taken a few steps when he saw a nod from the captain. Captain Larsen and the next largest man surged upwards, charging into the guards and knocking them over. The other four moved at the same time, plates clattering to the ground, pelting towards the forest. The captain and the other bruiser followed closely on their heels.

On their first movement, Akal shouted, "Taviti!" Alarm raised, he started to chase the escapees. He heard the hue and cry behind him and felt the ground shaking with the thundering of many feet pounding towards him. Larsen, with his exceptionally long stride, was by far the fastest and had overtaken his crew by now, calling back instructions to them in his language. The young Fijian warriors ran past Akal, Taviti in the lead, leaning forward into his sprint. One by one, the warriors caught up to the sailors, tackling them and then struggling to subdue them, with much shouting from both the Fijians and the Europeans.

Taviti ignored the bodies crashing to the ground around him. He dodged left, then pivoted right to avoid the limbs that would trip him up. The whole time his entire focus remained on the captain. Larsen seemed to be gaining speed as he went, his imposing body propelling him forward as his arms and legs pumped powerfully—he was approaching the edge of the clearing and would be in the forest in moments. Taviti, for all his strength and speed, was losing ground.

Akal had stopped running when it was clear he couldn't keep up. Without thinking it through, he bent down and scooped up a rock that was by his foot. Rotating his shoulder through a well-worn pattern, putting his whole body weight into the movement, he bowled the rock towards the fugitive. The rock sailed through the air, over the men wrestling on the ground, past Taviti, and landed squarely between the captain's shoulders. He stumbled forward. After its long journey, the rock didn't have enough force to knock Larsen off his feet, but it was enough to cause him to break his stride—which, in turn, was enough to allow Taviti to catch up to him and tackle him to the ground.

A roar erupted around the village as Taviti subdued the captain with the assistance of some of the other men. Ratu Teleni ran up to Akal and pounded him on the back, shouting something jubilant in Fijian, seeming to have forgotten to speak English in his excitement.

It took some time, and all of the able-bodied men in the village, to restrain the sailors and return them to their hut, dishevelled and covered in dirt and scrapes. Then it took some time for the captors to congratulate each other and Akal on the heroics of the evening. This story was sure to become a feature of the *yaqona* drinking sessions for the village for a long time. After the commotion had died down, Katherine approached Akal.

"Well done, Sergeant Singh! What a fantastic throw! Who knew your cricket skills would come in handy like that?"

Akal flushed with pleasure. "Yes, well, thank you, *mem*. I suppose it is a good thing I have been practicing."

"That's not just practice, that's skill. On a more serious note, I noticed something I think you should know about. I can't tell you definitively whether the sailors are Norwegian or not, but I can tell you this. When they were trying to escape and they were shouting at each other, they were definitely shouting at each other in German."

THE HUT WHERE the sailors were being held now had two guards on it. Akal approached apprehensively. He didn't have Taviti with him as his translator, as Taviti and a couple of his cousins were escorting Katherine and Mary back to their hotel. But he needn't have worried. Akal was now a hero in the eyes of the young men of the village, and they allowed him access to the sailors without needing a conversation.

Captain Larsen came out of the hut looking defeated. A

bruise was forming on his right cheek, visible even in the moonlight. He moved stiffly, favouring his right side. "Was it you who threw the rock?" he asked Akal.

Akal nodded, not wanting to gloat and risk getting the man further offside, jeopardizing his mission.

"Well, it was a good shot," the captain said grudgingly.

Akal inclined his head, graciously accepting the compliment.

"So, what have you come to tell me? Is there some further punishment coming our way for our attempt to escape?"

"That is a good question," Akal said. "I will check in the morning. Perhaps it will make matters even worse for you. No, I am here on a different matter."

The captain looked at him warily.

"Your men were heard speaking German during your escape attempt. Do you continue to insist you are Norwegian?"

The captain remained silent. Akal tried a different approach.

"It is obvious from your escape attempt that you are trying to avoid this flogging, so you clearly don't want yourself or your men to be injured or die. But even if you survive this punishment, you will surely be convicted of Sanjay Lal's murder. What do you imagine the penalty is for murder in Fiji?" Akal paused for a moment to allow that to sink in. "Of course, if you were German, you would be considered prisoners of war, and our government would intercede on your behalf with Ratu Teleni. And you would be far more valuable politically. I suspect we would be pushed to find an alternative theory for the murder as well."

Akal could see the calculation in the captain's narrowed eyes.

"Now, are you sure you are not German?"

The captain threw his shoulders back and straightened, seeming to add an inch to his already formidable height. "Very well. In any case, it seems that you already know who I am. I am Count Felix von Luckner, captain of the SMS *Seeadler*. These men are my crew, known as the Emperor's Pirates. We proudly work to defeat the enemies of the German Empire."

The C.S.R. Company

Attitude of Planters' Association

Mr Witherow was of the opinion that the matter left very little to be done except endorse it. Everyone knew that the C.S.R. Co. were making tremendous profits out of the war. Up till now they had refused to let the producers participate in a penny of that profit. They had asked the Company—almost begged them—for a bonus, but had been unable to get anything out of them. He would have thought that such a company would have come forward of its own accord and suggested that the Colony should have ten per cent out of its profit, at any rate the planters, who produced it for them.

Mr Powell: You are entering into a war with the C.S.R. Company. People have tried this before and it has ended disastrously on every occasion.

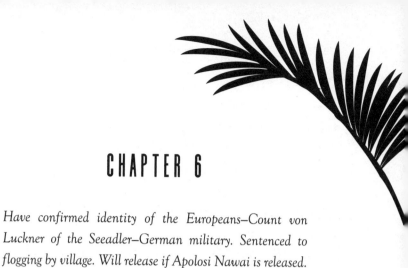

CHAPTER 6

Have confirmed identity of the Europeans—Count von Luckner of the Seeadler—German military. Sentenced to flogging by village. Will release if Apolosi Nawai is released. Need answer by tomorrow PM.

AKAL HANDED THE NOTE over to a scowling John.

"Please send this on your most reliable pigeon, if there is such a thing."

John merely snatched the paper from him and jerkily rolled it up to insert into the cylinder attached to the pigeon's leg.

Akal had earned the boy's ire by refusing to allow John to write the message this time. This one was too inflammatory. While Akal had been writing the message, Constable Kumar had been trying to soothe the strange, angry boy. Thanks to Constable Kumar's efforts, John was calm enough that he could do his job, but he was still visibly agitated.

The pigeon was dispatched to Suva. Akal had a fair idea of the shouting and cursing that would be coming from the inspector-general's office as a result and was glad he wasn't there to be on the receiving end of it. No doubt he would get his fair share the next time he saw the inspector-general in person.

"We are expecting a response, John," Akal said to the boy,

who had sat on the ground with his arms folded once the pigeon was away. "It is urgent. It is extremely important that any message you receive is given directly to us."

John continued to stare out to the ocean and gave no indication that he had heard Akal.

"Constable Kumar, could you stay with him? I need the inspector-general's response as soon as possible."

"Yes, sir."

Akal and Taviti left the pair as they were, the young boy sullen and near tears and the only slightly older police officer sitting quietly by him, both looking out to the water.

THEY WALKED BACK towards the police station, where Akal was going to leave Taviti to man the front desk for the morning, in case the people of Levuka needed to speak to a police officer, something they really hadn't been able to do yesterday. Akal was going on to Hugh Clancy's house to check in on Katherine and Mary. But as they approached the police station, they heard the drumming of footsteps coming nearer. A young Indian boy was sprinting down the street, a cloud of dust billowing behind him. He was wild-eyed, terrified, ashen. He approached at full tilt, seeming to have forgotten to slow down until the last minute, when he tried to skid to a stop. The boy would have taken a fall and seriously hurt himself if Taviti hadn't swooped down and caught him around the waist as he started to tumble.

"Ooof," Taviti grunted at the impact. He placed the boy back down on his feet and started to scold him. "What are you doing, you rascal? You can't run like that through town—you are going to get yourself hurt, or somebody else!"

At this, the boy seemed to crumple to the ground,

hugging his knees into his chest, and burying his face into his legs. He was wailing in Hindi, incoherent, but Akal caught the word *khoon* a few times. Blood.

Taviti went to comfort the boy, his face horrified at this response to his sharp tone.

"Leave him, Taviti. Let me," Akal said.

He crouched down next to the boy and spoke to him in Hindi.

"It is all right, you are safe now," he said, repeating similar phrases until the boy stopped rocking. "Can you look up?"

Taking a shuddering breath, the boy looked up.

"You are safe now. You can see we are both police officers."

The boy stared at Akal, who was still crouched next to him, and Taviti, who was standing back a little bit, giving them both space. He continued to take shuddering breaths, but these were also evening out.

"Now can you tell me what happened?"

The boy took a gulp and tried to speak, but instead, as he thought of whatever he needed to say, he started sobbing—not the terrified wails of a few moments before, but actual grieving sobs.

"Master Thakur . . ." he said between sobs.

Akal had a sense of foreboding that had him tensing up, ready to run himself.

"Master Thakur . . . *khoon*." This was all the boy could manage, once again. Blood.

Akal looked up and said to Taviti, "Something has happened to the teacher. Go get Kumar."

Taviti nodded and ran.

After a couple more minutes of soothing noises, during

which Akal had to fight to keep his voice low and calm, instead of shouting and bolting in some direction, any direction, finally the boy calmed enough to tell Akal what had happened.

Master Thakur had not arrived for lessons that morning, so the young boy had gone to fetch him from his home. When he arrived, he had found something terrible. He became garbled again at this point, but Akal understood clearly that there was blood.

When Taviti and Constable Kumar ran back from the station, Akal was pacing by the boy, who was still sitting and crying, but more of a normal, snuffling sort of cry.

"Kumar," he said brusquely. "Where is the teacher's house?"

"Far up the hill, at the end of that road," Constable Kumar said, looking frightened, pointing at the road the boy had come running down. "What has happened to Sarvesh?"

"You take him to his home and tell his mother there is no school today. Then come to Master Thakur's house. Constable Tukana and I will go and check on Master Thakur."

"What has happened to Master Thakur?" Kumar asked, his voice squeaking.

"I don't know yet," Akal snapped. "Can you just take him?"

Constable Kumar nodded, looking shaken, and crouched down next to the boy. Akal and Taviti started up the road, dread forcing their feet faster.

THEY DIDN'T SPEAK as they hurried along the road, slowing when the hill got steeper and the road dwindled to a small track. The only sound was their ragged breathing. After a final push uphill, they reached the plateau where the dirt path ended. Akal paused, head hanging down with his hands on his knees, to catch his breath. When his panting had subsided, he looked up at the house built into the hillside. It was tiny, enough for perhaps two rooms. There was space on the plateau for it to be extended, and planks were piled up next to it.

The front door was hanging open. Akal ducked to enter the house and stepped directly into a blood bath.

The teacher was slumped over the small dining table in the kitchen, arms sprawled out above his head. There was blood all over the table, dripping down over the edge to splash onto the wooden floor. Akal took two strides to get to the prostrate man and shook him, calling his name, but Master Thakur was limp and silent.

"Help me lift him," Akal urged Taviti. They took a position on either side and lifted the teacher by the shoulders. His head lolled back and Akal could see where the blood was coming from. His throat had been cut, the deep wound no longer bleeding. It seemed the majority of his blood was already outside his body.

For the second time since his arrival in Levuka, Akal felt for a pulse, fingers slick and red, and found nothing. Master Thakur was cold. There was nothing he could do for him. He looked up at Taviti and shook his head.

"Are you sure?" Taviti asked, his voice heavy with dread.

"We should get the doctor to be certain," Akal replied, looking around for a cloth to wipe the gore from his hands.

"I'll go," Taviti said, but at that moment, Constable Kumar came running through the door. The young man balked when he saw all the blood. Akal, who had felt the walls closing in when there were only two men in the room, ushered them all outside.

"Kumar, go get the doctor. I don't think there is much hope, but in any case, the body needs to be taken to the hospital. Taviti, can you stay here until Kumar returns? I have to go meet Miss Clancy, I'm already late. We can meet at the station later."

Taviti and Constable Kumar did not respond to these rapid-fire commands. Instead of moving, they stared blankly at Akal.

"Go," he barked, the sound echoing around the trio.

Kumar jumped at this order and started down the hill.

"Is this really the time to go meet the ladies?" Taviti asked incredulously. "A man has been murdered."

"Yes, and why do you think he has been killed?" Akal asked, his stomach roiling at what he knew was the likely answer.

"Because . . . because we asked him to translate that letter," Taviti said, taking a moment to think it through.

"Exactly. It must be that damned letter. It is too much of a coincidence that he translates it for us one day and is dead the next. I need Miss Katherine to open that second compartment. Maybe something there will help explain all of this."

"You go, then. I'll stay here, take a look around the house, and see if I learn anything," Taviti said. "I'll find you at the station."

Akal nodded and followed in Constable Kumar's footsteps back down the hill. As he walked, he berated himself. He had asked Master Thakur to translate the letter. He had gotten the teacher killed. A man who had dedicated his life to nurturing young minds. A man who had reminded him of his father. Akal, suddenly furious, kicked at a clump of grass on the path. Whoever killed Master Thakur had made a mistake. Sanjay Lal's death was simply a mystery to be solved. Master Thakur's death hurt, and Akal would not be satisfied until he found the killer.

He turned his mind to the investigation. How had anyone known the teacher had translated the letter? Master Thakur had promised discretion, and he had struck Akal as a man who took his responsibilities seriously. The previous sub-inspector wouldn't have used him for translations if he had a habit of being indiscreet. The only people who knew the teacher was translating the letter were Taviti, Constable Kumar, Katherine, and Mary. Taviti had been with Akal the whole time and was consumed with affairs in the village. Katherine and Mary didn't know anyone in Levuka. Either the teacher had not been as discreet as expected, or Constable Kumar had let the information slip to someone. Either way, it seemed the letter may have gotten another man killed.

ANXIOUS TO SEE if a response had come from Suva, and not knowing how long he would be at Hugh Clancy's house, Akal stopped at the pigeon post first. John silently handed over a note without looking at Akal.

Prevent harm to Germans. Meeting with governor today re demands. Unlikely to agree.

Akal grimaced. He didn't know how to prevent harm to the Germans if the governor wouldn't agree to the demands. And now he had to tell the inspector-general about another murder, one which the Germans could not possibly have committed. He looked at John and sighed. But first he would have to convince the uncooperative boy to allow him to send another message.

AKAL HAD FOUND his bearings in Levuka. His feet had automatically taken him to Hugh Clancy's house without needing to involve his brain, which was a good thing, as his mind was still replaying the gruesome scene he had walked into at Master Thakur's house. He paused at the front gate and pushed the horror of the morning aside, refocusing on the task at hand. He was there at the request of Mary, who had pulled him aside at the *lovo* to ask if he would come to the house in the morning; apparently, she and Katherine needed help to translate some questions they had for the housekeeper.

Mary had seemed oddly furtive in this request, completely out of keeping with her normal serene demeanour, which had him wondering what questions they could possibly have. With all that was going on with the murder investigation and the diplomatic incident brewing around Count von Luckner and his crew, it had seemed like a burden when she asked last night. Now he was glad to have a moment away from bloodshed and betrayal.

Akal's knock on the front door brought a flurry of activity. He could hear brisk strides tripping down the hallway, almost a run. The door handle rattled, and he could hear Katherine mutter "For God's sake" as she unlocked and unlatched the door. Finally she flung it open with a rush of air.

"Come in," she ordered.

Akal trailed Katherine down the hallway, jarred by her

brusque demeanour. Mary furtive and Katherine brusque? Something was certainly afoot with the ladies. Now was probably not the right time to ask for her help, but with the teacher's death almost certainly being related to the letter, he needed to know what else was in the jewellery box.

"*Mem*, please, may I speak with you for a moment?" he called after her.

Katherine spun on her heel and looked at him impatiently.

"The jewellery box. You said there was a second compartment. If I bring it to you later, could you take another look at it?"

"Yes, yes."

She turned back and kept moving through the corridor. Akal followed, wondering at the fact that she hadn't asked a single question about why he wanted the second compartment solved now. At the end of the corridor, Katherine led him into the dining room, where Mary was kneeling in front of a sideboard, assorted crockery scattered about her. When Katherine immediately started to leave the room again, muttering something about getting things over with, her aunt admonished her with an uncharacteristic harshness: "Katherine. Stop racing around like a headless chicken. Go get some tea sorted out. We can show Sergeant Singh a little bit of courtesy."

Abashed, Katherine sent Akal an apologetic shrug and went to organise the tea. Mary pulled and pushed her way up to her feet, as Akal hovered nearby, ready to catch her if she fell. She invited Akal to take a seat, and then they both sat quietly, tension building in the room, until Katherine returned with the tea. Mary took a sip, squared her shoulders, and shared a solemn look with Katherine, before turning her gaze to Akal.

"We haven't told you the real reason we are here," she said, then paused as though unsure how to go on.

Akal gave the older lady an understanding smile. "I suspected there was something more bringing you to Levuka than just some household goods."

"Of course we are here to sort out the house, as we said. But we are also trying to solve a mystery of our own: what happened to Clara, Hugh's wife."

Akal frowned. "Was there something suspicious about her death? I hadn't heard anything. Mr. Clancy is a prominent man. If there was some impropriety around his wife's death, it wouldn't stay hidden for long."

"No, I don't think so. Oh, I don't know," Mary said, turning liquid eyes to Katherine, who took over telling the story.

"It's just that Uncle Hugh has been so evasive about the details. We didn't even know she had passed until my parents asked if I could come to stay, and we still don't know how she passed. Uncle Hugh won't say anything—it is like he has disappeared into himself. He was always a bit too involved in work, but now he's obsessed, almost like he's avoiding us, or avoiding *something*."

Now that Katherine had started the story, Mary seemed to find her feet and jumped back in. "When we first went through the house on the day we arrived, we found the pieces of a cot." Mary paused, looking at Akal as though expecting a reaction. When he looked at her blankly, she explained, "Hugh and Clara didn't have a baby."

"Ahhh . . . So why would they have a cot?" Akal said as understanding dawned.

"We thought perhaps there had been a baby who had died along with Clara, and that is why Uncle Hugh has retreated from the world," Katherine said, not one to be left out. "But then yesterday when we went to the cemetery, there was no grave for a baby."

"Ah I see," Akal said. "I wondered what you were looking for at the cemetery."

"Which brings us to the favour we would like to ask of you," Mary said with a beseeching look. "The housekeeper would have been here when Clara was alive. We hoped she might have some answers, but we can't communicate this with hand gestures and nods and the few words we have in common. Could we ask you to act as our translator?"

"I know this is deeply personal," added Katherine, her hands folded in her lap, the stillest Akal had ever seen her. "We tried to figure it out on our own and we just can't. We need your help."

Akal shifted in his chair, his uniform suddenly itching against his skin. It seemed he was about to lose this battle to maintain distance from Katherine and Mary both. He hoped that Hugh Clancy would not hold it against him.

"Of course. I will help in any way I can."

Katherine left the room and returned shortly with the housekeeper, whose eyes darted from one person to the next.

"I didn't do anything wrong. Tell them I didn't do anything wrong," she appealed to Akal, nearly wailing in her distress. She was wringing her hands and casting pleading glances at the two European women. Katherine and Mary looked on with bewilderment and concern for the housekeeper.

"Nobody thinks you did anything wrong. They want to

ask some questions about Mrs. Clancy, Clara, when she lived here."

The fear faded from the housekeeper's eyes to be replaced by a frown. "The *mem* was good to me and to Samir. I will not say anything bad about her."

"You don't have to say anything you don't want to. Please be calm," Akal said, holding his hand up in what he hoped was a reassuring gesture. He took a calculated risk, thinking that he had a better chance at getting the truth if he assumed that a child had been born than if he seemed not to know at all. "They want to know about the child."

At the mention of the child, the housekeeper sighed, the tension draining from her body even though she still looked troubled. "I don't know. It feels wrong to talk about the *mem*'s private business when she is gone."

"They are worried about Mr. Clancy. He is her brother," he said, nodding at Mary, then Katherine. "And her uncle. They want to help him, but they don't know why he is sad."

"He should be sad," the housekeeper said with some bitterness. "It was a hard pregnancy. The *mem* didn't like the doctor here. She wanted to go back to Australia, or at least move to Suva, but Clancy *sahib* kept putting her off, saying next week, next month. He didn't take her very seriously, and he kept telling her to talk to other women who had had babies before. Then one day, four months into the pregnancy, she started bleeding, and she didn't stop. The day after the funeral, he packed a bag and left for Suva. He has not been back since."

Akal handed the lady his handkerchief for the tears trickling unnoticed down her cheeks. He relayed the information to Mary and Katherine without inflection, as though by remaining expressionless he could remove himself from the situation. Katherine wept silently, staring down at her hands. Mary, pale but composed, mused absently, "Four months. No wonder there was no grave."

This matter-of-fact statement broke a dam in Katherine, who made a keening sound and squeezed her eyes shut. Mary put her arm around Katherine and rubbed gentle circles on her back. Catching the housekeeper's eye, Mary called her over with her free arm. The three women formed a circle, leaning on each other, tears mingling with the sweat on each other's necks. Akal quietly slipped out of the house and left the women to their grief.

TAVITI AND KUMAR returned to the police station about an hour after Akal. They walked in, eyes grim, shoulders hunched, and slumped into the chairs opposite the desk where Akal was sitting.

"He was dead?" Akal asked, more of a statement than a question.

Taviti nodded. They were silent for a moment.

"Well, no point sitting here. We now have two murders to investigate," Akal said briskly. He had been sitting there for a while and needed to move, needed to feel like he was doing something.

"What next?" Taviti asked.

"Miss Katherine is going to take another look at the jewellery box later today. We still need to interview Mr. Arvind Chand. Let's all get some lunch, and then Kumar, you can take us to his store."

"Good plan," Taviti said, visibly cheered at the idea of lunch. "I'll go get us some food. Kumar, I assume you are going home?" On Constable Kumar's nod, Taviti wasted no time in finding the door. As Constable Kumar turned to also make his exit, Akal stopped him.

"Kumar, before you go home for lunch, a few questions." The constable turned back. "Yes, sir," he said, returning to stand in front of the desk.

Akal looked at the young man, polite and deferential, unaware of the disturbing questions Akal was about to ask him.

"You are our local. Is there anybody who would want to harm the teacher?" Akal asked, starting with an innocuous question.

"No, sir. Everybody liked Master Thakur. He stayed out of local politics and gossip as much as he could. All he cared about was getting the school built and teaching the children."

"I see. So, no arguments, no grudges, no failed romances?"

"No, sir, nothing like that."

"In that case, it seems likely that Master Thakur was killed over the letter he was translating for us," Akal said, eyes trained on Constable Kumar's face.

Constable Kumar stared at Akal, ashen. "Really?" he said faintly.

"He translated it for us yesterday, and he is dead today. There isn't any obvious reason to hurt the man. In the absence of any other motive, I'm going to assume this was why he was killed."

Constable Kumar nodded, looking stricken. It seemed he knew what was coming.

"My question is, how did anybody know that he had translated the letter for us?" Akal asked. "I know it wasn't myself or Taviti. That leaves you or the teacher himself. Did you tell anybody about the letter?"

Constable Kumar's eyes slid to the floor as he shook his head. "She wouldn't have told anybody. I told her it was part of the investigation."

"Who did you tell?"

"A friend. Kavita. We grew up together. She likes that I am a police officer now."

"And you trusted her to keep it to herself?" Akal exploded.

Constable Kumar's guilty visage told Akal what he needed to know. He stood and paced behind the desk, unable to remain seated anymore.

"Was she impressed by what you told her?"

Constable Kumar looked back up, shrugged, and, after a pause, nodded. Akal stopped pacing and glared at Constable Kumar.

"I hope so. I hope she was very impressed, and you think it was worth it. Because now a man is dead." Akal dragged the last sentence out with a terrible emphasis. His anger at Master Thakur's murder had found an outlet. He vaguely knew, somewhere in the back of his mind, that Constable Kumar had not actually killed the man himself, but that fact seemed secondary at the moment.

Constable Kumar's breathing grew shallow, and tears gathered in his eyes.

"Truly? Did I get the master killed? He was such a good man. How could I make this mistake?" Constable Kumar asked, his voice muffled as he buried his face in his hands.

Akal contemplated the horrified young man, the red haze of fury receding, leaving a sick feeling in its wake. He was a boy, really. A boy who had made a fatal mistake. But could Akal truly judge him? He had made a similar mistake in Hong Kong: giving information to a beautiful young woman to impress her. At least for Constable Kumar, he had a chance of actually marrying Kavita. Emily had been so far out of Akal's reach that impressing her had been an exercise in futility—and yet he had tried. Luckily for him, nobody had died. His indiscretion had led to the loss of property, not life. Even so, the repercussions for him had been severe: dismissal or exile to Fiji. What would the repercussions be for Constable Kumar?

"We need to find out whom Kavita told. Where will she be?" Akal asked.

Constable Kumar led him to the Morris Hedstrom store on Beach Street, explaining that his girlfriend worked there in the mornings, doing some light cleaning and making tea and coffee for the other workers. They hurried there, Akal furious and tense, Constable Kumar still fighting back tears. They caught her just as she was leaving for home, having finished her work for the morning. A slight girl with dark features, she was wearing a neat, dark-blue cotton dress. A single thin plait fell over her shoulder to the faint swell of her chest. Kavita greeted Constable Kumar with a smile that brightened her otherwise plain face.

"Kavita, we have to talk to you," Constable Kumar barked at her.

At the urgency in his tone, her smile faded to be replaced with confusion.

"Hello, Kavita. I am Sergeant Akal Singh. I am working with Constable Kumar," Akal said calmly in Hindi, taking Constable Kumar's cue on which language they would have in common.

Kavita nodded, her eyes darting from Constable Kumar to Akal and back again. She seemed wary but not surprised by Akal's introduction, which made sense given how much Kumar seemed to confide in her.

"Constable Kumar has told me that he mentioned something to you about Master Thakur translating something for us. Who did you tell this information to?" Akal asked, maintaining his even tone.

Kavita's eyes continued to flick between the two men and she just shook her head, not saying anything.

"I know you told somebody. What have you done? I told you not to say anything. You've ruined my life! I'm going to lose my job!" Constable Kumar said, his voice raising as he spoke.

Kavita shrank back, thin shoulders rounding forward.

Akal turned on the young constable. "What are you shouting at her for? You did this, not her. You are the police officer. It was your duty to keep your mouth shut."

Rigid with anger and guilt, Constable Kumar nodded sharply. He stepped away and took a deep breath. As Constable Kumar calmed himself, Akal returned his attention to Kavita, who was now looking at him with gratitude.

"You are not in trouble, Kavita. I just need to know who you told."

Finally she answered, a mere whisper. "My mother."

"That's all? You didn't tell anyone else?"

Another tiny shake of her head.

The attack would have required enough physical strength that Akal didn't think a woman could have done it, but Akal's sense of relief was short-lived, as Constable Kumar groaned. "Her mother loves to talk."

"Would your mother have told anyone?" Akal asked Kavita. She nodded. "Whom would she have told?"

Kavita swallowed before whispering, "I saw her tell my father and my uncle. But I think she told some of her friends, too."

Akal sighed. Constable Kumar might as well have run through town telling everybody.

"Thank you for telling us, Kavita. Wait there a moment, I'll ask Constable Kumar to walk you home."

She shot Constable Kumar an angry, fearful look, but nodded and waited with her hands folded tightly in front of her.

"Go with her. Find out who the mother told," Akal ordered the constable.

"Yes, sir," Constable Kumar said, shuffling his feet as though he couldn't decide whether to leave or not. "Sergeant Singh, what will happen to me?" The words burst out of him.

"I will wait until we have concrete evidence that your slip-up led to our killer knowing about the letter. But I will have to tell the inspector-general at that point. Then it will be with him to decide your fate. I expect you will be looking at dismissal at the very least. In the meantime, don't say anything to anybody about this case or your mistake. Just keep your mouth shut."

Constable Kumar squared his shoulders and looked up at Akal with a determined expression. "Thank you, sir."

Akal pondered Constable Kumar's mistake as he walked to the station. The boy had likely gotten the teacher killed; it was something that was going to haunt him for the rest of his life. Akal couldn't help but feel for the constable, too young, too green, without anybody to mentor him. And such a grave consequence to what must have seemed like a small indiscretion.

ARVIND CHAND OWNED a prosperous shop in the middle of town. After lunch, Constable Kumar led Akal and Taviti there, giving them the suspect's background on the way. Like Vijay Prasad, Mr. Chand had also completed his indenture and tried to make a life for himself with a small plot of sugarcane on Viti Levu. He was barely scraping together a living with the meagre payment the CSR Company gave for sugarcane. When a friend who was returning to India had offered to sell him his store in Levuka, Mr. Chand had jumped at the chance.

As everything was close in Levuka, they arrived at the store in short order. Akal sent Constable Kumar back to the pigeon post to keep them apprised of any incoming messages. The young constable left with his hands in his pockets and his shoulders slumped forward. As expected, Kavita's mother, an inveterate gossip, had had no idea who she had told about any particular story, let alone who they may have told. She hadn't thought this a particularly juicy tidbit, not involving marriage or bad behaviour, so she really hadn't paid much attention. Constable Kumar had relayed this information with such remorse that Akal hadn't had the heart to reprimand him further. But he couldn't allow Constable Kumar to be any more involved in the investigation than was absolutely necessary.

Akal and Taviti entered the store, where Mr. Arvind Chand was serving a couple of shoppers. The gregarious merchant was laughing with the women while he packed up their purchases and made change. He did not acknowledge the two police officers. Akal and Taviti waited quietly by the back shelves, which were full of products, a stark contrast to Sanjay Lal's store. If the contents of these shelves were swept to the floor, it would have been impossible to walk through the mess. Finally, the short, portly man walked his last patron to the door, waving his farewells before turning his attention to the two police officers lurking in the back of his store. The genial businessman persona disappeared as soon as the women left, to be replaced by a man with folded arms and his jaw thrusting out pugnaciously.

"Sergeant Singh, Constable Tukana, I presume?"

Once again, the smallness of the town closed in on Akal for a moment.

"That is correct, sir. And you are Arvind Chand?"

"I am. And you are here to ask me if I killed Sanjay Lal," the shopkeeper said, putting his hands on his hips, as if daring them to challenge the statement.

Akal took the dare, but gently. The conversation was starting more aggressively than he would have preferred. "We have heard that you were not fond of Mr. Lal. Is that correct?" he asked.

"Humph. 'Not fond.' I didn't like him one bit. Is that clear enough?" Mr. Chand said, leaning in defiantly.

"Very clear, sir," Akal said evenly. "Why did you dislike him?"

"Nobody liked him," the shopkeeper replied. On seeing Akal's interested expression, Mr. Chand lowered his hackles enough to impart some gossip. "Well, except for Vijay, and honestly I'm not even sure if he liked him, or just liked that they came from the same village."

"But your dislike in particular? Is it because he was your competitor?"

Mr. Chand laughed heartily. "Competitor." He chortled, holding his arms out expansively to encompass his entire store. "The man was a fool. He put his store out of town, thinking that one day soon Levuka would expand and he would have all of those people as his exclusive customers. Vijay tried to tell him it wouldn't happen. Levuka isn't growing, the town won't expand."

"So why would he start his shop outside of town after all this advice?" Taviti asked.

"Sanjay Lal was not the type to listen to anybody else. So there you have it. His store is no competition for mine. I don't even know how he was still going," Mr. Chand replied. He leaned towards them conspiratorially. "I think Vijay has been helping him with loans."

"If he didn't take any business away from you, why did you dislike him?" Akal asked.

Mr. Chand seemed to have decided that the police officers weren't a threat. He leaned against the wall and settled in to tell his story.

"I had an employee in the past. The son of a friend. When Sanjay arrived in Fiji, he wanted to set up his store, but he had no contacts, no suppliers. The man seemed to think he would come here and money would grow on trees, business would flourish without any effort. Well, he soon found out that you have to work here as well. He came asking me for my suppliers. Why would I help him? Even if he wasn't my competitor, he was arrogant, slippery, lazy. So when I said no, he bribed that idiot of an employee of mine to get all the details of my suppliers. Not that it helped him much. After one or two orders, none of them wanted to deal with him either."

"And your employee?"

"Tried to get work with Sanjay. But Sanjay didn't give him a job—said he wasn't trustworthy. Can you believe the nerve of the man?" Mr. Chand said with a disbelieving laugh. "The boy couldn't get another job in Levuka. He had to go to Suva to look for work."

"Where were you on Wednesday afternoon?" Akal asked.

"Here, of course. I am always here, everyone knows that. I had a shipment of goods come in on the *Amra*, and any number of patrons to the store."

"Constable Tukana will get the details so we can verify your movements."

Mr. Chand snorted. "Certainly. But you are wasting your time. The man was an annoying mosquito. Not someone I would waste my energy on."

Akal stepped outside into the heat of the afternoon as Taviti got the details of Mr. Chand's alibi. He would give the details of the alibi to Constable Kumar to run down, but he doubted they would learn anything more.

He was starting to get a clearer picture of their first victim. He seemed a thoroughly unlikeable chap. Akal hadn't got a strong sense of grief from Vijay or his wife, despite their supposed closeness to Sanjay Lal. Arvind Chand was very clear on his dislike for the man. And with Lal's treatment of Chand's disgraced ex-employee, there was at least one more family in town who had a grudge to bear against Lal.

Taviti rejoined him outside and they walked back towards the station.

"Well, that was a waste of time," Taviti said as he tucked his notepad back in his pocket.

"Agreed. Everybody knows everybody's movements in this town. So surely Vijay Prasad would know that Arvind Chand would be at his store and would have lots of witnesses to his alibi. What puzzles me is, why did Vijay send us to talk to Mr. Chand in the first place?"

GOVERNOR SENDING AIDE tomorrow to negotiate with chief. Continue investigation.

On their return from interviewing Arvind Chand, Constable Kumar had been waiting for them with the response from the inspector-general. He was pathetically grateful to learn that his next job was to vet Arvind Chand's alibi. Akal supposed it was better than waiting for a message with the uncommunicative John.

"They are sending somebody," Akal said. "That's a relief. I wasn't looking forward to passing messages back and forth between the chief and Governor Huton."

"Yes, my uncle will be pleased. It shows they are taking him seriously."

As Constable Kumar departed to visit Arvind Chand's customers and verify his alibi, Akal and Taviti made their way to the Royal Hotel. They found Mary and Katherine seated at the same side of a small table on the verandah, both facing the ocean, watching the day fade. The lemonades on the table in front of them were full, the women silent.

"Good evening," Taviti boomed, breaking the quiet.

"Hello, Constable Tukana, Sergeant Singh," Mary said. She held Akal's gaze for an extra moment, a moment that felt pregnant with meaning. Exactly what meaning, Akal would have to sort through later. For now it was enough to acknowledge that he had been witness to their grief.

Katherine briefly looked in their direction and smiled wanly, before returning her gaze to the ocean.

Taviti looked from Mary to Katherine to Akal. When none of them were forthcoming with conversations or explanations, he prompted gently, "May we join you for a moment?"

"Oh, yes, of course. I apologise, Constable Tukana. It has been a long few days," Mary replied, a small flush heating her cheeks.

Taviti pulled seats over from a nearby table and they both sat with their backs to the ocean, opposite the women. Katherine still hadn't said anything and her gaze remained fixed on some point far away. Akal respected her desire for silence, and equally silently offered her the jewellery box, which he had retrieved from the police station on his way to the hotel.

Katherine slowly turned to look at the jewellery box, then at Akal. A spark lit in her eyes. "I'll just go upstairs and get my pins."

As Katherine walked away, a spring in her step, Mary said to Akal, "Thank you—she needs the distraction."

Taviti looked again from Akal to Mary and back. Getting no further information, he shrugged, and proceeded to ask Mary about her day and how it was going sorting out Hugh Clancy's house. As they spoke, Akal let his mind wander.

It had indeed been a long few days. The death of the teacher affected him the most. Akal had felt a connection to Master Thakur in a way that belied their one interaction. He reached into his pocket and felt the letter from his father, the coarse paper gritty against his fingertips.

His father had fallen ill when Akal was eighteen and had

been too unwell to work. It was the event that had put Akal on the path of becoming a police officer in Hong Kong, the best paid position he could attain at the time. His father had written in the past of his deep regret, not only that he couldn't provide for his family and had to rely on Akal's income, but that he could no longer teach, could not nurture a child's joy in learning and celebrate their successes. In his next letter home, Akal would write to his father of the young teacher he had met and of the focus of the Indians in Fiji to educate their children.

Akal was pulled from his musings by the return of Katherine. In the time it had taken her to retrieve the tin of pins from her room, she seemed to have found much of her natural energy again, but still not her voice. Standing, she put one hand on her hip and extended the other to Akal. He placed the jewellery box in her palm. Her smile brightened her face and she quickly moved to the adjacent table to work on the box.

Once more, they all watched as she concentrated on the puzzle before her. First she tapped on the sides of the box and then, with her eyes closed, felt the four sides and top. Finding nothing, she replicated her previous steps to reopen the concealed bottom drawer. Then, keeping the box upside down, she took the drawer out completely and felt along the inset where the drawer had been, lightly dragging her fingertips over it. She looked up with an exuberant smile on the last side of the inset. She picked the box up and tried to look inside, but the failing light of dusk on the verandah was insufficient. Katherine picked up the box and charged inside, taking her tin of pins with her. Before anyone could react enough to follow her in, she returned triumphant, another concealed drawer protruding out of the side of the jewellery box.

"You clever girl!" Mary exclaimed.

"Very well done, *mem*," Akal said, while Taviti clapped and whooped. Akal wished he could be as exuberant, but it was neither in his nature nor his circumstance.

Katherine placed the jewellery box on the table and carefully pulled the drawer completely out of its confines. It contained a single envelope, which she handed to Akal. Despite his restrained verbal congratulations, his admiration must have been shining on his face. She gave a curtsy, a flourish which somehow managed to convey her supreme satisfaction with her achievement, before stepping back behind her aunt's chair.

Akal opened the envelope and withdrew a folded piece of paper. He unfolded it to see it was a news article. The masthead read *The Bihari Times* and was dated fifteen years ago; the article was written in Hindi and featured a grainy photograph of a smiling young Indian man. Akal squinted at it and felt a flicker of recognition, but couldn't immediately place who it was, so he turned his attention to the text, looking for the secret that made this article worth hiding in such an elaborate manner.

SEARCH FOR REBEL CONTINUES

The search for Suraj Tripathi continues, going into its third week. Police are expanding their search across the state, but fear the rebel may have eluded them as the search drags on.

Suraj Tripathi is the suspected ringleader of a group of local rebels

who are agitating for Indian independence. They are responsible for a string of robberies perpetrated against prominent British business owners in the state. Tripathi's parents have denied that their son has anything to do with the rebel movement, saying that he was a good son who worked on their small family farm and didn't have any problems with the British presence in India.

The only connection Akal could make was with the letter that had been hidden in the first compartment: the writer of the letter had mentioned that his mother was still being harassed by the police. So it seemed likely that the writer of the letter was this Suraj Tripathi. But without knowing who Suraj Tripathi was, and what his relationship was with Mr. Lal, it didn't seem to help with the murder. On the other hand, Sanjay Lal's dying act was to draw the pattern that helped them open the box. There must be some connection.

"Thank you, Miss Katherine. This has been incredibly helpful."

"Well, what does it say? Who is it?"

Akal read the article out to the group and finished with, "I do not know who Suraj Tripathi is. I do not recognise either the name or the photograph."

"Oh, well, that is disappointing. But you do think it is important?"

"Mr. Lal would not have hidden it away so securely if it wasn't important," Akal said. "I just don't see the link yet."

Chop Chop by Chips

Mr Apolosi, of the Viti Company, seems to be much in demand just now. One District Commissioner recently gave a judgement against him and we hear all sorts of warrants. He will always be remembered as the man who made the Company too big—and I hope too Hot—for its European parents. It is undoubtably through his influence that it has alarmed its said parents by turning from a nice little business proposition (for them) into a most embarrassing political concern of the worst sort.

CHAPTER 7

CO . . . CO . . . RI . . . CO . . . ROOO . . .

Akal blinked his eyes open and sighed. It was his third morning being woken by the infernal rooster and he was so used to it now that he wasn't sure how he was going to wake up in time when he returned to Suva.

Akal closed his eyes again, but sleep eluded him. The day before had been full of trauma and surprises, and his mind would not stop racing from finding the teacher dead, to Constable Kumar's mistake, to finally snag on the least difficult incident—learning the real reason why Katherine and Mary were in Levuka.

Katherine's demeanour yesterday had been a startling contrast to her behaviour in the days before. In her agitation when he had arrived, in her grief when she had learnt of the cousin who had not been born, Akal had seen the truth of Katherine. Beyond the mischief and the teasing and the determination to be taken seriously as a journalist, she was a woman who felt deeply. His respect for her had grown, as had his desire for some kind of friendship while she remained in Fiji, despite the vast gap in their social statuses.

The futility of his musings left Akal restless. He quietly dressed and slipped out to greet the day by the river.

Ratu Teleni had arrived earlier than him that morning and wasted no time on frivolities. "I understand there is another dead Indian man in Levuka?"

"Yes, sir."

"And my nephew was there when you found him?"

"Yes, sir."

"I thought I told you to keep him out of your investigations."

"Sir, I'm not sure if you have noticed that he is substantially larger than me. How can I stop him?"

The chief chuckled as he accepted his plate of fruit. Akal warily accepted his from the same cousin who had been so coquettish two mornings earlier. Somebody must have spoken with her, because she maintained a polite distance and left immediately after delivering their breakfasts.

"Sir, honesty compels me to tell you that, even if I could stop Taviti, I wouldn't," Akal said, staring down at the vibrantly coloured fruit on the plate in his lap. He absently batted away a gnat hovering around the papaya, but still didn't pick up any of the fruit. "He is a constable in the police force, he has a good mind, and he wants to learn. It is my duty to teach him."

Akal looked up at Taviti's uncle, hoping for some sign that the chief understood his position. He found it.

"I understand duty. My duty is to this village, as is Taviti's. But I understand that you cannot help me convince my nephew. I will continue to persuade him to give up policing on my own."

Akal gave a sigh of relief. He picked up his papaya and started his breakfast with at least one of his troubles lifted.

"I HAVE NEVER been to Sigatoka."

"Sing-a-toka."

"But I've seen it on reports. There is no 'n.'"

"Still, it is 'Sing-a-toka.'"

"Just like it is 'Nan-di' despite it being spelled 'Nadi.'"

"Yes."

Akal stared at Taviti in disgust. "That makes no sense."

Taviti shrugged. "Makes sense to me."

The two men were waiting at the wharf for the ship which was bringing the aide. The SS *Amra* was still doing its rounds, so a sailing ship had been hired, supposedly arriving at ten, but Akal hoped it would be earlier. The Fijian version of early was almost—but not quite—on time. It was now eleven. To pass the time, Akal had asked Taviti to explain some of the other towns in the colony, now that he had seen the difference between Suva and Levuka.

Half an hour and many more lessons on Fijian pronunciation later, Akal could see the ship appearing on the horizon.

"Who do you think they've sent?" asked Taviti.

"You would probably know better than me, given the work you do for your uncle in Suva," Akal replied.

"I just hope it isn't John Lewis. That man is so fussy, he makes my teeth ache."

Akal looked at Taviti with some surprise. Taviti was renowned for getting along with everyone.

As the ship came closer, they could see two men standing at the prow, eager to arrive. Akal recognised one of them.

"That is Dr. Holmes!" he exclaimed. "I wonder why he is coming here?"

"That is good news. The doctor is a good man to have around. And that with him is John Lewis," Taviti confirmed gloomily. "I am not surprised. The governor trusts him above everyone. He is good at making things happen."

John Lewis was a short, thin young man who was prematurely losing his hair. He had grown the hair on the side of his head longer, so he could comb it over the top to try and hide the bald spot. The longer pieces were streaming on the breeze behind him, defeating their purpose, for the moment anyway.

As the ship came closer, Akal could see that the doctor was scowling—it seemed at life in general, but with particular venom whenever John Lewis said anything. When the ship was moored, Dr. Holmes was the first passenger to disembark, nimbly jumping down, retrieving his case and his medicine bag from one of the deckhands, and briskly striding up the dock. His face brightened when he saw Akal and Taviti.

"Well, thank God, some sensible people to talk to."

Taviti grinned. "John Lewis talking to you about his stamp collection, is he?"

"That bloody bureaucrat is the reason I'm here. He convinced the governor that he needed me to certify that our prisoners of war are being treated correctly. Nobody else could do it. It had to be the chief medical officer for the colony. As if I didn't have enough to do."

"Maybe the governor thought you needed a holiday?" Akal suggested. "Visit somewhere new, spend some time with good friends."

"Well, it isn't new for me—I have spent some time here before, doing work at the local hospital. But your version of things sounds much more appealing," Holmes said, grinning at Akal before the scowl reasserted itself. "But no, they haven't sent me out here on a jolly. The administration doesn't want to hear about the health of the coolies and doesn't want to do anything about the malnutrition, all the suicides, all the babies that die. But six Germans? This, they think, is more important than the health of every man, woman, and child in this colony. Hmph!"

John Lewis was being helped down from the ship by the crew. When one crew member tried to hand him his enormous case, John Lewis just stared at him until the man disembarked, placed the case next to Mr. Lewis's feet, and walked away.

Taviti groaned. "I'd better go help him before somebody hits him."

As Taviti jogged away, the doctor turned to Akal. "I hear you have two murders on your hands as well. I don't think I'll invite you to visit my family back in Blighty. It seems wherever you go, bodies start to drop."

Akal spread his hand helplessly. "It is not me, I promise. This was not the case before I came to Fiji, Doctor *sahib*."

"Tell me what has happened. And for God's sake, let's go to the hotel. Taviti can deal with John. I've had enough of him for the day."

As they walked towards the hotel, Taviti and Mr. Lewis trailing along behind, Akal filled the doctor in on the details of the murders, focusing on the state of the bodies.

"So you think the first man was tortured and the other killed immediately?" Dr. Holmes asked.

"I think so. The second man—his throat was cut, and that was the only wound. But the first man, there were many wounds. It looked as though he had been whipped. I couldn't tell what actually killed him. The doctor here in town said he had died from the whipping, but that didn't seem right. I've seen men beaten much more badly than that without coming close to dying."

"Was his neck broken, perhaps? Or was he strangled? Any bruising around the throat?"

Akal reviewed his mental images of Sanjay Lal's dead body. "No, Doctor. The only strange thing was that his lips were blue."

"Ah, good catch, Akal," Dr. Holmes said. "It is possible that the beating may have inadvertently triggered a heart attack. That kind of pain and stress has been known to cause heart attacks."

"And perhaps that is why the store and the house were ransacked. Whatever they were looking for, Mr. Lal died before they could get the whereabouts from him. And perhaps what they were looking for was the letter that the teacher was killed for translating."

Before the doctor could respond, they heard a querulous voice calling out from behind them: "Dr. Holmes, Sergeant, please, slow down."

This request was echoed by Taviti in even more irritated tones. Akal and the doctor gave each other a conspiratorial smile but complied. When the two men caught up to them, Taviti glared at Akal, but not the doctor, who looked about innocently. It seemed that this sort of behaviour was to be expected of Akal but not the doctor. Akal accepted the glare with resignation.

"Mr. John Lewis, this is Sergeant Akal Singh. He is currently the senior police officer on the island," Taviti said, gesturing with his free hand. The other hand was full, carrying the aide's case.

"Sergeant Singh. The governor's office received very little information from the police force. Inspector-General Thurstrom blamed this on the deficiencies of the pigeon post. I simply cannot do my job under these conditions. Can you please confirm what the situation is with our prisoners of war?" Mr. Lewis asked with a pomposity that left Akal wondering whether it was for effect. Behind him, Taviti rolled his eyes.

Akal told the story again, this time focused on Count von Luckner and his crew. By the time he finished, they had reached the Royal Hotel.

"Excellent. Thank you for the efficient summary, Sergeant Singh. However, I will need much more detail. Once I have checked into the hotel, we will meet to review the pertinent information."

Still out of Mr. Lewis's range of vision, Taviti slumped his head down.

"Very well. We can meet in the dining room downstairs," Akal suggested.

"No, no. That is far too public. We will meet at the police station. Dr. Holmes, you will also attend in case we need to go directly to the village."

It was the doctor's turn to heave a silent sigh.

"Very well, gentlemen. We will meet here in half an hour."

With that pronouncement, the young official made his way inside, gesturing for Taviti to follow him. With a final baleful glare at Akal, Taviti trailed after Mr. Lewis. The doctor and Akal were left outside, trying not to laugh.

AKAL WALKED INTO the dining room, planning to wait for the other men there. The doctor had also gone to check in, and Taviti was still acting as porter for Mr. Lewis. He was pleasantly surprised to see Katherine and Mary sitting at a table. Mary was knitting, and Katherine was ostensibly reading a book. She leapt up, book abandoned, as soon as she saw Akal. Mary put down her knitting and laid a gently restraining hand on her niece's forearm to prevent her from rushing over to Akal. Instead, he walked quickly over to them.

"We've been waiting for you," Katherine said by way of greeting. "Where have you been?"

"Good morning, Sergeant Singh," Mary said dryly.

"Never mind all of that," Katherine said, waving her hand as though to brush away the need for niceties. She leaned in closer and asked quietly, "What did you find out about the article?"

Mr. Lewis cleared his throat loudly from behind them. Akal and Katherine, their heads bent closely together, started from their position and turned to see Mr. Lewis glaring at Akal, and Taviti standing behind him sporting a cheek-splitting grin.

"Sergeant Singh, it is not appropriate for you to be bothering these ladies," Mr. Lewis said, looking horrified.

Katherine jumped in, face flushed with outrage. "Sir, I do not know who you are, but Sergeant Singh is not 'bothering' us. He was our escort to Levuka at the behest of my uncle, Hugh Clancy. We were having a perfectly lovely conversation before you interrupted."

Akal intervened before Katherine could dress the man down further. "May I present Mr. John Lewis, who is an aide to the governor, and here to negotiate with Ratu Teleni for the release of the sailors. Mr. Lewis, this is Miss Katherine Murray and her aunt Miss Mary Clancy, recently arrived from Australia."

"Charmed, I'm sure," Katherine said, her voice heavy with sarcasm.

"Hugh Clancy. The editor of the *Fiji Times?*" Mr. Lewis asked, his face lighting up with interest. "Well, it is lovely to meet you. I apologise, I misunderstood the situation."

Apparently, Katherine's uncle's position in Fijian society overcame any concerns about social impropriety. Katherine merely nodded, one eyebrow raised in a cynical expression.

"All right, gentlemen," boomed Dr. Holmes as he entered the dining room. "Oh, and ladies." He stopped short when he saw Katherine and Mary. John Lewis introduced the two women, and the doctor nodded his greetings. He seemed shyer, more tentative than Akal had ever seen him.

As Mr. Lewis engaged the ladies, largely Katherine, with some social niceties, asking how their journey from Australia had been and how they found Fiji so far, Akal noticed that Dr. Holmes's eyes often strayed towards Mary, who maintained her usual serene demeanour. The doctor noticed Akal noticing and cleared his throat, frowning at Akal.

"Shall we get going?" the doctor asked, abruptly interrupting the tedious small talk. "The sooner we get done here, the sooner I can get back to my real job."

Mr. Lewis frowned, tore his gaze away from Katherine, and reluctantly nodded. "Yes, yes, we should make a move. Constable Tukana, can you please go to the village and alert them that I have arrived at Levuka and will come to the village shortly?"

Taviti nodded. "I will let my uncle know."

"Excellent. We will meet you there. In the meantime, Dr. Holmes, Sergeant Singh, let us adjourn to the police station," Mr. Lewis said. He bowed to Katherine and Mary.

"Ladies, I am afraid we must go tend to some small matters. I would be honoured if you would join me for dinner here at the hotel tonight?"

With a hunted expression, Katherine turned to her aunt for a way out. Unfortunately, Mary politely accepted, much to Katherine's visible chagrin. She brightened when Mary also extended the invitation to Dr. Holmes, who accepted with ruddy cheeks. With the plans set, the men departed for the police station and the ladies for a stroll around town.

CONSTABLE KUMAR WAS manning the police station's front desk with a tense look on his face. He seemed even more confused when the two European men walked in the door. Akal realised that they had not kept the inexperienced constable up to date with the situation— somewhat through negligence, but largely because he no longer trusted him. After some hasty introductions, Akal sent Constable Kumar out of the station to continue verifying Arvind Chand's alibi. The younger officer diffidently suggested that perhaps they could accept the alibi, as he had already spoken to a few witnesses, but Akal ushered him out the door anyway.

He then settled in to answer Mr. Lewis's questions. The first round of questioning was about the conditions the European sailors were incarcerated under. It turned out Mr. Lewis had sent Taviti off to the village to get him out of the way as he didn't know where Taviti's allegiances lay. Akal had to grudgingly admit that this was well done on Mr. Lewis's part. No matter how hard he tried, Taviti could not possibly remain objective in this situation.

The questioning then turned to the investigation of the two murders. Akal laid out the information so far,

excluding the newspaper article which he hadn't figured out
yet, answering Mr. Lewis's frequent and incisive questions.
At the end of it, Mr. Lewis leaned back in his chair and
nodded slowly.

"I understand your logic and agree that it seems unlikely
that the sailors were the perpetrators of either murder. However, in order to strengthen our position on the negotiations
with Ratu Teleni, we must continue down the path to arresting the sailors for the murder of Sanjay Lal."

"But sir, the chief will surely know that we don't believe
the sailors committed either murder. If he didn't figure it
out himself, Taviti will have told him."

"Nevertheless, from a legal perspective, we are within
our rights. We will maintain the fiction," Mr. Lewis replied,
unperturbed.

"I was instructed by Inspector-General Thurstrom to continue investigating," Akal argued.

"Ah, yes. I have your new orders here," Mr. Lewis said,
rifling through the papers in his folder and withdrawing an
envelope, which he handed to Akal. "You will see that I am
in charge for the duration of this particular incident."

Akal's heart sank as he read the missive. It was from the
inspector-general, and it did indeed instruct Akal to follow Mr. Lewis's orders until further notice. It was a simple
instruction, with no room for interpretation.

"So, we will go to the village, and I will conclude the
negotiations with the chief and the village council. When
I've secured the sailors' release from the village, you will
arrest them for the murder of Sanjay Lal. A fairly simple
plan. Any concerns?"

Given Mr. Lewis wasn't perturbed by arresting men for

a crime they didn't commit, Akal didn't think he had any concerns that the civil servant would be interested in.

AKAL LED MR. Lewis and Dr. Holmes to the village, happy that he knew the way well enough now to be the guide. The first stop when they arrived was to meet the chief, who was holding court with Taviti and a couple of the older men of the village.

"Ratu Teleni, this is John Lewis, aide to Governor Huton. And you know Dr. Holmes. Mr. Lewis, this is Ratu Teleni, the chief of Tabenu village."

"Mr. Lewis," the chief said with a nod. Ratu Teleni was more reserved than Akal had seen him before, bordering on hostile. He thawed when he greeted the doctor, shaking his hand and asking after his journey.

Mr. Lewis eventually interrupted. "Ratu Teleni, thank you for meeting with me. Governor Huton is eager to see this situation resolved."

"I have explained the conditions under which I will release the sailors," Ratu Teleni said, with a small shake of his head, his jaw set.

"Yes, well. Before we discuss that, I'll see the prisoners," Mr. Lewis replied, his hands folded primly at his waist.

"You have no need to see the prisoners. They have already admitted their guilt in eating turtle without my permission. Your business is with me."

"Dr. Holmes is here to see to their welfare."

The muscles bunched in the chief's jaw. "Their welfare? What are you suggesting?"

"This is a sensitive situation," Mr. Lewis replied, seeming

blithely unconcerned about the chief's bad humour. "If we must explain something to their government at some point, I want to be sure we have done all we can to ensure the well-being of these men, including having the foremost doctor in the colony tend to them."

After a few moments of silence, Ratu Teleni barked an order at Taviti and walked away, back to the group of older men. He must have filled them in on Mr. Lewis's demand, as they started to glare over at him.

The European sailors filed out of the storage hut, their hands tied with rope in front of them. Their heads were hanging down, except for Count von Luckner, who strode out with his usual swagger. He sported a scrape that went from cheek to chin, and the skin around it was purple and green. The other men lifted their heads and Akal could see that they all had an assortment of scrapes and bruises, though none as severe as their captain's.

Mr. Lewis gasped. "You were told to ensure they weren't harmed!" he exclaimed to Akal.

"Sir, these men were completely unharmed, unrestrained, and being fed the same food as the rest of the village. Then they tried to escape. I expect these injuries were sustained in their escape attempt," Akal responded evenly, as Taviti bristled beside him.

"They've clearly been beaten after they were recaptured. Look at their faces! How did they all get the same injuries?" Mr. Lewis argued.

"Because they were all tackled to the ground," Taviti responded. "My uncle did not have them beaten. After they tried to escape, he had their hands tied up and stopped allowing them out of the hut to eat. That is all. Why would he hurt them when he wants this negotiation to go well?" Taviti was glowering at the fussy aide, who continued to shake his head in disbelief.

Count von Luckner had been observing this exchange with a small smile playing on his bruised face. "It is as the police officers have explained. We have not been beaten. These little injuries are all from the ground when we were wrestling against our captors, not from fists. We made a valiant attempt to escape, and all of my men fought hard to get away," von Luckner said, pride ringing through the speech.

Akal quickly stepped in to introduce the captain to the aide and explain that John Lewis was there to negotiate for their release. Meanwhile, Dr. Holmes went to examine the men's wounds.

"I'm pleased to see that your British government is acting. When can we expect to be released?" Count von Luckner asked.

Mr. Lewis gave a noncommittal politician's answer. "The negotiation has not yet commenced. Ratu Teleni is making some very serious demands. It is going to take some time to work through it."

Akal inwardly winced at this bland non-answer. The captain's scowl gave a clear picture of what he thought of Mr. Lewis's response.

"Your safety and the safety of your men is of the utmost importance to Governor Huton," Mr. Lewis assured.

The scowl eased from the captain's face, but his brow remained furrowed. Before Count von Luckner could question any further, Taviti, at the prompting of the guard, stepped forward.

"My cousin is getting restless. He wants the men back in the hut."

"Doctor, are you finished?" Akal asked.

"Of course I am. What a waste of bloody time," Dr. Holmes grumbled, snapping his medical bag shut. "Nothing serious. The local doctor could have tended to them. You certainly didn't need me, Mr. Lewis." He glared at the offending bureaucrat.

"As I said, we need to tread with care," Mr. Lewis responded. He seemed wholly unconcerned about the various glares and glowers being sent his way.

"Well, I've taken care of it," Dr. Holmes declared, hoisting his medical bag up and scanning around the village. "If you don't have any other pointless errands for me to do, I'll go back to Levuka and check in with the local doctor. Where the hell is that path?"

As the guard ushered the restrained men back to their improvised prison, Taviti called a young boy over and instructed him to guide the doctor back to Levuka. Dr. Holmes followed the boy into the jungle without a backward glance.

Mr. Lewis turned to Taviti. "Now, let's go speak with your uncle."

AS THEY APPROACHED Ratu Teleni and his coterie of advisers, they abruptly stopped speaking. Akal noticed that they were eyeing Taviti with some suspicion. His friend was stuck between two worlds, his loyalty being questioned by both sides.

"So, are you satisfied now that we did not mistreat them?" Ratu Teleni asked John Lewis.

"Yes, thank you, Ratu Teleni. I had to be sure, you understand," Mr. Lewis replied.

Ratu Teleni arched an eyebrow, looking very much as though he did not understand, but he didn't comment. He led them into the *bure* where the village council had been held, and his informal court followed them in. They all sat cross-legged on the mats in the middle of the room, Ratu Teleni with his men around and behind him on one side, with Akal and Taviti flanking John Lewis on the other side. One of the chief's men must have been dispatched to call for some others, as a short while later, four warriors appeared and stood behind the chief's men, spears forming an intimidating circle.

"Thank you for coming from Suva, Mr. Lewis. We are here to discuss the fate of the European men," Ratu Teleni said to open the conversation.

"Thank you for receiving me, Ratu Teleni. Please could you clarify the reasons you have incarcerated the European sailors?" Mr. Lewis responded.

"They have killed and eaten turtle. They have admitted this. Turtle is for the chiefs only, unless we permit others to eat it."

"So, it is in your control whether it is permissible for them to eat the turtle?" Mr. Lewis asked, his head cocked as though he had caught the sound of something intriguing.

"It is," Ratu Teleni replied with an incline of his head. "But they came like thieves onto our land and stole from us. They didn't ask for permission, and even if they did now, I'm hardly going to give it after the fact."

"Hmm . . . I do not believe that this traditional custom has been written into the law of the colony. In fact, I believe the chiefs have been arguing for this, but have not been successful. Is that correct?" Mr. Lewis asked.

Ratu Teleni's voice deepened into a growl. "You would come to my land and tell me which of my traditional laws I may follow?"

The rest of his men shifted and muttered to each other and, most notably, the warriors straightened, their eyes darting around, looking for danger. Akal didn't think these men necessarily knew the content of the conversation, but they certainly understood the chief's change in tone.

Mr. Lewis delicately changed the topic. "Are you aware that these men are believed to have killed a shopkeeper? The people of Levuka want them brought to justice."

"As do I," replied Ratu Teleni. Behind him, the rest of the Fijian men relaxed at his even tone. "I want justice for their crimes against my people first, then the crimes against yours."

"And the punishment for their crime against your people— could you tell me what that will be?"

"A flogging," the chief responded with an implacable tone that sent a shiver down Akal's spine.

"That is a harsh penalty for men who could not possibly have known your laws."

"Mr. Lewis, is ignorance of a law a defence in your British justice system?"

Akal silently cheered for this legal wrangling that put John Lewis on the back foot, however briefly. Clearly Ratu Teleni had not confined his perspective to his Fijian culture; he also had a deep understanding of the British system under which his people were living, though not without some chafing.

"Do you not believe that the killing of a man is a more serious offence than the eating of turtle? On that basis, will you hand them over to us?" Mr. Lewis asked, without responding to the chief's question.

"The killing of a *kaivalagi* is the business of your police, and I make no judgements on the seriousness of that crime," Ratu Teleni said. His brow lowered and each word was delivered as a blow when he continued, "You would try to judge the seriousness of their crime against me when you know nothing of our culture? No, I will not simply hand them over."

"These men are German. They must be treated as prisoners of war, and this form of corporal punishment is forbidden by all civilised societies."

The chief responded implacably, not rising to the bait implied in the term *civilised societies*. "Again, this is the concern of the British."

"Do you not consider yourself a British citizen?"

"I am *kaiviti* first."

In his time in Fiji, Akal had learnt little of the Fijian language, but enough to know that *kaiviti* translated to "of Fiji," where *kaivalagi* translated to "of the land of the foreigners." Akal could imagine how this distinction would have gained prominence in recent years, with the influx of Europeans and Indians into Fiji.

"I understand there are conditions under which you will release them to us."

"The release of Apolosi Nawai."

"Apolosi Nawai has been jailed for embezzling funds from Viti Kabani. He was stealing from the people who trusted him."

Ratu Teleni snorted. "Don't insult my intelligence. We all know why he has been imprisoned. The Britishers were losing too much money."

"This was not the motivation, sir. There was evidence of

his embezzling," Mr. Lewis said. When Ratu Teleni laughed at him as though he was simple, Mr. Lewis tried a different approach. "He was disturbing the relationship between the people and their chiefs, telling people not to provide their labour to the chiefs in the traditional ways. We must keep him imprisoned to protect your people, to ensure they don't lose their culture to his corrupting influence."

"In one breath, you deny our traditional laws, in the next you say you want to protect our culture. Our people are not as children to be protected from their own choices."

The room was silent for long enough that people started to fidget. Somebody coughed. Akal could hear the mats rustling as people shifted in place, trying to get relief from the strain of sitting on the floor. Neither Ratu Teleni nor Mr. Lewis seemed the slightest bit perturbed.

"I am authorised to agree to removing the hard labour component of Nawai's sentence," Mr. Lewis said, after what felt like an eternity.

"That is not sufficient. He must be released."

The silence resumed. An interminable length of time later, Akal, for all that he had grown up sitting cross-legged on the floor, could feel his backside growing numb. He joined the chorus of rustles, subtly lifting one leg and buttock, then the other.

"Very well. We will release him, and he will be exiled to Rotuma. He will have nothing more to do with Viti Kabani," Mr. Lewis finally said. He continued in the same even tone, as though the decision was of no great consequence to him. "This is as much as I am authorised to offer. If you don't agree to this, and if you hurt these Europeans, I don't think you will like the outcome."

For a third time, silence descended. Akal thought it was over, that the negotiation had failed. But finally, the chief nodded.

"Please wait outside. I will confer with my men and tell you of our decision."

Akal, Taviti, and Mr. Lewis all rose to their feet with some relief. Mr. Lewis and Akal started to walk towards the door. When Akal realised that Taviti hadn't followed them, he paused and looked back. Ratu Teleni and Taviti were staring at each other, appearing to be in some silent communication. After a long moment, Taviti tore his gaze away from his uncle and strode out of the *bure*. Once outside, Taviti continued his internal struggle, walking away to brood at the river, hands on his hips.

"Can you really have this man released, or are you just stalling?" Akal asked Mr. Lewis in a lowered voice, glancing around to ensure he wouldn't be heard.

"Yes, I already have tentative approval. Exile to Rotuma will curtail Nawai's actions, and releasing him will quieten people like Ratu Teleni who have been saying that his imprisonment is political," Mr. Lewis replied. "This may work out well for everyone."

There was movement at the door of the *bure* as Ratu Teleni emerged into the sunlight. The rest of his men followed and dispersed in various directions. The chief joined Akal and Mr. Lewis and waited for Taviti to come back. He returned from the river somewhat subdued, but calm. The chief gave a triumphant smile as he announced, "We agree to your terms. I will surrender the European sailors into your custody."

Local and General News

A pair of boots has been found in the Upper Rewa. They are, we believe, in excellent condition and are supposed to be of German manufacture. The owner can have same by applying to the authorities in person.

CHAPTER 8

RATU TELENI LED AKAL, Taviti, and Mr. Lewis to the storage hut and instructed the guard to release the prisoners. All six men emerged blinking into the sunlight, the five subordinates laughing and chatting animatedly to each other in their own language. Their faces fell when Akal and Taviti approached to place handcuffs on them. They protested to their captain, who stopped their complaints with a single finger in the air.

"Mr. Lewis, I presume you have secured our release?" Count von Luckner asked. On Mr. Lewis's dignified nod, he continued, "I am in your debt. And yet, we are being handcuffed?"

"Count von Luckner, you and your men are being arrested for the murder of Mr. Sanjay Lal," Akal replied.

"We have discussed this in the past. We strenuously deny these allegations. What reason did we have to kill that man?"

"You will have a chance to defend yourself in a British court," Mr. Lewis responded evenly.

"You have saved us from the Fijian system of justice, only to have us face execution within the British system," the captain said with disgust.

Taviti recruited some men to assist with moving the

prisoners back into Levuka. They made an odd procession, John Lewis and Taviti in front, the handcuffed prisoners in the middle, and burly Fijian warriors, armed with spears, on either side. Akal was walking by Count von Luckner, who was at the front of his men. They attracted a lot of attention as they came into town. Shopkeepers and shoppers alike abandoned their transactions to stand on the store front porches and gossip with each other as they marched the prisoners along Beach Street towards the police station. Taviti's cousins enjoyed the attention, waving and shouting out to people they knew.

There was one bystander who seemingly didn't want any part of this spectacle. Vijay Prasad walked out of the Morris Hedstrom department store onto Beach Street. When he saw the motley assortment parading down the street, the colour drained from his face.

As Akal watched, Prasad turned and tried to return to the store, but the door was blocked by an elderly woman who was trying to exit at the same time. In his rush, he jostled her, knocking a bag out of her hand. He was forced to stop and pick it up, along with the items that had fallen out.

Akal looked from Vijay Prasad to Count von Luckner. Prasad's strange reaction had to be about the captain. He had been perfectly calm when they had interviewed him previously.

"Do you know that man? The one trying to go into that store," Akal said to Count von Luckner.

The captain squinted in the direction that Akal was pointing and shrugged. They continued to watch as Vijay handed the woman the bags and she finally exited onto the street. Taking her place in the doorway, Prasad looked over his shoulder with a hunted expression before disappearing inside.

"Oh, yes, now I recognise him," Count von Luckner declared. "I had forgotten about him! He is the man who helped deliver the first round of purchases to our boat—he didn't seem important."

"He came directly to your boat? So he knows the way there?"

"Correct. Two rounds of goods from the beach to the boat. The shopkeeper said he was a friend, but I don't think he was. He was very angry to be there."

THE PROCESSION ENDED at the police station, where the five sailors were unceremoniously split between the three cells, each of which was intended for only one person. These shed-like structures had small windows, too high and small for any mischief, but for the men who had been locked in a dark room for days, at least this allowed in some light.

The captain was taken into the main room of the station for questioning. When Akal had entered this room on his first day in Levuka, it had seemed small with himself, Con-stable Kumar, and Taviti. Now, with the addition of Mr. Lewis and the captain, it was positively suffocating. This was partially alleviated by excusing Constable Kumar from the room, who left with a now near-permanent hangdog expres-sion on his face.

"I believe I have the honour of addressing Count Felix von Luckner?" John Lewis asked.

The captain stiffened for a moment, as though unused to responding to that name. But then he sighed and responded in the affirmative. "Yes, that is I."

"Captain von Luckner, also known as *Der Seeteufel*, the Sea Devil. Captain of the SMS *Seeadler*, the Sea Eagle, whose crew has earned the moniker 'The Emperor's Pirates.'"

Count von Luckner laughed at all of these monikers. "Indeed."

The interrogation of Count Felix von Luckner continued for another hour, as John Lewis, in his very thorough way, learnt all the details of the SMS *Seeadler*'s movements. It seemed that the story he had given Akal had many elements of truth. The ship had been struck by a tsunami and wrecked on a reef near the Society Islands. Captain von Luckner had taken a few men in a longboat to Fiji, while the rest remained stranded on the wrecked *Seeadler*.

He had been evasive on what he hoped to achieve in Fiji, stating he had come for supplies. Mr. Lewis suggested that he was hoping to steal or capture another ship, which von Luckner denied, but with a smirk that made Akal think that perhaps Mr. Lewis had struck on the truth.

When it became obvious that Mr. Lewis had an inexhaustible list of questions, Count von Luckner crossed his arms, leaned back in his chair, and stopped answering. When Mr. Lewis also stopped speaking, the captain looked at Akal and asked, "Do you believe we killed the shopkeeper?"

Akal looked inquiringly at Mr. Lewis, who was effectively his superior officer at this time. Mr. Lewis nodded.

"No, we do not believe this," Akal said. "You are not under arrest for this crime. Instead, you will be transferred to Suva and held as prisoners of war."

"Thank you, Sergeant Singh. Didn't I say from the very beginning that I knew that you would be able to solve this?"

Mr. Lewis resumed his questioning, but at this point,

Akal was more interested in pursuing his murder investigation. He stepped outside, leaving Taviti with Mr. Lewis to
guard Count von Luckner. He found Constable Kumar sitting on a bench, looking downcast. He scrambled to stand
when he saw Akal.

"Sergeant Singh, what did they say?"

"We are at liberty to continue investigating both murders," Akal said, intentionally being somewhat evasive.

"May I help?" Constable Kumar asked hesitantly.

There was something Akal needed his help with, but
would it be foolish to trust him again? "You will not say
anything, not a single thing, to anyone?"

"I swear, I won't say anything, not after what happened to
the teacher," the young man said, near tears.

Uneasy, but with little option but to rely on Constable
Kumar's local knowledge, Akal withdrew the envelope with
the article from his pocket and handed it to him. "Do you
recognise that name, or the photograph?"

Constable Kumar shook his head. "No, sir, I don't know
the name. But that photograph . . ."

"I have a thought on who it might be," Akal said, "but I
do not want to influence you."

Constable Kumar squinted at it, moving the paper around
to get better light. His face paled and he looked up to Akal
with dread-filled eyes. "Could it be Mr. Vijay Prasad?"

Akal took the newspaper back from Constable Kumar
and stared at the grainy photograph. Looking at it afresh,
Akal could see faint hints of the features of a younger, slim-
mer, less careworn version of Vijay Prasad.

"For different reasons, I also thought it may be Vijay
Prasad. Though if we are right, that is not his name."

They were both silent, Akal waiting for Constable Kumar to tell him what had horrified him so much, the young constable staring at the ground. The longer Constable Kumar remained frozen, the more Akal dreaded what he was going to hear. Finally, he could bear the suspense no longer. "What is it? Clearly something is bothering you."

Kumar swallowed convulsively before replying, "Kavita, the girl I told about the letter. She is Mrs. Prasad's sister. Vijay Prasad is her brother-in-law."

"Ah," Akal said heavily.

"How can we find out if it is him? I have to know. I have to know if I got the teacher killed."

"I have an idea. Remember how I said not to say anything to anyone? I take it back. One last time, you should be indiscreet."

A SHADOWY FIGURE slipped into the slumbering Kumar house on unshod feet. He knew where to step to avoid the squeaking floorboards; he went straight to the sideboard, a prized possession in the Kumar household. Easing the top drawer open, he rifled through, peering at the contents in the faintest of moonlight, until he found what he was looking for. He started to make his exit, but only took one step before the door was flung open and Taviti's authoritative voice cried out, "Stop where you are!"

The man turned in a blind panic but found his way to the bedrooms barred by Akal, who had a gun trained on him.

"Vijay Prasad, you are under arrest for the murders of Sanjay Lal and Master Thakur."

Editorial Comment

The position of a newspaper is a very difficult one in these times. Our readers will understand that we are acting in the best interests of the Colony and of the Empire in not publishing particulars of recent stirring occurrences.

CHAPTER 9

THE SHED-LIKE CELLS IN the courtyard of the police station had become even more crowded with the arrest of Vijay Prasad. The five sailors were now crammed into two cells with the final cell containing Mr. Prasad on his own. In recognition of his rank and title, Count Felix von Luckner had been moved to a room in the hotel, where he was being guarded by Taviti.

In the morning, Akal brought Mr. Prasad into the main station to question him. Constable Kumar stood in the doorway, posture alert in case Vijay Prasad tried to escape. It was not necessary, as the fight had gone out of Mr. Prasad, and he sat slumped in the chair with his eyes closed.

"Mr. Prasad, or should I say Mr. Tripathi?" Akal began.

The man in question opened his eyes and regarded Akal with a look of exhaustion. He remained silent.

"You should know, we will not be charging the German sailors with either murder. We will be charging you with both."

"You have no proof that I killed anybody. All you can prove is that I broke into the Kumars' house."

"And retrieved an article that makes us suspect that you are actually a man named Suraj Tripathi, who is wanted back in India. If we truly can't prove murder here, my inspector-general will send you to face those charges in India instead. Far from your pregnant wife."

This had an impact. The suspect straightened up, the exhaustion in his face replaced with alarm.

"What would you prefer, Mr. Tripathi?" Akal asked.

"I am Vijay Prasad now—that name no longer means anything to me."

"But it was the name you were born with?"

"Yes, it was the name my parents gave me. Even they are dead now, so I no longer have any ties to that life."

Akal breathed a silent sigh of relief that the spectre of the Indian justice system had been an effective threat. He thought they had enough to convict the man of both murders, but it would be much easier now that he had admitted who he was.

"Tell me about your life as Suraj Tripathi. What let you to be part of the rebellion?"

"I was never part of the rebellion!" Mr. Prasad insisted.

"The police in India certainly thought you were," Akal replied.

"They were wrong."

Akal leaned forward in his chair and rested his forearms on the table. "Why don't you tell me your side of the story. Perhaps it will help with your case if we understand why you committed these murders. Tell me about your life."

"Very well. I do not believe it will make any difference with the Britishers, but perhaps you will believe me, Sergeant Singh," Vijay Prasad said. He paused for a moment, looking out the window as though he was looking into the past.

"I am from the south of Bihar. My parents were farmers, successful enough to ensure I was educated and could speak English—something neither of them could do. Though I went to school, I wanted to be a farmer like my father, so after I completed my education, I went back to work on the family farm.

When I was about twenty, some of my former school-mates became involved in a violent rebel movement. I stayed well away from them. But somehow, the authorities decided that not only was I involved, but that I was a ringleader. I don't know whether it was simply a mistake, or if my supposed friends implicated me to throw the police off their scent. However it happened, a warrant was issued for my arrest. I know what the British justice system is like for Indians: execute first and never ask any questions. So I ran. I fled Bihar, changed my name to Vijay Prasad, and signed the indenture contract on the next ship to Fiji."

Did Akal believe that Mr. Prasad was the innocent victim of mistaken identity? He wasn't sure. But either way, that wasn't his priority. He was seeking the truth about the deaths of Sanjay Lal and Master Thakur.

"What about Sanjay Lal? He has some connection with your past in India?"

"I barely knew him in India. He lived in my town, but he was a little older than me and younger than my parents, so our paths didn't really cross. When I came out of indenture, I made contact with a friend at home and started sending him letters for my parents. Well, my father had died by then, which I learnt when the first response came, so they became letters to my mother. Without my knowledge, when that friend moved out of town, he arranged for Sanjay Lal to receive my letters and read them to my mother. Sanjay now knew all the details of my life in Fiji. When my mother passed away, he kept my letters. Some time later, when things weren't going well for him in India, he decided to come try his luck in Fiji. He saw I was doing well here after indenture, so he thought there must be plenty of opportunities out here."

"But he didn't come under indenture?" Akal asked.

Vijay's face twisted with a bitter smile. "Of course he didn't want to go through indenture. Who would, if they had the option? He scraped together what money he had and paid his way out here. Imagine my surprise when he arrives and comes to my house, greeting me as though we were long-lost friends, expecting me to help him get established. I told him to go away—I didn't know him and I wasn't going to help him just because we were from the same town. That is when he showed me the letter and the article and said he would go to the police with my identity if I didn't help him. I had no choice."

"What sort of help did he want?" Akal asked.

"He had some money to get started but he needed more, and he didn't have any contacts. So I helped him get the store set up. I thought that would be the end of it. But he wouldn't give me back the documents."

"What went so wrong that you had to kill him?"

"What went wrong for him is that he did not know the first thing about running a store. He did all sorts of stupid things. I told him not to put the store outside of town, but he wouldn't listen. He thought that people would soon be building homes that way and that people from the Fijian village would come to him, but neither thing turned out to be true. The village had no need for his goods and the town didn't grow. Every time I turned around, he had run some scheme or another and kept making things worse for himself. Then the demands for more money started coming."

"The blackmail continued?" Akal asked.

"Yes. If I wanted to keep my life here in Fiji, I would have to give him money until his business became profitable. That was two years ago. I knew his business would never be profitable, but I had reached a point where supporting Sanjay seemed like a small price to pay for my otherwise wonderful life. And then he decided he wanted to move to Suva."

"Surely that would be a good thing. Get him out of your life?" Akal suggested.

Vijay gave Akal a sardonic look. "You strike me as a smart man, Sergeant Singh. I think you know that he was never going to be out of my life. Here or Suva or back in India, he was always going to hold that letter and that article over me. But the issue with moving to Suva was that he needed yet another infusion of money to get set up. I must have seemed too comfortable because he decided that I could afford more than I had been giving him. It was the last straw."

"So you decided to kill him."

"It was not as simple as that. I had to get those documents first. What if somebody found them after he died?"

"And when the Germans came, you thought you had a scapegoat?"

"A smart man, as I said, Sergeant Singh. Yes, I knew when they were taking their final delivery and I arrived immediately after that. I had my whip with me. I knew how to use it—I had been a *sirdar*, an overseer, after all. Sanjay may not have wanted to go through indenture, but he learnt what the *sirdar*'s whip felt like that day," Vijay ended, his face fierce.

Akal shuddered. "You wanted to punish him?"

"I wanted the documents. He must have known he was going to die—I don't know why he didn't just tell me where they were. Maybe he was trying to hold on, thinking help would come. But then, he seemed to become confused and stopped saying anything at all. I don't know why. I had not whipped him that hard."

Akal recalled the livid whip marks on Sanjay Lal's face and body. If that was Vijay Prasad's version of not hard, he would not have wanted to be a coolie on a plantation where he was overseer.

"Dr. Holmes said that the fear and pain likely caused a heart attack," Akal said pointedly, unable to keep the judgement from his voice, losing his sympathetic pose. But it didn't matter; the release of confession seemed to have taken over for Vijay and he continued.

"I gave up on questioning him. I tore the house up looking for the letter and the article. I felt like I was searching forever. I couldn't find them. And when I came back to the kitchen to force Sanjay to tell me, he was dead. I heard someone coming and slipped out the back."

"You almost got away with it. If you only had to deal with Constable Kumar, no doubt you would have."

"I was shocked when I realised that you were a sergeant from Suva. I never thought they would send anyone from Suva. I knew Sanjay had reported the Germans, but I thought it wouldn't be taken seriously. Why did they take it seriously?"

"They didn't. We were sent for another reason, and the

follow up on the report of Germans was a futile search, a joke. And yet, here we are, with a group of German sailors in custody. You know you did a good job making them look guilty, with that whip and the money on their boat. The captain told us you had been there before, helping Sanjay Lal deliver goods. Is that how you knew where to go?"

"Yes. He forced me to help him, of course. So when I had to get the whip out of my house, I thought of the boat. I knew they were being held and I thought you would prob-ably find the boat eventually. Even if you didn't, at least the whip wasn't in my house."

"And the money?"

Vijay Prasad groaned. "All that money. I thought I could keep it, make up for all the money Sanjay had taken from me over the years, slowly spend it elsewhere. But I had to put it on the boat as well. It had to look as though they had stolen it back from Sanjay. I thought I was safe."

"But then you killed Master Thakur."

At the mention of the second murder, Vijay Prasad pinched his eyes closed in an expression of regret. "I am sorry about the teacher. I went to ask him about the letter, and he wouldn't say anything, didn't confirm, didn't deny. At first he looked confused about why I was asking, but then his face went blank. I knew that he had figured out who I was. I couldn't let him tell you. After Sanjay, it wasn't so hard."

Akal forced his muscles to unclench. It should still have been hard to kill a man.

"How did you know he had translated the letter for us?" Akal asked.

Vijay nodded at Constable Kumar, who was still standing

in the doorway, taking notes. Constable Kumar took this like a blow to the gut, leaning against the door.

"I suppose you already knew that. That is why he told Kavita where to find the documents? So that you could catch me?"

Akal nodded. Vijay turned and looked at Kumar.

"How could you put your family in danger like that? You didn't know who would come."

"We knew a murderer might come. That is why Constable Kumar's parents were staying at the hotel for the night," Akal responded for Constable Kumar, who still looked sick at the final confirmation that his indiscretion had gotten the teacher killed.

"I see. It seems you thought of everything. But I object to being called a murderer, Sergeant Singh. I had good reasons."

Akal replied softly, "Killers generally do."

WHILE AKAL HAD been conducting his interrogation, Taviti had been sending and receiving messages from Suva, keeping John's pigeons busy. A ship had been organised to come from Suva to take Akal, Taviti, and the six German prisoners of war back to Suva. A contingent of police officers was coming over on the boat to assist with the prisoners. There was one passenger coming from Suva who would not be making the round trip: the new officer had finally arrived from Australia and was coming to Levuka as his permanent post.

Until the ship arrived with the reinforcements, Taviti had convinced his uncle to lend a few of his warriors to assist Akal and Taviti. Akal, Constable Kumar, and Taviti's cousin

Peni were at the police station guarding the German crew and Vijay Prasad. Taviti and another warrior were at the Royal Hotel, guarding the captain. Yet another of Taviti's cousins was at the wharf, awaiting the arrival of the ship from Suva.

"What will you tell him?" Constable Kumar asked. He had asked Akal to step away from the cells, leaving Peni to guard the prisoners. Now Akal knew why.

"The new sub-inspector? I won't tell him anything." Constable Kumar brightened, but his face fell once again as Akal continued, "It is only a brief reprieve. I will have to put everything in my report to the inspector-general and I am sure this will come back through to your sergeant the next time the mail is delivered. I suggest you tell him yourself."

"What exactly will you put in your report?" Constable Kumar asked, his voice low and tight, as though he was forcing the words out.

"That you told Kavita about the letter. If I don't, somebody will ask how Vijay Prasad knew that the teacher had translated it for us. But I will make it clear that your performance was excellent otherwise, and that, with your local knowledge, you were the one to recognise Vijay Prasad in the article. I'll say that I believe you have learnt your lesson, whatever my opinion is worth. The inspector-general is extremely short on men. He might have to keep you."

They stood outside for a few more moments, Constable Kumar contemplating his fate while Akal recollected being on Constable Kumar's side of this conversation. He wondered if his inspector-general in Hong Kong could have done more to protect him from the consequences of his mistake. Perhaps not. The fact that high-profile, wealthy families had been affected by Akal's mistake made it impossible to give him any more leeway than he had received.

Just as they were about to return to Peni, a group of police officers turned off Beach Street and appeared from around the building in front of the station. Akal recognised the six Fijian and Indian officers, but not the European officer striding briskly in the lead.

"Sergeant Singh, I presume? I'm Sub-Inspector Bob Cuthbert," the European man said, extending his hand, his broad accent immediately identifying him as Australian.

Akal shook Sub-Inspector Cuthbert's hand, surprised at the warmth of his greeting. He was new. Perhaps he didn't know that Akal was out of favour.

"Yes, I am Sergeant Akal Singh, and this is Constable Raj Kumar. He was born and raised in Levuka. I think you will find his local knowledge helpful."

Constable Kumar stepped forward and shook his new senior officer's hand, flashing Akal a grateful glance.

"Can I give you a hand getting your prisoners squared away for the journey back to Suva?" Sub-Inspector Cuthbert asked.

"Yes, please. The sooner we get them back to Suva and they stop being my responsibility the better," Akal said with feeling.

The Germans were being transferred to Suva, but Vijay Prasad was staying in Levuka for the moment. Eventually he would end up standing trial in Suva, but the immediate priority was the Germans. Akal had argued that there might have been some risk in transferring him with such high-profile prisoners who had attempted escape before. While this was true, Akal's real reason was to give Vijay a bit more time in Levuka, near his family.

Cuthbert and the officers from Suva transferred the five sailors to the ship, while Akal went to the Royal Hotel to pick up Taviti and Count von Luckner. As he approached the hotel, he was dismayed to find Katherine and Mary waiting for him on the verandah, their bags at their feet. Mr. Lewis was also sitting with them, a furrow between his brows as he peered at Katherine out of the corner of his eye. He had handled Ratu Teleni and negotiations which affected the security of the colony with aplomb, but it seemed that a conversation with Katherine may have ruffled his feathers.

"Good morning, Sergeant Singh. Is the ship here?" Katherine called out as Akal walked up.

"Good morning. Ah, the ship taking the prisoners back to Suva is here," Akal replied.

"And will you and Constable Tukana be on this ship?" she asked pointedly.

"Yes," Akal said, drawing the word out.

"Well, you are our escorts, so we will also be on the ship."

"I've tried to explain to them that it won't be safe," Mr. Lewis interjected.

"We saw the police officers march past here, the officers who came from Suva. They will be on the ship, correct? There is an entire regiment of them. What could possibly happen?"

"It is unlikely that anything untoward will happen," Akal agreed, before continuing in a less positive note. "But we can't guarantee your safety. The SS *Amra* will be back in Levuka in a few days and will return straight to Suva. This will be a much more comfortable journey for you both."

"I'll feel safer on the ship with you than being here without you for a few days," Katherine said, looking at him with wide eyes. Akal merely raised one eyebrow up to his turban. She abandoned her innocent look and laughed. "It was worth a try. Look, we've done what we came here for, so Aunt Mary and I would both like to get back to Suva. We've got a few things to clear up with Uncle Hugh." The last sentence was said with a wry twist of her lips.

Before Akal could continue to argue, Dr. Holmes walked out the front door with his medical bag in one hand and his duffle bag in the other to join them on the verandah. "Akal, excellent. Ship is here?" Once again, Akal didn't manage to answer before the doctor smiled and nodded, ostensibly to both of the ladies, but his eyes were only for Mary. "Good morning. Are you joining us on the ship?" he asked with delight as he noticed their bags.

"Mr. Lewis and I have been encouraging the *mems* to wait for the SS *Amra*. Constable Tukana and I will be busy guarding the prisoners, and I have some concerns for their safety," Akal responded, frowning at the older man.

"Oh, not to worry," Dr. Holmes replied, dismissing Akal's concerns with a wave of his hand, as though Akal was being a fussy old woman. "John and I can take care of the ladies, can't we, John?"

"Well, I suppose we'll have to. Logic doesn't seem to be having any impact," Mr. Lewis replied, throwing his hands in the air in a gesture of both surrender and frustration.

Akal shook his head as Dr. Holmes shared a conspiratorial grin with Mary and Katherine. Leaving the Europeans to their small talk, Akal went inside and headed upstairs to the room where Taviti was guarding the captain. When Akal entered the room, Taviti was seated in the armchair while his prisoner was sitting on the bed.

"Captain, the ship is here to take yourself and your crew to Suva."

They made their way downstairs, collecting the entourage of people Akal had not expected to be responsible for, and walked to the wharf. Once they had all boarded the ship, the Germans were moved to the aft, where they were guarded one police officer to one prisoner. All of them were kept restrained except for Count von Luckner, and they had been admonished not to speak with each other. All was quiet, the restrained men sitting with their backs against the hull and the captain standing by himself, looking out over the ocean.

At the fore of the ship, Mary and Dr. Holmes were talking and laughing together, the doctor blushing when Mary touched his arm. Meanwhile, Mr. Lewis seemed to be holding court with a reluctant Katherine. He didn't seem to notice that she had her arms crossed and was not looking at him. Again, Akal marvelled that this man, who had read the situation so well when it came to political negotiations, was so blinded by the lovely woman in front of him that he stopped seeing her as a person. Katherine caught Akal's eye and gave him a pleading look.

"I think she wants you to rescue her," Taviti observed.

"Miss Katherine would be better off talking to Mr. Lewis. I would certainly be better off if she kept talking to him," Akal responded with a sigh. "Besides, we have to keep an eye on the prisoners."

"They are restrained and well guarded. And even if not, where are they going to go?" Taviti asked, gesturing to the open ocean around them. "Let's go. I'll distract Lewis, you talk to Miss Katherine."

Taviti nudged him with his elbow, once, twice, three times until Akal knocked Taviti's elbow away.

"All right, fine. Just stop doing that."

After casting another eye over the constables who were guarding the prisoners, Akal and Taviti moved to the fore of the ship, dodging the sailors who were doing mysterious things with ropes and sails. As they approached, Katherine immediately moved to allow them access and stepped back away from Mr. Lewis, who only faltered momentarily before continuing to pontificate about the negotiation with Ratu Teleni.

Akal maneuvered himself to be by the hull, so he could keep an eye on the prisoners. After Mr. Lewis made a particularly stirring point in his story, Taviti stepped forward to ask him a probing question, effectively cutting Katherine out of the conversation. She immediately took a few strides to the other side of the fore of the ship, away from Taviti and Mr. Lewis. As she brushed past Akal, Katherine rolled her eyes at him, urging him silently to join her. Akal was more furtive than Katherine but casually strolled over.

"Thank God we got away," Katherine said with a gusty sigh. "That man will not stop talking."

"I believe Dr. Holmes had the same problem with Mr. Lewis on the way over."

"It seems I owe Constable Tukana a favour," she said, watching as Taviti asked Mr. Lewis a question which seemed to agitate the man greatly, causing him to speak faster and lean forward. "He's very good at distraction."

"People underestimate Taviti. His size and his charm, that's all they see. Sometimes this is an asset for him, but I think most of the time, it's not."

They stood quietly for a while, Akal facing inwards and watching the prisoners, Katherine facing outwards and watching the waves.

"I'm not like Emily, you know," Katherine blurted out.

Akal stopped breathing. He desperately cast about for something to say but his mind had gone completely blank.

"I'm sorry. I've shocked you. I just thought that you should know that I know."

"How?" Akal choked out.

"Aunt Mary. Uncle Hugh told her. She saw me teasing you and she thought I should understand why you might be wary of being friendly with me. But I'm not like her."

Akal squeezed his eyes shut, his whole face tight, and tried to remember how to breathe. Once the initial shock cleared, he realised he was glad that Katherine had said something. He never could have.

"I know that. I could tell from the first time I met you," he finally responded.

"So, can we be friends? At least while I'm in Fiji, until I go home to my proper marriage," she said, eyes rolling on the word "proper."

"I wish we could," Akal said.

"But we can't? Because of what happened with Emily?"

"What happened with Emily happened because the world doesn't want an Indian man and a European lady to be friends. That hasn't changed in the last year. That hasn't changed going from India to Hong Kong to Fiji. Just look at Mr. Lewis now," Akal said. He himself wasn't looking at Mr. Lewis directly, but had caught the aide periodically frowning at them out of the corner of his eye. Katherine looked over just as Mr. Lewis was glowering at them again.

"Hmph. Well, I'm not one to do what the world tells me," Katherine declared, glaring at Mr. Lewis and tossing her chin in the air. She glanced up at Akal and continued with a sad, soft smile, "But I would not want to make your life any harder."

Akal held her gaze until his heart was too full to allow it any more. He looked down at the deck below his feet, feeling the ocean churn under them. He and Katherine stayed in their positions for what felt like a lifetime to Akal. The world seemed to be suspended, the shouts of the sailors far away. Akal could feel the weight of his mistakes, the weight of his yearning for Hong Kong, slipping from his shoulders and into the Pacific Ocean, to be lost among the waves.

"Friends," Akal said, with a slow, small nod.

"Friends," Katherine replied, smiling to the ocean.

THE DAY AFTER they all arrived back in Suva, life was getting back to normal. The German sailors were under guard in the cells at the police station, awaiting a ship to New Zealand, where they would be interned in a prisoner of war camp. Akal had written and submitted his report that morning, including the truth of Constable Kumar's mistakes. He wondered whether the inspector-general would manage to make Constable Kumar's error in judgement Akal's fault somehow. But, as with the last time he wrote such a report, Akal wrote the truth, no matter what might come of it. At least this time he didn't have to find a way to expose those truths to the wider world.

In the early evening, in keeping with the theme of getting back to normal, Akal was at a desk on the ground floor of the

Totogo police station, reading a report of the latest Night Prowler sighting. While they had been in Levuka, the Night Prowler had made another nocturnal visit to the windows of a family home on Berry Road. The senior constable who had taken the report in Akal's absence had happily thrust the file at Akal as soon as he'd walked into the station that morning. As usual, the report featured a hysterical mother, a confused child, and a complete lack of any new information on the man's identity.

"Singh, with me."

Akal started and looked over his right shoulder toward the source of the peremptory command. Inspector-General Thurstrom was waiting for him in the doorway, tapping his pace stick against his thigh. Glancing through the grimy, louvred window at the rapidly disappearing sunlight, Akal realised the time. In the evenings, the inspector-general always had an early dinner and then went for what he called a "constitutional," a brisk thirty-minute walk in whichever direction he fancied that day. Sometimes he took an officer with him—either to dress them down away from prying ears, or to praise them. It seemed that today was Akal's turn. Thurstrom had never shied away from dressing him down in the station. Could it be that he was going to praise Akal? Surely not.

"Come on then, Singh. Let's go."

Akal hastily packed away his files and joined Thurstrom outside. They walked down to Victoria Parade and joined the citizens of Suva as they went about their business on the main shopping street of the town. The journey to Albert Park was made in silence, the inspector-general's brisk pace forcing them both to dodge around slower pedestrians.

When they reached the corner of the park, Thurstrom executed a sharp left turn and started to walk along its edge, up the slight slope.

"You managed to follow instructions this time," the inspector-general observed out of the blue.

"Yes, sir," Akal said, with some trepidation. He couldn't tell whether this was a positive sign or an opening for a reprimand.

"And look how well it turned out. You got the real murderer and we got a dangerous group of German privateers into a prisoner of war camp. You don't have to disobey orders to achieve the right outcome."

"No, sir," Akal replied once more. A backhanded compliment, then. Of course, it was easier to obey orders when those orders did not include covering up exploitation and abuse. He didn't mention this to Thurstrom.

"John Lewis has submitted his report to the governor. It reflected well on your performance and on Constable Tukana's. He seems to feel you both assisted him ably. The governor is happy."

"Yes, sir, thank you, sir," Akal replied. This was unexpected. He had thought the aide would take all the credit for himself, or even worse, report on Akal's rapport with Katherine and Mary, a friendliness that Mr. Lewis had volubly disapproved of.

"This situation with Kumar doesn't reflect well, though," Inspector-General Thurstrom continued.

Akal silently groaned. He had started to hope for exclusively good news, but here was the bad news, as expected.

"I'll have to let him go," Thurstrom continued. "It's a shame—he just got through training, and from all accounts he showed promise. God knows where I'll find another junior officer for Levuka."

Akal felt a pang of disappointment. He wasn't surprised. Constable Kumar's mistake had had dire outcomes, and the response was warranted, but he had still held out some small hope for the young man. As for himself, Akal waited for the recriminations about his own failure to prevent Constable Kumar's catastrophic mistake. When this wasn't forthcoming, he ventured to express a few thoughts of his own. "I thought he showed promise also. And his knowledge of the people of Levuka was crucial. Perhaps if he had had a more senior officer to learn from, as he does now, he wouldn't have made this mistake."

"You were there," Thurstrom said, his voice hardening to a tone Akal was more familiar with. "You were his senior officer. Why didn't he learn this from you before he got the teacher killed? I suppose you aren't exactly known for your discretion when it comes to women, are you, Singh?"

And there it was. Akal would have kept his mouth shut, but he owed Kumar some assistance. "We had one day with Constable Kumar before this all occurred. One day is not enough to be an influence, good or bad," Akal replied, some heat creeping into his tone despite his best efforts. He took a moment, then continued more calmly. "Could Kumar be given a second chance? Perhaps be made a probationary officer who will not be promoted for a very long time?"

They had reached the top of Albert Park by now, and the inspector-general paused for a moment. Akal couldn't tell whether he was deciding on a direction to go next, or on Akal's suggestion, or simply pausing to catch his breath. For a red-haired Britisher, the colony's senior police officer seemed remarkably unaffected by the heat. In similar circumstances in Hong Kong, Akal had seen British officers turn beet red, eyes smarting as they were stung by the sweat pouring down their faces. Akal himself could feel the sweat trickling through his beard, and had to suppress the urge to rub it away. But Thurstrom, while slightly damp about the forehead, wasn't even flushed. Probably not pausing to catch his breath, then.

Without a word, Thurstrom started moving again, crossing the road towards the botanical gardens. Akal followed a pace behind, lengthening his strides to catch up.

"What did you tell Cuthbert about Kumar's cock-up?"

"I didn't have a chance to discuss it with him, sir. I only met him for a moment. We were very occupied with getting the prisoners secured on the ship."

"He will need to be told. I'll give him the choice: a junior officer who needs to be kept on a short leash, or no junior officer at all for God knows how long. I suspect he'll keep him. But the instant it is in the papers, none of us will have any choice. He'll be gone. We already get enough bad press as it is."

Akal felt his face go slack, stunned. It had worked; Constable Kumar had been granted a reprieve. He had the feeling of coming full circle, the chance to help the young man the same way he had been helped by his superior officer when he'd made a similar mistake in Hong Kong. Not to mention the fact that the inspector-general had taken his advice. Akal wanted this promenade to end now before anything came along to ruin it.

They were walking along a path through the botanical gardens now, back towards Victoria Parade, back towards the ocean. The path wound between the trees, somehow managing to avoid the trees with actual foliage which might have provided some shade. Instead, the shadow of the occasional tall, skinny coconut palm crossed the path. It would be as though somebody was trying to take shelter in his own shadow, Akal thought. They'd get some relief, but not an awful lot.

"Hugh Clancy sent along his thanks. It seems you managed to escort his sister and niece without getting yourself into trouble there. I'm surprised. Given your record on this, I thought you would be the one I'd be considering dismissing."

Thurstrom stopped short of saying he had been hoping for that outcome, but Akal was sure that this was the case.

"Perhaps I have misjudged you, Singh. Perhaps it is time I gave you a second chance as well."

Akal was mid-stride when Thurstrom uttered this incredible statement, stopping him in his tracks. He finally managed to put his foot down on the ground, which felt like it was moving under him, and then hurried to catch up with the inspector-general.

"Sir?" Akal said, unable to produce a more coherent response.

"Yes, yes," Thurstrom said, waving off anything more Akal might have said about this change of attitude with a dismissive flap of his hand. "You've still got the Night Prowler case to sort out. Don't get ahead of yourself."

"No, sir," Akal replied, unable to suppress a smile.

They were at the water's edge now, and evening had properly descended. Thurstrom stopped to look out over the Pacific Ocean, his hands clasped at his back. There was a strong breeze flowing over their faces and shoulders, but not enough to disturb the vast expanse of water.

Akal closed his eyes and breathed in the briny air, allowing the spark of hope to permeate through his bones. Perhaps nothing was going to change immediately, but if Thurstrom's attitude towards him was thawing, maybe the other officers' might as well. Maybe he could prove himself enough to be a respected, valued police officer in Fiji. And maybe, just maybe, he could find his way back to Hong Kong.

A COUPLE OF afternoons later, Akal walked into the Totogo station dusty, dishevelled, and dispirited. Taviti wasn't at his usual spot at the front desk. Akal sighed. He really just wanted the day to be over. Scouting around for somewhere quiet to sit, Akal slumped into a chair in one of the smaller interview rooms, where he could keep an eye on the front counter to catch Taviti as soon as he returned.

After the conversation with Inspector-General Thurstrom, Akal had attacked the Night Prowler case with new determination. He had read all the witness reports again and spoken to all of the police officers who had attended the scenes. He had even re-interviewed some of the parents of the victims, though nobody would let him talk to their children again for fear of reopening the trauma. Nothing new had shaken loose for him.

There was nothing fantastical about this case; the dratted Night Prowler was no criminal genius. There was just nothing to grab hold of. Unless they actually grabbed hold of *him* mid-act, they might never catch him, Akal thought, slumping further into his chair. The sound of Taviti humming jerked Akal out of his reverie.

"Are you ready to go?" Akal asked, poking his head out of the door.

Taviti started. "Man, don't do that. You just appeared out of nowhere."

"What kind of police officer are you, getting scared when somebody talks to you? No wonder they keep you behind the desk."

Taviti scowled.

"Sorry, sorry. I know that isn't funny for you," Akal said, giving his friend a wry smile. "Anyway, shouldn't you be finished with your shift by now? We should go. Though I should freshen up first."

"Oh, yes, wouldn't want Katherine to see you with dust on your face," Taviti said archly, humour restored.

Hugh Clancy had invited Akal, Taviti, and Dr. Holmes over for dinner to thank them for escorting his sister and niece to Levuka. Akal suspected that Katherine and Mary were actually the driving force behind the invitation. The preoccupied editor had not seemed the type for dinner parties.

Ten minutes later, they met outside the station and started the short walk to Hugh Clancy's home, near the newspaper office. The friends had not had a chance to talk outside of the police station since their return from Levuka, and Akal took the opportunity to broach a topic he had been wondering about since they got back.

"How did you leave things with your uncle?"

"I . . . don't know," Taviti said on a heavy sigh. "He's not happy with me. I think the only reason he hasn't told me to come home is because it might cause trouble, me and him in the village together obviously disagreeing on so many things."

"If he told you to go back, would you?"

"I would have to. He is the chief."

They walked a few moments in silence, before Taviti continued in a low, contemplative tone. "You know, when I was young, I didn't think too much about these things. I was more like Peni. Not serious and quiet like him, but not questioning. I would have thought as my uncle thought. He was the one who sent me here—to learn more about how the Britishers do things, to make connections we could use. So I learnt about the Britishers and made connections—and learnt how to think for myself. He doesn't like that last part. He wants me to think as he does. But I can't do that, Akal. I can't forget how to think for myself now."

"In some ways, it is the same for me. I'm not sure how it will be when I go home. Not with my father—he and I write letters to each other. He knows my mind and I know his. And he knows the world is changing. But my mother, she is frightened of the world changing. She only wants what she knows."

"Frightened?" Taviti said, frowning. "I never thought my uncle could be frightened of anything. I will have to think about this."

"Later, though, yes? First we have to manage dinner with Katherine. Who knows what she will say," Akal said in mock horror as he picked up the pace a little bit.

"Oh, yes, you and Katherine had a long talk on the ship coming back," Taviti said, twitching his eyebrows suggestively.

"Do you know why I was sent here from Hong Kong?" Akal asked, not looking at Taviti. He was almost certain Taviti knew the story of Emily, but they had never addressed it directly. He had been dreading having this conversation,

but now that it was here, now that he had heard some of
Taviti's stories, it had a feeling of rightness about it.

"Yes."

That one word seemed to cover a wealth of meaning.
Yes, Taviti knew, and he had invited Akal into his home
anyway. Taviti's easy acceptance left Akal wondering—would
he have had the compassion if the roles had been reversed?
Certainly not before his own tribulations. For all his friend's
jocularity, Taviti had an innate wisdom that Akal was only
just starting to recognise.

"Well, so does Katherine. Despite this, for some reason,
she wants to be my friend. I'm not sure if it is possible, but
we will see."

"Oh. That's very sensible. And very boring. Man, you
couldn't have let me have some more fun with this before
making it all sensible?"

"Oh, my apologies. I forgot that your entertainment
should always be my first priority."

"Always. How could you forget?"

They had arrived at Hugh Clancy's house, and Akal
blinked in surprise.

"Well, that garden has been given a haircut," he remarked
to Taviti as he walked through the gate. "Last time I was here
I had to fight my way through."

The bougainvillea vines had been cut back, so they were
graceful rather than overburdened. Light filtered through
the leaves and flowers, dappling the ground below. The mass
of leaves had been raked away, leaving patches of grass and
rather sad-looking areas of exposed dirt. Years of dilapidation
couldn't be repaired overnight, but it was clear that some care
had recently been put into this long-neglected garden.

As they walked up the stairs, Katherine appeared at the front door. She looked like the elegant young society woman that she was, wearing a pale-green silk dress which draped modestly to a sash at her waist, then fell gracefully in soft pleats to her calves. Her smile was the barest twitch of her lips as her eyes darted between the two men.

"Miss Katherine, you look lovely."

As her smile expanded to her usual beam, Akal silently cursed Taviti for saying what he was too dumbstruck to say.

"Hello, Sergeant Singh, Constable Tukana. Please come and take a seat," she said, gesturing to some chairs on the verandah.

As with the garden, it was clear that some effort had been put in to make the home more welcoming, with the mismatched chairs arranged around a table covered in a white tablecloth, a vase of flowers set in the centre.

"I hope you don't mind being outside. We are waiting for more furniture to arrive from the house in Levuka so it is a bit bare inside, and it is just a bit cooler out here. Aunt Mary is cooking and Uncle Hugh—well, I don't know if he will be here in time for dinner. Some last-minute disaster at the newspaper." She paused the flow of information, took a deep breath, and continued more calmly. "Now, how about some gin and tonics?"

Katherine hovered until the two men sat, then went back inside. She returned a few minutes later with a tray of drinks, Aunt Mary following behind her.

"Hello, gentlemen. No, no, stay seated, please. How are you both?"

They exchanged pleasantries as Katherine handed the drinks around.

"You have been gardening?" Akal asked.

"Yes, now that Katherine and I are here for a little while, we've started sorting out the house."

"You are staying for a little while?" Akal asked, hoping that the bloom of joy he felt wasn't too obvious.

"Yes, we are," Katherine said. It seemed to Akal that her smile was just for him. "I've still got some articles to get published, and Aunt Mary isn't ready to go home yet either." She threw her aunt an arch look that left Akal puzzled.

"Well, Mr. Clancy must be pleased that you are staying. And that you are putting the house in order," he said, some doubt creeping into his voice for the latter statement.

"He hasn't objected, in any case, which is an improvement from before," Mary replied with a laugh. "I have enjoyed sorting out the garden—I do love my garden at home. I am a bit stuck, though. There are some plants that I've never seen before, and I just don't know what to do with them. I had to hire a man for the heavier jobs, but he doesn't have great English and I haven't been able to ask him what they are."

"I might be able to help," Taviti said. "Do you want me to take a look?"

"Oh, yes, please, that would be wonderful."

Mary and Taviti walked down the stairs of the verandah and into the front garden, drinks in hand, leaving Akal and Katherine somewhat alone, though always within glancing distance.

"How did your uncle like your recipes?" Akal asked Katherine. "Did he love them as much as you thought?"

The peal of laughter from Katherine had Mary looking their way, but she must have decided it was innocent, as she remained in the garden with Taviti.

"He *actually* loved them. He is planning on printing them. So I will have my first articles printed and we are both thrilled. What a result!" she exulted.

"I am very happy for you. Did you ask if you could report on Captain von Luckner, given you helped in the investigation?" Akal asked.

Katherine leaned in, her eyes alight. "Haven't you noticed? There are no reports in any newspaper about our German friends."

Akal started. She was right. He had been so focused on the possibility of Constable Kumar's mistake being reported, and so relieved that it hadn't been, that he had failed to make the connection that nothing was being reported about the Germans.

"The government has gagged the newspapers," she said, lowering her voice as though somebody might be eavesdropping. "They are saying it is for security reasons, even though everyone knows about it! Of course everyone does, it's such a tiny country. Uncle Hugh is furious."

Hugh Clancy may have been furious, but Akal was relieved. Perhaps Constable Kumar's second chance would actually have a chance to stick.

"I wanted to thank you again for helping us find out what happened to Aunt Clara," Katherine said, looking out at a spot in the garden.

"You are welcome," Akal said automatically. He wanted to tell her that she didn't need to thank him or talk about it at all if she didn't want to, but he didn't know how to have such a conversation with a young woman. She continued before he could find a way to express himself.

"Aunt Mary had a long talk with Uncle Hugh the night

we got back from Levuka. I don't know what she said to him, but I presume she talked to him about the child. Ever since then, he has come back to us a little bit. He seems lighter somehow." She finally looked at Akal and gave a small, lopsided shrug. "At least I've got my uncle back."

The creak of the gate broke the silence, as Dr. Holmes arrived. Mary greeted him in the garden, both of their faces lighting up upon seeing each other. This must have been why Katherine was teasing Mary about not being ready to go home yet, Akal realised. Taviti jogged back up the stairs to the verandah, the older couple trailing after him, already deep in conversation.

"Come inside and I'll fix you a drink," Mary said to Dr. Holmes after he had greeted Akal and Katherine. "And perhaps you could give me a hand with dinner?"

Akal watched as Dr. Holmes opened the door for Mary, and followed her in, his free hand hovering at her lower back as though she were precious. He was happy for his friend, for this simple romance that seemed to be blossoming, though that happiness was somewhat tinged with envy.

Was this in his future? It felt impossible. Akal knew that if he went home, his mother would have him married as soon as his feet hit Indian soil. But it wouldn't be this. It wouldn't be of his choosing. If he hadn't left, he wouldn't have known any different; he probably would have been happy, just as Taviti had said about leaving his village and coming to Suva. But, like Taviti, he *had* left, and now he had seen too much.

It probably wouldn't make any difference. It wasn't as though there were women in Fiji he could marry. He glanced at Katherine, her face glowing with delight at whatever

Taviti was talking about. If he wanted to marry—and really, what else did one do?—then he had to return to India. And he would have to make that choice soon. He was already twenty-six.

Akal turned his attention back to the conversation flowing around him. Taviti was telling Katherine the story of the end of their previous case. It had been a dramatic incident the way Akal remembered it, but the way Taviti told it, it had reached epic proportions. He smiled to himself and took another sip of his drink. His future could wait.

AUTHOR'S NOTE

HELLO DEAR READER,

I hope you have enjoyed Akal's second adventure in Fiji. He is certainly having a better time of things than he was in the first book. But how long will it last?

In this note, I wanted to discuss a few things that are on my mind, and that maybe you will find of interest. I will cover a question I'm often asked: Why set a book in Fiji? I also wanted to talk about my depiction of the indigenous Fijian people, the iTaukei people. Finally, the all-important section about the historical aspect of the novel—the research, the characters and plot points which are based on real people and events, and where I've taken some liberties.

The short answer to "why set a book in Fiji" is to explore my heritage. But who wants a short answer? Not I, dear reader, and I assume not you. So I will start at the beginning. I was born in Fiji of Indian descent, and my family moved to Australia when I was three. Growing up in North Queensland in the 1980s, I was focused on fitting in and didn't want to know anything about my heritage. All I vaguely knew was that my Indian forebears went to Fiji to work in the cane fields some undefined amount of time ago. It was on a trip to India in my twenties, where I witnessed the poverty in my ancestral homeland, that I became more interested in learning about how my ancestors escaped that cycle of poverty to go to Fiji.

I was traveling a lot at the time and everywhere I went, I looked for cool libraries (that's a thing) where I could research the history of Indians in Fiji. I found resources in unexpected places: the Bodleian Library at Oxford University, the New York Public Library, the Library of Congress in Washington, D.C. Finally, and most importantly, the Sir Alport Barker Library at the National Archives of Fiji and the University of the South Pacific Library in Suva.

What I learnt was that Indians were taken to Fiji as part of an indentured servitude program set up by the British government in India. The program provided cheap labour to the British colonies, something they were crying out for after the abolition of slavery in the British Empire. It was the next evolution of slavery—not as egregious but still exploitative and degrading.

The Indians who signed up for this program were poor and generally illiterate. They would sign contracts to work for five years in a particular colony; they theoretically signed these contracts of their own free will, but of course their illiteracy and their often desperate circumstances left them vulnerable to exploitation. Add to this the fact that the agents who were recruiting them to the indentured servitude program were paid depending on the number of people they signed up; they were incentivized to lie to those they were recruiting.

The Indians who went to Fiji as indentured labourers, the *girmityas*, signed a five-year contract called the *girmit*. On a side note, apparently *girmit* is a mispronunciation of the English word "agreement," which came into common usage as the name of the contract.

After five generally very difficult years on the plantation, the time-expired Indians, as those who had finished their contract were called, had options. First, they could sign another contract. Given the abuses in the system and the misery of indenture, very few did. Second, they could return to India if they could afford to pay for the journey home. Most couldn't. So—third—they could stay and try to make a life in the colony of Fiji as free people.

After another five years living in Fiji, a return journey was paid for by the program. Sixty thousand Indians went to Fiji as indentured labourers; twenty-four thousand of the return journeys home were taken up.

Now, for the world of fiction! Akal has been sent to Fiji against his wishes and he's pretty miserable when he gets there. In *A Disappearance in Fiji*, the first of the Sergeant Akal Singh Mysteries, he goes to a plantation and witnesses the degradations of life for the indentured labourers. In *A Shipwreck in Fiji*, he moves much more in the world of the "time-expired *girmityas*." Akal learns that life outside of indenture isn't without its challenges. In the next book (at time of writing, just a sparkle in my eye), the story will somehow revolve around the question of staying in Fiji, or going home.

In this book, I've taken a risk I wasn't brave enough to take in the first book. I've added a lot more about indigenous Fijian culture, the culture of the iTaukei (literally meaning "owner") people. I avoided this in the first book because I was concerned about writing about a culture that I didn't feel like I was authentically in a position to talk about. I grew up around Fijian Indians, but not many iTaukei people. On the other hand, how can I write books set in Fiji, with an emphasis on historical issues of race and exploitation, with the iTaukei people only ever relegated to bit players? So I took a deep breath and took a chance on putting Taviti's family centre stage.

I researched as much as I could, devouring books and essays and pamphlets at the University of the South Pacific Library, Pacific Collection. I consulted with academics at the university to confirm my understanding of questions around the chiefly power structures, how village politics worked, how villages were laid out, traditional punishments, traditional lore and laws. Finally, I had the privilege of being hosted in the village of Lovoni in Ovalau (see the Acknowledgements for more details), which brought all of my research to light in one of the most beautiful places I've ever seen.

The iTaukei culture is complex and varied, with different traditions prevailing in different areas of Fiji. I did not attempt to faithfully represent one area's traditions. My intention was to give a sense of the types of traditions that existed. For example, the rule about turtle flesh being reserved for the chiefs seems to have been traditional law in some parts of Fiji, but by 1915, when this novel is set, this custom had fallen into disuse.

I also invented a village. The name of the village, its location, and its setting are all fictional, and an amalgam of places I saw in my travels in Fiji.

To any iTaukei people reading this, I did my best— please excuse any errors. I hope I represented the best of your culture.

Now let's talk about what is fact, what is fiction, and where do the lines blur? I had so much fun writing this second book. Before I put pen to paper, I knew that it was going to feature Count Felix von Luckner, the swashbuckling German privateer whose exploits were so legendary in Germany that they made a television series about him. I had read about the story of his capture near Levuka during World War I, an event which I wanted to incorporate somehow. This also meant that I could set the book in Levuka, a town which had captured my imagination when I spent a few days there in 2016.

Count Felix von Luckner was a minor German noble who had run away to sea as a young man and had a colourful and audacious early career. During World War I, he was the captain of the SMS *Seeadler*, a German raider which had escaped the British blockade disguised as a Norwegian ship, complete with faked correspondence in the Norwegian language. After terrorising and scuttling ships all over the South Pacific, the *Seeadler* ran aground on a reef near the Society Islands (about 3,400 miles away from Fiji).

Captain von Luckner then took six of his men in a longboat, with the intention of capturing another ship to rescue the rest of his crew, fifty-eight men who stayed behind with the ship. He eventually arrived in Fiji without achieving his goal, landing on the island of Wakaya near Ovalau. Here he came into contact with some of the locals, one of whom didn't believe his story of being Norwegian and called the police. On September 21st, 1917, the police, on board the steamer SS *Amra* (the ship Akal and his companions travel to Levuka on), bluffed von Luckner and his crew with a non-existent weapon. They surrendered, and were eventually taken to New Zealand as prisoners of war. Of course, the ever-intrepid Count von Luckner's story didn't end there—there was an inevitable escape attempt from New Zealand—but if I keep writing about him, this author's note will never end!

After reading about this story, and knowing I wanted to somehow incorporate it into this novel, I went looking for newspaper reports of this situation. I checked September 21st, 1917. Nothing. Then I checked the following week. Still nothing. I wondered, could this story have all been a myth? Much later, in an academic text, I learnt that the government had suppressed reporting of the incident for reasons of national security. Knowing this, I went back and found oblique references to "not publishing particulars of recent stirring occurrences." (This article appears before Chapter 9 of this book.) Later articles made it clear that the editors were not best pleased about this censorship!

Another feature of this story is the setting of Levuka. Levuka is my favourite place in Fiji. It is charming and beautiful, everyone knows one another, and, as the original capital, it is crammed full of history. Taviti covers some highlights of this history as he guides our cast through the town.

A major point in Levuka's history where I deviated from historical accuracy was the pigeon post. I fell in love with the idea of the pigeon post, which did exist and was initially set up by the *Fiji Times* to relay shipping information and other news between Suva and Levuka. However, it was defunct by 1915. I've kept it in place, as it seemed like such an elegant way to communicate.

The Indian school that features in the story is fictional.

The teacher, Master Thakur, has been brought out to Fiji by the British Indian Association of Fiji, which was established in 1911 to advocate for the improvement of the Indian community. While I didn't find any direct evidence that they assisted teachers to migrate, one of the founding members was Totaram Sanadhya, who was noted as encouraging Indian teachers to migrate to Fiji.

Ratu Teleni negotiates for the release of Apolosi Nawai towards the end of the story. While Ratu Teleni and this negotiation are both fictional, Apolosi Nawai was a significant figure in Fijian history who was imprisoned for political reasons. In the early 1900s, economic power in the colony was held by the Europeans. Nawai established Viti Kabani (Fiji Company) in an attempt to put power back into the hands of the Fijians, giving them more bargaining power when selling their products. This was a direct challenge to the European settlers, who pushed the government to do something about the upstart.

In the book, Ratu Teleni is advocating for Nawai, but in reality Nawai also represented a challenge to the power of the traditional chiefs, supplanting their role. In 1915, Nawai was convicted of embezzling funds from Viti Kabani and was sentenced to eighteen months hard labour. When he was released, he resumed his activities and started to become drunk on his own power. After making statements such as "I am the enemy of the government," he was arrested again in 1917 and exiled to Rotuma for seven years and finally to New Zealand in 1940.

Phew, I've gone on a bit. If you are still with me, then I must thank you for your perseverance, dear reader. You may be wondering: What is next for Akal? I don't quite know yet, but I think he might be up for some romance and a big decision. Whatever happens, there are sure to be some laughs with Taviti and Dr. Robert Holmes as Akal explores his new home in Fiji.

ACKNOWLEDGEMENTS

NEVER ONE TO SHY from stating the bleeding obvious: writing a historical novel is HARD! (Forgive me for the textual equivalent of yelling at you, dear reader.) It takes a lot of work and a lot of help. Here are some of the people who have helped me the most.

My beautiful editor Taz—when I started writing my first novel, it was a pretty lonely experience. This one was different. I felt like I had a partner on this caper. Thank you for loving Akal, for your brilliant insights on the manuscript, and for all the pep talks. Every email from you gladdens my heart.

Ratu Petero Rogoyawa and the Lovoni people for welcoming me into their beautiful village. It is truly paradise, both from the exceptional physical beauty of their home in the heart of the crater and from the warmth and the kindness of the people. They seemed to adopt me almost immediately. In particular, I'd like to thank Joanne for organising the stay and for opening up her home to me. Over endless cups of lemongrass tea on your verandah overlooking the village, you gave me an invaluable insight into the history and culture of the Lovoni people.

The people of Levuka who shared their history so

generously. Manhar Lal Vital, who has an amazing collection of old photos of Levuka, rebuilt painstakingly after his original collection was washed away in a storm. Suliana Sanders, for chats and biscuits fresh from her tree. Thanks to Vonda at New Mavida Lodge for helping me get in touch with people in town and taking such good care of myself and my parents.

My cousin's cousin (yep, that's a thing) Deven, for sharing all his Levuka connections with me.

A lot of my research was done at the University of the South Pacific, at the beautiful Suva campus. Many thanks to Dr. Nicholas Halter for introducing me to the right people, and Dr. Paul Geraghty for his responsiveness to questions about Fijian culture.

I love the library at USP. Walking in there gives me a sense of excitement and purpose and calm all at once. It feels like time stands still when I'm there and I'm in this beautiful bubble of learning. The Pacific Collection is an invaluable resource, an absolute treasure trove. And the librarians are a wonder. In a country where things are not always efficient and service oriented, the USP library was a haven where everything was achieved quickly and with a genuine desire to help. Thank you so much to the team of librarians, in particular Jade Moore and Gwen Cousins.

Last, but by no means least, Juliet and the rest of the Soho team, thank you for your unwavering support and for putting your faith in me and in Akal for a second novel.